Praise for Car

SUMMONING

3

Moon Wolf
Book 1: Summoning
Book 2: Binding

"What can a werew
Only the need to save
planet-shaking power of the world Snake. And where else to
do it but Darkest Los Angeles? In *Summoning* Carol Wolf gives
us a story rich in mythic lore and as tightly woven as
the mesh of fate itself."

—Douglas Rees, author of *Vampire High*

"A fast-moving adventure full of surprises and delights
including several richly imagined women of power. Our heroine,
Amber, is convincingly tough, confident, and resourceful, no
bluster but plenty of heart, which makes her a pleasure to spend
time with or, rather, try to keep up with. The story *moves*, like
its protagonist, boldly, unhampered by any emo blithering, to an
unusual and satisfying conclusion. I hope there's more coming!"

—Suzy Charnas, Hugo, Nebula, and James Tiptree Jr. Award-
winning author of *The Bronze King* and *The Ruby Tear*

"Lone wolf Amber is a character any reader will enjoy discovering."

—Linda Wisdom, national best-selling author
of *A Demon Does It Better*

"Carol Wolf's *Summoning* is a fast-paced, colorful romp
through a supernatural Los Angeles full of demons, witches,
soul stealers, and plenty of supernatural hi-jinks to delight
lovers of Urban Fantasy."

—Matthew Kressel, World Fantasy Award nominee
and founder of *Sybil's Garage*

First Edition

ISBN 978-1-59780-398-4

Night Shade Books
Please visit us on the web at
http://www.nightshadebooks.com

Summoning

BOOK ONE OF THE MOON WOLF SAGA

CAROL WOLF

NIGHT SHADE BOOKS
SAN FRANCISCO

For the pillars of my house, with my love:
for Bill, for Riva, for Rebecca,
and for Eric.

"And you can tell everybody this is your song."

CHAPTER ONE

I wasn't going to get involved.

I heard the drums start up at sundown. When the wind was right, I caught a hint of smoke. But there was more than that: a hum in the air, a tremor of power gathering. Well, that pissed me off. There's no way I was going to allow someone to raise power in the territory I had marked out as mine, without at least finding out who it was, and what they were up to. And then do something about it.

A muddy haze on the horizon caught the last glint of sunset as I slipped past my landlady's window. I'd made a point of not letting her see much of me since the day she rented me my place four months earlier, the day before the big earthquake. My I.D. says I'm nineteen, and that I stand five foot four. I'm five foot nothing, lean like a runner. I didn't try to look taller, or older. I just looked her right in the face as I handed it over. My eyes are green with flecks of gold when I'm easy. When I'm angry, you'd almost think they were gold, if you dare look close. My landlady looked away. Maybe it was the smile. You don't see my teeth when I smile like that. But you know they're there.

The lights of Los Angeles were visible to the west, softened by the haze. Half of a waxing moon was high in the sky. Traffic was light on Greenleaf as I trotted up towards the hills to the north of Whittier. No one could see me. Why not make a night of it? I changed.

It felt so good to stretch out my full length, all four paws hitting the ground. I opened my jaws slightly to take in the wave of scents. My ears pricked forward, categorizing the new range of sounds. The night looked suddenly brighter, the edges sharper, and distracting distances blurred as my wolf mind focused on scent and sound to describe the world.

I went easily till I made Hellman Park and got off the pavement, then I opened up, streaking straight up the hillside. A small herd of deer bounded out of my way, gasping in terror. One let out an adorable shriek. My head skewed round, following them, the compelling scent calling me to the glorious chase, the promised victory. For a moment I lusted for that flying mortal leap, my jaws ached for that first gripping tear that brought up flesh and blood and life all at once... I let them go. I had other game afoot that night. In retrospect, it would have been better if I'd gone after the deer. Well, not for everyone.

They had set up wards in a dozen places along the trails of the park, little wispy spells like tiny suggestions appearing suddenly in your head: "There's nothing here, go away, you're not hearing anything." They don't work on me. At least, these didn't. Maybe they weren't expecting anything like me to show up at their party.

I found my intruders in a hollow beyond the crest of the hill. They'd laid out their circle out of sight of the fire station that's up on the west end of the ridge. That was smart, because they'd built a bonfire. About two dozen women danced widdershins around the fire to the pounding of drums; a couple of djembes, and a big round buffalo drum. They all wore long dark robes that swung in heavy shadows in the firelight. There was purpose in the dance, the drumming, the chanting, the ceremonial clothes. And I was going to know what it was.

I laid up on the hillside overlooking their circle, invisible in the shadows and the brush. I could feel the charge in the air from the power they were raising, like the pressure of a coming storm. They sang, clapped, danced, and drummed, raising a charge of chaos and turning it on the spindle of their dance, the pattern almost printed on the air.

At the west edge of the circle they had built an altar of stone and wood, where candles burned among various crystals and pots and branches of herbs, pieces of fruit and flowers. The leader stood there with her back to the circle, holding a sword across outstretched hands. Her voice rose in a different song—a summoning? So this was not a random power raising. Not an experiment. These people knew what they were doing, and they had a purpose. And I was going to know what it was.

Her lone voice, high and strong, wove a counterpoint with the drums and the chanting, and the beat of the women's feet on the broken grass and dirt. The leader raised the sword in the air, and the drumming changed, reverberating in the darkness. The hair rose all down my nape. I crouched uneasily. The circle chanted aversion, protection, deflection; the altar working summoned— what? Help?

The leader's gaze rose my way, met my eyes briefly, and returned her concentration to the working. I bared my teeth for an instant. Frankly, I like a little more respect than that.

The drums hammered imperatively; the dancers wove among one another, their voices rising to a clamor. My head came up in wonder as I sensed a new flare of energy. I got up, turned about, tasting the air. There were other circles in other strong places to-night, near and far, raising power as well. The working here had just connected up with the others. What was going on? It wasn't one of the eight holy nights; I knew that. The equinox was more than a week away. This was something else, something unusual. I settled down again, uneasily, to watch.

The chanting changed as the connection of their energy to the power of distant workings solidified. They wove it together quite nicely with their own; this bunch knew their stuff. The moon began to fall toward the west.

I sensed him as he topped the ridge and raised my head. He walked down the slope and straight to their fire, a young man, not tall, straight-backed and fair-haired, in an old leather jacket and worn jeans. I got up when I smelled his fear, trailing along behind him like blood from a wound. Not a new fear, but something he had carried with him for a long time. He made his way into their circle, breaking up their working and bringing it to a halt, as though he were under a compulsion. Curious. I wondered what he thought he was doing. The drums and voices stopped so sharply that silence opened up like a sound of its own. As the women turned on him, his fear bubbled up fresh and new. I could taste it where I stood. I moved closer down the slope, parting the brush like a shadow.

"It is not your business," I heard one of the dancers tell him.

"It is," he insisted. "I can help, if you'll let me."

"You?" she said scornfully.

The leader came forward, and the others made way for her as though their movements had been choreographed. She stood before him and looked him over, and he bent under her regard as though he stood in a strong wind.

"This is no place for you." Her voice was grand and strong. She was middle-aged, heavy-set, and carried her years as she wore her power, with authority and grace.

He made an effort to stand his ground. "Listen, I just want to know what's going on, what you've heard."

She held out a hand toward him, as though feeling a fire for its warmth. "I know what you are, Dark One. I command you to depart."

While the celebrant spoke, the women moved up to surround him, the fire burning at their backs. Some of them took hands, touched shoulders, reinforcing each others' power. He swayed, and braced himself against them.

"I'm not what you think. Really." His eyes seemed to burn in his narrow face, but that could just have been the intensity of his desire.

"No?" the celebrant asked.

"No, I mean yes, all right." He looked down, "But it's different than you think."

She studied him for a long moment. "Can you prove it?"

He raised his head and met her gaze. "I'll bear any trial you care to name." He added, "If you command me."

"If I command you?" the celebrant asked, surprised. "Can I command you?"

"Yes," he said. He bent his head to her. Some of his fear and tension left him. That was strange. The women surrounding him shifted. Their force changed, no longer pressing him out, but something else, probably more dangerous. What was he thinking? I moved up a little closer.

The celebrant studied him, her hand again feeling the air between them. "You aren't one thing or the other. Dark or light, where is your place? Have you come here to find out?"

He shook his head. He looked even younger than I'd thought, not even in his twenties. "I know what I am," he said. "I'm willing to prove my good intentions."

The celebrant did not seem impressed. "Are you?"

"To you, yes."

"Even to your death?"

He smiled a little, and shrugged. "If that is your wish."

A shock of excitement went through the group. I decided it was time to step in. I didn't know what they thought was wrong with this guy, except maybe his gender, but I wasn't going to stand by and see murder done.

When I stepped into the circle the group froze, electrified. I felt the trance of power and self-assurance lift right away from a lot of those women. I almost grinned. Now that's respect.

The leader turned her head to me. She didn't back up even a step. "Sister, welcome." She nodded regally. "Do you have business here?"

I stood up. I may not be as impressive on two feet, with my short dark hair, jeans, and a black sweatshirt, but there's nothing sillier than an animal dumb show when you're trying to have a conversation. Besides, when I change, it's impressive, whether you believe you saw what you thought you saw or not.

I folded my arms and nodded in return. "Lady."

She asked, "Is this one under your protection?"

I looked over at the young man. He stared at me, wide-eyed. I could sense his shock, but he wasn't feeling any more fear, like a lot of the women were. Funny—he smelled calmer now.

"I'm just here to see fair play done. Seems like you were ganging up."

"He has agreed to the trial." She looked over at him for confirmation and he nodded. But he was still staring at me.

"Very well." I gave them permission to continue.

Someone brought her the sword from the altar. Very low, very sharp, very slow, the drumming began again.

They called on the powers of light. On purity, rightness, right action. When they called on the powers to give one straight answer, one right truth, I started to feel uncomfortable. What would one straight answer or one right truth make of me? I had a thousand of them. I thought of voicing a question, or an objection, but the circle, as I said, was strong and practiced, and this new working borrowed power from the pattern of energy already flowing across that hill. I was too much a part of it myself by then to break away. The celebrant raised the sword. She sang, and the women answered, and they collected all the power of their working and directed it into the blade of her sword. She turned to the young man she had called the Dark One, and raised it over him. He bowed his head, and she lowered the blade. When it touched his skull, he changed.

I leaped, huge with sudden rage, changing instantaneously, and had him on the ground, his head in my jaws, on instinct at the scent of it. He screamed then, and he was just a guy again, my forepaws on his shoulders. He writhed under me, the sword fallen feet away in the dirt. I got off and backed away, head still down. My flanks were heaving, and I snarled involuntarily. The taste of his blood and his scent were human, now. But what had that thing been as the sword touched his head?

It had been shapeless, but deep, like a writhing hole into nowhere, or some place from my nightmares, or beyond death, a dark mass of potent otherness. It had will, and consciousness, I'd felt it clearly, a will so powerful I could taste it. The memory of it kept my hackles on end. He lay on the ground, shivering. He smelled of blood where I'd broken his skin, and fear all over him.

The Wiccans re-gathered themselves. Their collective power, broken at the appearance of that thing, whirled and drew itself together again.

The celebrant stepped forward, bent with dignity, and recovered her sword. They stared at the young man on the ground uncertainly. I snarled again.

The celebrant turned to me. "You have claimed him, Sister. We recognize your claim. He is yours to dispose of."

What? I shook off my other nature, something I almost never do so awkwardly, and asked again. "What? I didn't claim him!"

She looked sideways to her sisters, a little smile on her lips. "Who are we to come between our lupine sister and her lawful prey? No, he is yours."

"I don't want him. You take him. Do what you want." I backed off. I thought they could zap him to another somewhere, where we wouldn't have to look at him again. The gods knew I wasn't going to *taste* that thing. Not for anything.

The celebrant gathered her sisters' assent with a glance. She stepped forward and put the point of her sword to his throat. He lay quite still, staring up at her.

"Do it," said one of the women, shakily.

"It'll break the raising," another one cautioned.

"No," someone answered. "It will seal it, make it stronger."

There was a murmur of assent, and they closed in, supporting her action.

The celebrant looked at me again, as if to say, You can stop this if you want. I thought maybe she wanted me to stop it. After all, this isn't the Middle Ages. She'd probably never taken a life in cold blood before. I folded my arms, waiting to see if she'd actually go through with it.

She spoke to the sword. "Gray Maiden, Daughter of Fire and Earth, taste this blood and release this creature into Hell, where it belongs."

"So mote it be," the others responded.

He still didn't move, just lay there looking up at her.

All right, I can't say I haven't killed. I am what I am. Maybe the sword called me. Maybe the working would have been spoiled. Or maybe it's just that I still had his blood on my lips, and that really did make him mine. I leaped. She drew back in a hurry. I stood on four feet between him and the sword and snarled, as much at myself and what I found myself doing as at them. It was all the same to them. They broke up and fell back.

The celebrant was obviously relieved. I didn't think she could do it. She put up the sword, cradling the blade over one arm. She bowed to me regally. "Sister, he is yours, as I said before. Do with him what you think good. Gray Maiden will drink no blood tonight. Sisters, friends, the moon is down. Our work for tonight is finished."

They thanked and dismissed the powers they had called. They put out the fire. They dismantled the altar. They kept a respectful distance from the young man on the ground, stepping cautiously when they got anywhere near him. He still lay there, his eyes closed, breathing long and hard. When they had undone the wards, they had a little conclave. They chanted briefly, and then they all turned in our direction with a shout and a gesture, setting up another ward, I realized, between whatever that thing had been, and themselves, wherever they were. They tied it up, and then they broke up and set off down the hill, dragging drums, robes draped over their shoulders, lugging props, as the moon turned red in the haze on the horizon and slipped into the sea. I followed them a few paces, listening to their footsteps, pricking my ears as the phones came out, and their voices sharpened to tell someone where they were, and that they were coming home. The conversations faded off down the hill.

He got up behind me. I turned, head down, and growled at him. He was a wiry, compact young man in black jeans, serviceable leather boots, a long-sleeved t-shirt under his leather jacket. None of the clothes he wore were new, and none of them had been his when they were new. A medley of previous owners wafted tiny traces in the air, only discernible if I paid attention.

He looked at me a long moment. I'm not yet full grown as a wolf. My shoulders came to his hips. But my wolf eyes are yellow, and not many dare to meet them. I was still in my winter coat—it must have looked all black to him now that the fire was gone, and there wasn't enough light to pick out the highlights of amber, gray, and brown. My point is, he stood there ten feet from a wolf. Most people, this close to me, would have fear spiking off of them. But then, he wasn't people, not entirely. I'd seen that.

He dropped his eyes, and then knelt down.

I stood up on two feet, sputtering, "What are you doing?" And then his tension rose. Now that was strange. He wasn't big, but he was taller than me. And he was beautiful, despite his shabby clothes. His body was like a knife, as perfectly made. His jaw line was taut with tension. He would of course assume that he was stronger than me. It's one of my favorite assumptions. But now, facing me in my human form, his fear was spiking. What was going on?

"I owe you my life," he offered.

"Yeah, maybe."

I tried to see, or sense in any way, the dark writhing form he'd been. It wasn't there. But the memory made the hair on my neck stand up.

He glanced up at me from under his brows. He gestured down the hill, where shapes were still visible in the darkness. "She said…" He trailed off. He looked after the disappearing figures as though with regret, and then looked up at me. "What are you going to do with me?"

I could still smell his blood, though it wasn't running anymore. He'd been human again by the time I'd knocked him flat. I'd taken his head in my jaws—all right, I'd wanted to kill that *thing*—just on instinct. But he was a man between my teeth, his scream had been a man's, and I don't kill men, unless I mean to. Was that thing in him? If I took him apart now, would I find it? Even more to the point, would I want to?

"What the hell on Earth are you?" I asked him.

He sat back on his heels. "Does it matter?"

"Yes, it matters!"

He turned his head away from my rage, and after a moment he shrugged.

"Are you human?"

He shrugged. "'If you prick me, do I not bleed?'"

"I think you would bleed rather a lot, really." I stepped forward, smiling my not-nice smile, just to make him lean back, which he did. I found my rage comforting and opened up to it. "And what the hell did you think you were doing, walking into their circle like that? You're lucky they were reasonable people."

"I know."

"What were you doing up here in the first place?"

He shook his head, and I stepped forward again. Somehow he took that as a threat—well, so he should have. I like sensitive people. He answered, "I sensed the raising. I let the call guide me.

I think I can be of help, if they let me." He looked up at me, his eyes troubled. "If you let me."

I shook my head. "This has nothing to do with me."

"No?" He smiled, and something in me suddenly ached. "Then what brought you here tonight, Lady?"

I stepped forward into my wolf nature. I walked onto him, flattening him to the ground, put my two forepaws on his chest and sniffed him up and down, starting with his head, where I left smear trails across his face and in his ears, and where I could still smell his blood and my saliva. I snuffed him up one side and down the other, trying to scent his true nature. I smelled nothing but man. He lay still, though tense, not curling up or protecting himself. He lay flat on his back with his throat, his belly and his groin in my reach. And that pissed me off, that he thought he could trust me not to hurt him. He didn't know me well enough to know that. I took hold of his leg at the thigh, hard, and I let one tooth pierce the skin on the inside of his leg where it would hurt, and how. He started to scramble up and pull away at that, but stopped himself. I could have bitten through to the artery in a second, and the taste of his blood in my mouth again all warm and sharp really made me want to do it. What the hell was he thinking? I changed back. "What the hell is the matter with you?"

His eyes widened. "What—?" he began.

"Why are you lying there? Why aren't you running?"

He took a breath, the first full one in a long while. "You want me to run?"

I shook my head to clear the bloodlust from it, and stepped back. "I just don't understand you. Why aren't you trying to get away?"

He sat up, touched the notch I'd made in his leg gingerly, then pulled at his jeans and pressed the cloth to where the blood still leaked a little. "The sorceress said," he explained slowly, "I was yours to dispose of. I thought... you were doing that."

"And that's all right with you?"

He shrugged. "That's the way it works."

"So, I could have you for breakfast, and that would be okay with you?"

He shifted again, onto his knees, and that pissed me off, too. I stepped up and knocked him flat again. He lay on his back and took two deep breaths, one after another. "I didn't make the rules," he said. "But I know them. All too well."

Why is it that when someone cringes, it makes you want to kick them harder? There he was, lying flat... I shook my head again and let his words distract me. "What are you talking about? What rules? And what the hell happened when that woman touched you with the sword? What are you? Answer me!"

He lay still, looking up at the sky. It was not quite dark up here, though the moon was gone. It's never quite dark in the city. I could see his pale, sharp face illuminated by the lights from below. He closed his eyes. "I'd rather not have my head bitten off, thank you very much."

I thought about that. "You think if I know what you are, I'll kill you?"

"Isn't that what the sorceress wants?"

He was right; she had left it to me. She had shrugged off the fallout of her working onto me, and hoped I'd do the dirty work. Well, that pissed me off too. "It sure looks that way. All right. What if I promise you I won't kill you? Tell me what you are."

He closed his eyes for a moment as though he was awfully tired. "A lot of people don't think they have to keep promises to... what I am. As though I don't count."

I was getting tired, too. Dawn was only a few hours away, and back in my apartment was an alarm clock already set to go off. "What if I promise that if you don't start talking, I'll go ahead and take your head off and find out what you are that way?"

He turned his head to me. "Damned if I do—"

"And if you don't, that's right. What did she call you? Dark One? What are you?"

He sat up on his elbows and looked up at me. "I'm a demon," he said. "Summoned out of Hell. And now, by the rules, I belong to you."

❧☙

CHAPTER TWO

F at chance. In the first place, I don't keep pets. For obvious reasons. In the second place, I don't take on obligations that I don't choose. Not ever and, especially, not now. That's a principle of mine, and I'm sticking to it. So obviously I wasn't going to let this creature, whatever it was, follow me home. On the other hand, I was starving.

We went to the donut place on Hadley, because it was the only place handy that's open all night. He looked even rattier under the lights than he had up on the hill, like he'd been on the streets for quite a while. His blond hair was clean, but his last hair cut had probably been done without a mirror. His skin was unusually pale for California, almost milky, like in fairy tales. His face reminded me of a Greek statue, but his cheeks were hollow and the set of his mouth was hard. He still radiated tension, but it wasn't the same as when he'd first appeared on that hill. He must have been hungry. He ate more donuts than I did.

I downed a buttermilk bar and a glazed while I studied him. He was formed like a piece of art, where every detail, his wrist, his throat, the line of his jaw, drew and held the eye. He scarfed up two chocolates and an old-fashioned. I realized, annoyed, that he knew I was looking at him. I started on another glazed and said, "All right. Let's have it. What were you doing up there? And what's the whole story, where you come from, what you are, and why the hell do you think for a second that it has anything to do with me?"

He put down the donut he'd started on. He was wary of me, but not afraid now. That was strange. Maybe he was on a sugar high. He didn't look at me directly, but said, "Where should I begin?"

"At the top. What were you doing up there?" I took a drink of coffee. It was loathsome.

"I sensed the working. I went up to see if I could talk to them." He glanced at me briefly and amended, "To talk to the sorceress." He licked sugar off his thumb as though he had to concentrate on it.

"You can sense a working in advance?"

"No, of course not. They've been up there Thursdays for five weeks now."

"You're kidding." What had I been doing last Thursday? What did those bitches mean by doing a working in my territory, which I had plainly marked out when I got here? They should have known better. The celebrant hadn't been surprised to see me, so she knew it was my territory, and if it weren't so late I'd get up, follow her home, and prove it to her.

"They are a strong coven." He was staring at the remaining donuts. I pushed the box toward him and he took one. "I couldn't find my way to them through their wards until tonight. Something changed. They must have reworked the wards to make a gateway, to guide the ones who heard their call."

"What are they calling for?" I asked. The coffee was really ghastly. It wasn't even hot.

"For help," he said.

"I know that. I heard them. Help, protection, deflection. What is their problem?"

He put down the donut, turned it on its napkin, picked it up again. "It's not just them. All the Wiccans, all the pagans, all the power raisers are out. Even the Buddhists are chanting protection up on Mount Baldy, though they probably don't know why."

"But you know." I gave him a moment, but he just pulled the chocolate donut in half and started on it. "So tell me," I prompted. "Why?"

He swallowed hard. He looked up and his eyes, blue and troubled, met mine. He looked old then, old enough to have seen Hell, even. He said quietly, "The World Snake is coming. She's turned."

"The World Snake?" I'd never heard of it, but the hair along my nape rose at the name.

He nodded. "There was an earthquake, some months ago, in November."

"I remember." My first night in my new apartment. My skin had been tingling all day, and I couldn't sleep that night. I was not surprised early the next morning when I heard the rumbling begin, and then felt the quake jump beneath me, and roll on by. I didn't have anything breakable. I went out onto the landing above the steps down to the street. In the predawn darkness, my neighbors emerged, some of them yelling and screaming. My building is across the street from the Whittier College campus. It's old and ramshackle, and relatively cheap, but I chose it mostly because lots of students live along here. It gives me more cover. You could tell how recently my neighbors had come to California by how much noise they made, while we watched the showers of sparks as the transformers on the power poles flamed out. The power came back on the next day.

"And what has that to do with the World Snake?"

His eyes widened at my ignorance. "Herakleitos? Thrace? Helike?"

I shook my head.

"Those are some of the cities she's swallowed before. Atlantis?"

"Oh, yeah, right."

He shrugged. "It doesn't matter if you believe me. The power raisers know it. That's why they're working deflection and protection all around this basin, from the Primrose Dragons down in Irvine, to the Black Robes out in Claremont, to the Thunder Mountain Boys up in West Hollywood, and all the diviners and lone shaman with their backyard altars in between. I've been to some of them, for help. Help I can give, and..." He fingered the napkin. "Help I need myself. Well, not the Thunder Mountain Boys. They think they own something like me." He met my eyes briefly, and I couldn't tell again if he was young or old. Either way, he'd seen more trouble and care than he was good for.

I leaned back in my chair, folded my arms. "So this city is going under. No one's going to be surprised. Why not head for Colorado?"

He shrugged. "I can't. I'm bound here." He glanced at me again. "Oh, yeah? Well, I'm not."

"What they don't know, but I know, is what comes before." He leaned forward now, speaking in earnest, the donut pushed aside. "Before the World Snake?"

"Yes." He didn't like to hear the name, anymore than he liked saying it. He lowered his voice again, and I had to listen sharply to hear his words. "Before her, in her bow wave, will come the Eater of Souls." He eyed me now with a whole world of trouble in him. "That's what I'm afraid of. And I don't think they know, or they wouldn't be calling so openly. But they won't—they won't listen to something like me. I can't even get near most of them." He smiled a little, tightly, and opened his hand. "Somehow they don't trust me."

"And you think I will?"

He looked straight at me. "I am not allowed to lie to you."

My turn to smile. "Uh huh. And why do you say that?"

He avoided my gaze again, and looked down at the table. He turned the donut on its napkin once more, pushed it away. "You don't believe me."

"No, I don't."

"But you saw what I am."

The memory raised the hair on my neck again. "I saw," I told him, "what I want no further part in. Namely, you, whatever you may be. Thank you for your information. I'm sure it will be a big help. Now, I want you out of this town, out of my territory, and out of my sight." I got up to loom over him, but he scrambled to his feet as I stood. "Do you understand me? Good."

I left him there and went home at a jog trot. When I got out of the shower, my alarm clock was already screaming. My kind don't generally need much sleep, but I was not pleased at having had none.

I rolled my black Honda Civic out of the carport and turned down the alley that led to the street. Damned if that guy wasn't leaning against the side of the building by the dumpster! I saw red for a minute, and took my foot off the gas. I was going to get out and chase him out of town right then. After a couple of heartbeats, I thought, All right, he didn't believe my implied threat; we're even. I didn't believe almost anything he said. Then I thought, what the hell. I can always run him off later if he bothers me. There's a lot to be said for having a secret identity.

I slogged through the traffic to the 605, hopped on the freeway, drove along the River Where the World Was Made—according to the original inhabitants—and down to La Mirada. I clocked in at Arches Auditorium only ten minutes late, got a bucket and a handful of cloths, and joined Brad, Marcus, Tepio, and Yvette on the scaffold in the second-story lobby.

Arches Auditorium was a hundred years old that year. The whole building was being cleaned, refurbished, and repainted from the attic dressing rooms to the tunnels under the stage to the scene shop. We'd started upstairs in the dressing rooms months ago, opening cupboards where things had died and even more name-less things had been stored for decades, until they left nothing but a smear on the walls and floor and the smell of their passing.

I'd gotten the job through the lucky chance of overhearing a conversation in a coffee shop in Whittier. The guy at the next table was telling a friend that he was blowing off his job so he could take an extra class. I went down to Arches the next day and told Pete, who was in charge of our crew, that I was there to take Conner's place, and Pete took me on that day. I liked earning money. Even more, I liked having something worthwhile to do all week. Days can get pretty long, otherwise.

Today we were in the upstairs lobby, cleaning the section of paneling we could reach from the scaffolding, then applying a first coat of linseed oil to the wood. While that dried, we washed the cornice above, working around the hand-painted watercolors in each panel.

I'd been the first woman hired on the team. Marcus, Brad, and Tom had been the rest of the team then, guys in their twenties who banded up like dogs when I showed up. They did their best, in their stupid, unimaginative way, to make me feel unwelcome. I don't care if people don't take to me. I don't, for the most part, take to people. But I won't stand for disrespect. Tom was the worst of them, with a big neck and small eyes, mean in the way he worked, and in everything he said. Strangely, the lights went out in the tunnel not many days after I started, while Tom was down there. I chased him up one side and down the other, making the kinds of noises you only think you hear in nightmares, till he tripped and fell flat out in a pool of slimy water. That's when the lights came back on. He finished the day in the bathroom, and he didn't come back. After that, the other guys were sweet puppies. Yvette was hired in Tom's place. She's big and strong and kind, and she could handle herself. Tepio came a week later. I don't know where he was from. He was quiet when the others were, and the first to laugh when someone made a joke. He was okay. I listened to their banter all day, and their laughter.

Late in the day as we were cleaning our brushes, Yvette said to me, "Hey, Amber, you hear any drumming last night?"

My I.D. says my name is Elizabeth Beaumont. I still forget to answer to it. I tell people I'm called Amber, which makes it easier. I turned to her. "What's that?"

"You live in Whittier, right?"

"That's right."

"So do I, up on Beverly. You hear drumming in the hills last night?"

"Is that what that was?" I wanted to hear what she would say, but I didn't want to commit myself.

"Yup. I've heard it before. One of these days I'm going to take my drum up there and join the party." She beat out a rhythm on a couple of paint cans. Tepio, coming into the sink room joined in, clicking with his brush handle against the edge of the sink.

I headed home through the rush hour traffic, ready for a big dinner, a short evening of loafing, and then bed. I parked my car in the carport and turned up the stairs to my apartment.

He got to his feet where he had been sitting on the steps below my landing. I stopped. His fear was flaring. His tension was back. Despite that, he moved with the grace of an animal. I had forgotten how beautiful he was, despite being thin, despite his old clothes. His eyes were haunted, wary, almost desperate. My response to his attractions fed the surge of anger I felt on seeing him. "Do you have some kind of death wish or something? I told you to get out of town." He was afraid now, no doubt about it. I could smell it. That was good.

"Please. I need to talk to you."

I stood looking up at him for a long minute, tired and hungry and pissed off. "What if I don't want to listen?"

He shrugged. "I'll wait. I'll wait until you do." He met my eyes and said levelly, "I have to."

His outward form was beautiful, but that wasn't all he was. If he wasn't human, would it count if I took him out? I mean, would anyone even know? But his blood had been human. I still remembered the taste of it.

I decided that eating took priority. I'd had a hamburger for lunch a long time ago. And in this form, he wasn't going to take me. "All right," I said, walking past him. "Come on up."

He stood near the door while I went into my room and changed out of my paint clothes into some clean ones and used the bathroom. Then I went into the kitchen and pulled the big plastic bin out of the fridge that I keep full of marinade and slabs of meat. I heated up a pan of oil and threw on as many as I felt hungry for. I got out a plate.

"What did you want to talk about?"

He kept his hands jammed in his jacket pockets. I could see he was salivating involuntarily at the smell of the frying meat. I was myself, as a matter of fact. I tried not to look at his throat as he swallowed. I wondered if he'd eaten anything since the donuts early that morning.

"There are things you need to understand," he offered, "about what's going on."

"No, I don't," I replied, flipping the meat in a hail of spitting oil. "All I need is food, and sleep, and an occasional night out, and to be left alone."

He ventured another step toward the kitchen, and spoke louder, so I could hear him over the sounds of sizzling. "You are involved in what is going to happen. That's true. And it remains true, whether you want it to be, or whether you like it or not."

I smiled at him, showing my teeth. "Didn't I tell you, I'm moving to Colorado? Probably tomorrow."

That gave him pause for a moment, but then he shook his head. "No. That isn't how it works."

I turned off the gas and speared the meat onto my plate. I got a bottle of cider from the fridge, sat down at the table, and started in on my steak. Yummy. Gods, there's nothing like meat when you're hungry. "All right," I said, over my mouthful. "You tell me how it works."

He took a few steps forward to stand by the table. I could see his jaw working as he swallowed the saliva in his mouth. I cut myself another big bite, forked it around the plate to soak up all the red juices, and put it in my mouth.

"Go on," I said around my mouthful. "Tell me all about it."

"All right." He swallowed again and looked away. "They had a working. They called for help. And you came. That means you're involved."

"Oh, yeah?"

"Yes. I'm involved already, but what is important—"

I got up, put the pan back on, and put some more meat into it. "Yes? Go on, I'm listening." I picked up my plate, and kept working on my dinner, as I cooked seconds. I was hungry.

"What is important is that you stepped between me and the sorceress."

"Okay," I said. "You're welcome."

"Listen. Please. I am not a free agent. I am never a free agent. It's part of the conditions of my being here. I always belong to someone. That's the way it works."

"Uh huh." I pressed the meat down in the pan, just to hear it sizzle louder. "And now you belong to me? Because the Wiccan lady said so?"

"Not only that."

I spooned some of the marinade into the pan. The smell was heavenly. I glanced back at him. "All right. What?"

"You claimed me from her. You did."

I turned to him. For a minute I thought he would step back, but he got hold of himself and held his ground. I said, "The last thing you want on this Earth is to be close to me. That is a promise. You can say your piece, and I'll listen, but then you go, and you don't come back. Understand?"

"That isn't…"

"It's that or nothing. Understand?"

He raised his hands briefly, I thought, in surrender. He said,

"This is what I know. I am bound to the events that are going to come to pass here."

"The World Snake, and all that?"

His hand went up again, as though to still my voice on that name. I'd said it to see what he would do. He went on after a moment. "Yes. And since last night, I am also bound to you."

"So you say." I turned the meat. My kind of cooking never takes long, just enough to put an artistic bit of browning around the edges of the meat.

"Yes. And I've been through this enough times... I know how it works. Look." He took something out of his pocket and held it out to show me.

It was a deck of cards, larger than most, and so old and worn that the pattern on the back had worn off to a pasty white almost everywhere that fingers would normally touch them.

"Cards?" I said. How cute.

He shook his head, turned them over, and fanned them. The other sides weren't faded at all; they were livid with color, pulsing with life, flaming with symbols, and full of meaning. "It's a tarot deck."

"I can see that." I said.

"It's how I know," he said earnestly, "that I'm in service. They don't work for me. I'm only able to use them on behalf of my master." He was flushing, the delicate color rising to his cheeks and his ears. He lowered his head in embarrassment, cut the cards, and turned over the one at the top. "Look," he said. "This is you."

It was the Moon, and below it a wolf stood, drawn in a Medieval style, with its head back, howling. "Oh yeah?" I said. "That's me?"

He made an impatient gesture. "It symbolizes you. Your nature—your true nature—is guided by the moon."

"That's a myth, you know."

"No, that's not what I mean. The moon is your sign because, like the moon, you are changeable. You have more than one aspect."

"I've got lots of aspects," I said gently, "and most of them you wouldn't like."

He shook his head. "I know it's you, because until today, that card in that form never appeared in my deck before. And I've had these a long, long time."

I forked the meat onto my plate. After a moment, I got out a second plate and put some meat on that, too. I got out some cutlery and put it on the table across from me with the other plate, and sat down to the second half of my supper. "Sit down," I told him, pointing. He didn't have to be told twice, but he waited till I had my first mouthful before he started in. Then he ate faster than I did. Boy, he must have been hungry.

I leaned back in my chair when I'd finished. "All right, demon. Let's have the rest of the story. What are you doing this side of Hell?"

He'd been finished for a while, looking at his plate as though he'd like to pick it up and lick it. But he raised his head and took a breath. "I am here because I was summoned by the most ignorant practitioner of the magical arts in the history of the craft, who called my name, commanded me into human form, this form, and set no limitations in time or space for my durance here. None!"

"Uh huh." I thought about this. "Okay, there's some magician who can call up demons, make them human—"

"Make them wear human form, pardon me."

"All right. But he's supposed to put an end time on how long you stay, and he didn't. Is that right? So—don't tell me. Now that you belong to me—as you say—you want me to kick his ignorant ass."

He smiled then, and for a moment I saw the ghost of the beautiful boy he had been commanded to be. "I wish it were so simple. John Dee has been dead more than four hundred years. I am good and stuck here...." He looked away, his mouth hardening.

I didn't let him help with the dishes, or even clear them. I didn't want him to feel that much at home in my place. He wasn't staying. He didn't seem to know that yet. While I cleaned up, I made him tell me the rest of the story. He didn't tell it all, but I guessed that.

"I thought when John Dee died, I would return to my true form and be free to go. When he found he could not use me as he hoped, he gave me to his daughter, who kept house for him. She was never at a loss to find me something more to do. Then John Dee died, and I went on as before.... I thought when Katherine died, then I'd be free, but it wasn't so. She sold me to pay a debt, and I found myself still bound."

"They had to die while you were still working for them. Is that it?" I turned off the water and hung up the dishrag.

"I thought so, too," he said. "But I once consulted with a master of the magical arts, who interested himself in my case. He told me that because I was summoned and bound here in this form without end, that this is my fate. I have been in servitude to one master after another ever since."

"Yeah? So last night, when you headed up the hill, who was your master then?"

He blushed. The rose color was awfully pretty on his pale skin. I watched him flail around for a lie that would work for him. He held out his hands again. "That was... different. Things have changed since then."

"Oh, yeah?"

"Look." He put the deck of tarot cards down on the table in front of him. "Will you cut them?"

"All right." I like card tricks. I cut the cards and pushed the deck across the table toward him. He didn't touch them.

"Turn over the top card," he said.

I did. It was the Moon again. "Good going!" I pushed the deck toward him.

Again he shook his head. "Will you shuffle them?"

I put the card back in the deck and shuffled them idly for a while, wondering what trick he would pull next. Then he said, "Whenever you like, choose a card from the deck."

I simply turned the deck over to reveal the bottom card. It was the Moon. I dropped that card on the table where I could see it,

and shuffled again. I looked a challenge at him, but he only nodded. "Whenever you like, turn over the card of your choice."

So I cut the deck and turned over the top card. It was the
Moon. When I looked over at the card I had dropped on the
table, it seemed I had mistakenly dropped the Knave of Wands
there instead. Except I hadn't.

I handed him back his cards. "Cute trick," I said, but he only
shook his head again.

"I have cast the cards a hundred times today. Every time, you
appear in the central place, balancing the issue between of the
fate of this city, the coming of the Eater of Souls, and the Great
Snake." He lowered his head and added, "And of my fate, as well."

I cracked a smile at that. "That's real funny. What do you think
I am, some kind of superhero?"

He said, "I only know what I am told. We are at the outset of
catastrophe, and you are the vital player."

"And with you at my side, we will prevail? That's rich. I always
liked those stories too, but just now, these days, I'm just hanging
out on the outskirts of L.A., doing my thing, living my life, know
what I mean?" I backed him across the living room toward the
door. I was about to reach past him and open it for him, when he
held out the cards again.

"I am not without my uses." He sounded like a hawker in the
marketplace, only this guy was selling himself. "I can offer you
what it is you want, what you have been longing for." He fanned
the cards in his hand.

"What are you talking about?" I said, low and dangerous.

He turned the cards over and fanned them face up, so the bright
strange shapes writhed before my eyes. "I am, as I said, the tool of
my master. I can read the cards for you. I can find what is lost to
you. I can discover what it is you want to know."

"Out," I said. And I bit off the word as my four paws hit the
floor. He backed toward the door, still talking.

"Only if you want, Lady… your tool to use… if in return you

would aid me…"

I walked him to the door, my head low, my mouth open. I get bigger when I'm angry. So they say. I almost didn't fit in the doorway, so I think it must be true. He backed out onto the landing and down the stairs.

I slammed the door on his last words, took two turns around the living room as his footsteps retreated to the foot of the stairs and he stood hesitating. After a while, I heard him walk away. I got up on the big chair and curled up. How did he know? What did he know? He can't have read my mind. Could he have read my heart? And I'd thought, for the longest time, that mine was dead.

ഇൻൽ

CHAPTER THREE

When I got to L.A., I'd chosen Whittier because of the hills. They aren't very high, but they go on quite a ways, and if you're willing to cross a road, they go on even farther. There are no trees to speak of, and the traffic noise never ends, but there is space, and many trails, the scent of grass and the web of the creatures' lives that live there, and at night there are almost never any people. I took off for the hills when the moon was high, trying to run my way back to peace of mind, trying to run from thoughts I thought I'd escaped months ago, when I left home, the home of my mother, and her new mate.

Up in the hills the air was cool and almost fresh. The California grasses and herbs were sweet and damp from the dewfall. I climbed the hill beyond where the Wiccans had had their working—nothing there tonight, except the wards that whispered, Go away, there's nothing here, you don't want to be here. On the next rise I stood with my back to the city lights, looking out into the darkness of the hills beyond. Down the rise where the park abutted the houses, a family of raccoons made a ruckus in the trash cans. A snake had passed here not long before. Four deer stood in the hollow below, not moving, not making a sound, waiting for me to go.

My coyote cousins began to sing across the way. I sat down to listen to them.

Everything changes. The days turn. The moon rises and falls. My dad was gone, and I didn't know what happened to him.

I wore a new name now, though I was not yet used to it. My family name is Hunter. I left my puppy name, the one my brothers called me, the one I was called at school, behind me when I went away. My dad called me Amber. I use it these days, because I like to hear the word.

I had two brothers of my own. When I was fourteen, Carl, my older brother, went with my mom and my dad to the Gathering. My younger brother Luke and I, not being of age, stayed home with my Aunt Dora. When my mom came home, she brought Ray with her. Her new husband. My dad and Carl never returned. Ray moved in to my mom and dad's room. My dad's stuff was packed in boxes, down to the coffee cup he always used, and sent away. Carl's room was cleared out, and my four hated stepbrothers moved in. Life at home was insupportable from that point on.

My mom wouldn't talk about it. She wouldn't answer questions. She said, when I was older I would understand. Well, I was older, and I did not understand. How could she let that bastard, that monster, into her house, in the place of my dad? And why wouldn't she tell me what had happened to Dad and to Carl?

No one I knew would talk to me. They were all afraid of Ray. I didn't blame them. I was afraid of Ray, too.

All right, it pissed me off that I wasn't the darling of the house anymore. I'd always been my dad's favorite. I knew it, everyone knew it, but my brothers were sweet about it. I was their favorite too. I knew what it meant, among my family, to be my mother's daughter, the Daughter of the Moon Wolf. When the clods invaded, they tried to make me into their servant.

They'd done me a favor in a way, I tried to tell myself once more. Because of them, I'd learned to fight. I'd grown into my powers early, and made them sorry. I'd had to fight for Luke as well as myself, which gave me twice as much to do. I'd put my oldest stepbrother in the hospital the last time he bothered me. Unfortunately, that brought me the attentions of his dad.

How could my mother put up with someone like that? That was the question that made my fury rage. But what that did was cover my little-girl question, which was, how could she let him do that to me?

I learned not to be beaten down by him. I learned how to fight back. He was too strong for me, but his sons were not. The next time he bothered me, I went after his youngest boy. He only did it one more time before he got the message.

They knew I'd take off as soon as I came of age. So I took off even earlier, as soon as I possibly could, so they couldn't stop me.

My dad was wise. He looked out for me. When I rode the surge of my blood in blind passion and for the first time made the twist that brought forth my wolf nature, when I fell onto four legs, stunned by new senses, crippled by a different throat, a different height, a different brain, my dad was there. He changed in front of me, nosed me onto my feet, and led me up the pasture, into the meadow, up into the woods. Slowly, exploring every trail, every scent, every sound or motion, we gamboled and tracked, leaped and played, until I fell into an exhausted heap, too tired to move. He carried me home. It is easy for the two-natured to make a mistake, when we first learn to change. My dad was there, and he saw that I didn't.

When Dad didn't come back from the Gathering, I held all his lessons close. He showed me the old family caches, some of them dating back to when we first settled the area more than a hundred years ago. I emptied them, and hid them anew, obscuring my track with every trick he taught me. My mom must have known about the caches, but she said nothing. I hoped that meant that at least in this small way, she was still on my side.

One of my cousins also planned to leave. Ray brought trouble to a lot of people. She found out how to buy new I.D.s, and she got one for me. I left tiny little hints, like mistakes, that I was planning to hide in the mountains. I spent more time in the woods, hunting, learning to be invisible. I left trails, and then crossed and re-crossed them, so I would be hard to track.

When the time came, I emptied all my caches and I left with my cousin in her car. We drove down and picked a car she bought for me with my money, and then we drove off in different directions. I headed into the mountains. There are a lot of mountains in California.

You can hide in the wild, in your true nature. You can hide in the mountains, in the woods, where the trees are indifferent. In the city, the people, like the trees, are indifferent, but there your trail is obscured every day by a million cars and a million people.

I made a big loop out into the desert, then doubled back and drove south. I chose Los Angeles, rather than San Francisco, because it is not only big, really big, but there are fifty ways to get out of there, if you have to.

All right, I had questions. Questions I had been longing to hear the answers to for more than two years. Where was my dad? Was he all right? Was he dead? Did Ray kill him? What happened to my brother? Why was Ray able to come in like he did, and why did he suddenly have such power over everyone, over my mother, over me? Where was he from, what did he really want? In time, I swore on my soul that is the same in both my natures, that I would know the answers.

But for the time being, I was too young, and not yet strong enough, to fight back. I needed to wait, I needed to grow, I needed to find all my power. And meanwhile, I needed to stay hidden. So I had a policy. No ties, no alliances, no contacts. Just me, and I would take care of myself.

My mom didn't know where I was. All right, true. But she gave up her right to know my whereabouts when she stopped taking care of me. I was hoping the family would think my stepdad had done for me. That would bring him a lot of trouble, and it would serve him right. But if he was not yet defeated, when the time came, I would do it. I swore it.

Out across the way, the coyotes yapped and bayed. I stood up and raised my head and sang my loneliness, betrayal, and loss. I silenced every living thing for ten miles around.

I sat and thought for a while, in the quiet. The traffic sounds were like the distant roar of the sea. It was true that if the city I had chosen was going to be destroyed, then I was involved. And I had claimed some territory, despite my policy of invisibility. It's in my nature, after all. And why else had I gone up the hill last night, except to see what was going on? My family hadn't found me yet. They weren't going to look here. They were out wandering all over the mountains, tracking the elusive wolf. And there are hundreds of miles of mountains in California. There were answers I wanted that would be worth having. And knowledge is power, and I like power a lot.

I stood up and howled one more time, to let everything that heard know that I was there, this was my city, my domain, I had laid my claim, and I would make my claim good. When I finished, I headed down the hill and went to look for the demon.

He wasn't hard to track. From my place, he'd headed down Philadelphia Street to the center of town. He was probably still hungry, and that's where people are, and food. It was still early enough for the restaurants and cafés to be open. I got up on my two feet when I came under the streetlights. I lost his scent in the dozens of others outside the disco on the corner where Nixon's office used to be. I picked it up again on Greenleaf, down near the church where the homeless guys get their soup twice a day, but it was old. I turned uptown and picked up his scent again, fresh and clear.

I spotted him standing on the curb by the little plaza beside the coffee shop where the musicians hang out. He was talking to a big guy, a biker, with large shoulders and beautiful, muscular legs in tight leathers. The biker kept reaching out to him, touching his hair, smoothing his jacket, I noticed as I walked towards them. I thought maybe this was how the boy made money for his keep, turning tricks. His head was down, though. He wasn't the one making the come-on. While his face was turned away, he caught sight of me. His head came up. His face was tight, his skin a little flushed. His eyes were haunted. If anyone ever called for help without speaking, that guy did. At the same moment, the biker got on his bike, and pulled him, unresisting, up behind him. I walked a little faster. While the biker put on his helmet, started up his machine with a roar, I thought the demon would just step off. He wasn't being constrained that I could see. But the bike started up, and the demon reached his hands around the biker's waist. He reached under his jacket in a gesture of practiced intimacy.

All right, I thought. I stopped. So much for him.

The demon caught my eye as they passed me, reached out with his hand, and dropped something at my feet. He torqued around on the bike and stared back at me, until the bike turned the corner, heading for the freeway. I picked up what had fallen. The biker's leather wallet. With his driver's license. And his home address.

I can take a hint.

I can't say I hurried, but I didn't waste much time, either. I got my car, checked the map, and headed down the 605 to Laguna. The biker's name was Thomas Fallahan. He was 6' 2" and weight 190 pounds. He had dark brown hair and brown eyes, and did not require corrective lenses, and he lived in a pretty green clapboard bungalow on a corner two blocks from the beach. I parked across the street. The biker's motorcycle was parked out front. The boy's scent was still fairly fresh.

The house was hidden behind a tall green hedge, with a fanciful iron gate in front, under an archway of climbing roses. The gate was locked, and behind the hedge was a fence. I walked the fence line along the front and side of the house to where there was a gap in the hedge at the end of the property line. I slipped behind the hedge and tested the pole that secured the fence. It wobbled quite a bit. I wobbled it some more until I was able to step around it. I was enjoying myself. It was fun to have an excuse to do some mischief again.

Most of the windows of the house were lit, but covered from scrutiny by curtains or blinds. I walked around three sides of the house. Behind the fourth was a row of trash cans and recycle bins, a pile of lumber, and some firewood.

I could break a window, but that would make noise. I could break down the door, same problem. Far easier if Thomas Fallahan came and opened the door himself. I walked up the front steps and knocked. Just on impulse I added the shave-and-a-haircut tattoo, and was rewarded by a big voice from inside calling, "Chris? That you?" There was a rattle of locks being undone, and the voice continued, "Forget your keys again...?" Then Thomas opened the door wide and found me outside it. He did look surprised.

His broad face was framed by a neatly trimmed beard. He stared down at me from deep set, tired old eyes. He was dressed in a long, brown, silk paisley robe, loosely belted at the waist, that hardly covered his big hairy chest, and draped all the way to the floor. He smelled of incense, sweat, sex, and... the demon.

I gave him a big smile. With teeth. "Hi. Thomas Fallahan? I think you dropped your wallet." I held it out to him while he instinctively reached for his pocket that wasn't there. I started walking forward, and I let myself grow larger as I came.

He stepped back as I approached him, on instinct. "Uh... yeah... thanks..."

"Actually," I said, as I crossed the threshold and stepped passed him into his living room, "I came here looking for someone." And then it occurred to me: I didn't know the demon's name.

"Hey, listen, thanks for the wallet, but—"

I ignored Thomas Fallahan and looked around his living room. The floor was hardwood, glowing with proper care. The walls were paneled with the same dark wood. A fire burned in the fireplace, beyond a beautiful fur hearthrug—no cousin of mine, or Thomas's luck would have run right out that night—a set of comfy leather furniture, and half a dozen candles set at strategic intervals around the room.

"Very nice," I said.

"Uh, thanks. You want to go now? Here. I'm kind of in the middle of something...." He opened the wallet, and pulled out a couple of bills. I ignored him.

Three doors led off the living room. One went to the kitchen, I could see that. One door was closed, the other partly open. Through this one emanated the smell of incense and lightly scented steam.

"Actually, I came here to get someone." I called loudly, "Hey! You in there?"

That's when Thomas Fallahan grabbed me. Poor guy. What he touched wasn't what he was reaching for. I should make it clear: there's no long, slow process when I change, like some Hollywood make-up job and time-lapse photography. I can change my nature as quick as I can turn my head. That night I may have done it quicker. He reached, I changed, and he backed up so fast, his mouth open almost as big as mine, that his heel caught on the hem of his robe, and he went down without my touching him. Really.

The demon emerged from the bedroom at the thump of Thomas Fallahan's fall. He was naked, pink with the heat of his bath, his fair hair plastered to his head, and scented with the steam and incense. He did look a tasty morsel. I shook myself mentally, and changed.

He stared at me.

"Hey," I said. "I came to rescue you. But if you'd rather stay, I mean, if this is your scene..."

"No," he said. "Thanks—"

"All right. Get your clothes and let's go. This guy's expecting someone."

"I know," the demon said. He dived into the bedroom.

After a few moments, Thomas Fallahan began to stir. "Hey," I called out toward the bedroom. "You coming?" I stepped over to look in. The demon had not dressed. He was on the floor, halfway under the bed. "What the hell are you doing?"

He came out fast, went swiftly to the wall of voluminous mirrored closet doors, pulled one set open and began rummaging through it. "I'll be right there—I have to find…"

I went back into the living room where Thomas Fallahan was sitting up, touching his head. When he saw me, he lunged—not at me, but toward the coffee table, where he grabbed a cell phone and flicked it open. I changed and jumped on his chest. He went down again. I picked the cell phone delicately from between his fingers, moved it back in my jaw, and bit down. Very satisfying crunching noises ensued. I dropped the parts on his robe. I got off him. While he was down and I was still angry, I stood up on my two feet and I turned the couch over on him. It was just his size.

I went back into the bedroom to find the demon tearing his way through a blanket chest at the foot of the bed.

"Will you get dressed already? I'm leaving."

"Yes… please. Just a minute…" He spotted something, and jumped up on the tall bed with the tousled red satin sheets and the drooping comforter. The headboard had a shelf in it. On one side, there was a little mirror, purely decorative, I thought. He pushed it with his fingers and a small cupboard opened. "Ah," he said. With gentle delicacy he withdrew a softly glowing little glass bottle. He turned, holding it to him with great care as though it were alive. His eyes had softened. He looked young. "I'll be right with you. Half a sec, I swear."

I went out. Thomas Fallahan lay resting peacefully beneath the couch. Outside I heard a car door slam and steps approaching. Company was coming. I listened another second. Company that had a key to the front gate. I heard it creak wide open. "Hey!" I called, but as I turned to the bedroom, he came out. He was wearing his own pants and jacket but had taken a blue silk shirt that belonged to Fallahan. And a laundered pair of socks.

"You got the wallet?" he asked.

"Yeah, I gave it back to him. Come on."

The demon saw the wallet, and the fallen bills, lying on the floor. He gathered them up, opened the wallet, and pocketed what looked like quite a lot of cash. He looked up at me with a mean little smile. "I'm worth it," he said. Then he followed me to the door.

I opened the door as the person outside reached out for it. Chris was also tall, also well-built, also good looking, with a trim little mustache over his full lips. He carried a grocery bag from which protruded a long loaf of bread and a bottle of wine. He looked up at me in surprise. I gave him another one of my big smiles. Funny, people almost never smile back.

"Hi," I said. "Thomas has had an accident."

"Is he all right?" He hurried past me. The demon relieved him of the grocery bag as he went by, and I don't think he noticed.

He looked around the living room and saw the turned-over couch. Tommy's feet were protruding from under it. "Tommy!" He called. "Is he all right?" He started heaving on the couch, trying to shift it. It was darned heavy, I know. "Tommy?"

The demon said, "Tell him that I won't be coming back."

Chris paused and looked up at him. "Look, man, it wasn't my idea. All right?"

"Just tell him." The demon walked past me out the door.

He sat relaxed and easy in the passenger seat as I found my way back to the freeway and headed for home. I had a couple of strong questions for him.

"Why did you go with him?"

"I had to," he answered quietly.

"Yeah? Was that your old master?"

"Not precisely. He only thought he was. He had something of mine. I had to get it back."

"What? The money?" I knew it wasn't that, but I said it anyway.

"No."

"That thing you found? In his headboard?"

He pulled it out of his jacket pocket. I saw the glow in his hand. "My soul," he said softly, leaning over it. "It's mine again. And now, everything has changed."

∞○○

CHAPTER FOUR

It wasn't that late when I pulled into my carport. The moon was still pretty high. He got out of the car after me, holding the bag of groceries I'd forgotten we'd stolen, that had sat on the floor between his feet on the drive. "Hungry?" he asked.

Just the sound of that word can make me hungry. This time I sat at the table listening to his light, pleasing voice, and let him do the honors. He emptied the grocery bag and brought two plates from the dish drainer. "Fresh bread, of course." He sniffed it. "Chris would rather die than eat day-old bread, ever since he spent a week in Paris. Brie, that's Tommy's favorite, and here's Chris's Gouda. Garlic olives. Oysters… hm. I wonder who those were for? Not me, I bet."

"You don't like oysters?" I was starting to feel my exhaustion.

He gave me a sideways look. "If you like," he said enigmatically. He dove back in the bag again. "Blood oranges. Now I know where he bought all this. And—Chris's secret vice: Belgian chocolate." He found a knife for the bread at my direction and cut us each a generous chunk. He spread cheese and dished olives and oysters and even peeled the oranges. He found a couple of mugs and decanted the wine with a flourish. All accompanied by his ceaseless running chatter, slipping along like a friendly brook in the spring. Finally he sat down. "Anything else?" he inquired, when I made no move for the food.

"What's your name?" I asked him. Suddenly I had his whole attention. I didn't know why that alarmed him, but he went taut like a bow. I added, "When I got to that guy's house I was going to call out for you. I didn't know your name."

He hesitated a second, then told me, "Tommy and Chris called me Stan."

"That's not your name?"

He shook his head, still wary.

I reached out to my plate for a piece of the bread and cheese. Really tasty. That bread was good.

He hadn't moved. Now he said, "What would you like to call me?" I continued chewing, so he added, "Almost every master I've had has given me a new name."

"Oh yeah?" I started on the olives. "What was your first name? What did John Dee call you?"

He hesitated again, but I didn't think that he had forgotten. "Phaedrus," he said, with obvious dislike.

"What kind of name is that?" Damn, those olives were good.

"He was a student of Socrates. He's supposed to have been beautiful."

"I'm not going to call you Phaedrus. Tell me another one." He relaxed again, and finally reached for his food. I suddenly realized why. "No, I know. Tell me your real name. Your true name." I leaned forward, pointed a finger at him. "Your demon name."

His hand stopped and withdrew. His face was tight. He didn't want to tell me, but I waited, and at last he did.

I tasted the strange syllables. "How do I know that's really it? You could say anything."

He shook his head. "I told you. I'm not permitted to lie to you."

"But you could be lying now."

He shrugged. "Ask me, by that name, to go play in the traffic, or swing on a powerline, or eat glass. What you command, by that name, I must perform, to the end of my existence." He shrugged again, but his eyes were bleak.

I said the name, tentatively. I certainly had his complete attention. It was as though I had my hand on a knife in his belly.

"If you please," he said quietly, "call me by something else. It is better that name should not be overheard. It's dangerous."

"Dangerous for who?" I said, smiling. But I let it go. "Give me another choice. Katherine Dee called you Phaedrus too? Who was next?"

"She sold me to a drayer to pay a debt. He called me Jack. His son's cousin had an inn. I was 'tapster' there, or 'you, boy,' for a generation." He began to eat.

"You're not telling me any good names."

"I was Philip after that. An officer's servant in the wars." His eyes darkened.

"But you don't like Philip."

He shook his head. "I was an earl's leman, from his boyhood in the wars to his death, after that." He glanced at me briefly from under his lashes. "He won me at cards."

"Still called Philip?"

"No. Amyas."

I took a sip of the wine. It was sweet and fruity. Not to my taste. My plate was empty then, and he got up to cut me some more bread, and added some of all the other treats as well. He opened the chocolate. What a heavenly smell!

"Didn't you have any good times?" I asked him.

"Some. For a short while. In places." But he had nothing more to say to that. He sat down again and gave more of his attention to his supper.

"How about Luke? You ever been called Luke?" He shook his head, but I had changed my mind already. That name had a certain flavor for me, a certain associated scent, and a horde of memories. I didn't want to cloud them. I bit in to one of the chocolates, a hard milk chocolate outside with a soft hazelnut center. Divine. I lapped it up and took another. "Richard," I said. "How about Richard? You ever been Richard?"

He shook his head again, smiling a little. "It's not a servant's name."

"Well, let's use that." I got up. "I'm going to bed, which I haven't seen nearly enough of for the last couple nights."

He was on his feet again instantly, and it suddenly dawned on me what he was thinking. I almost laughed aloud. I put my hands on my hips and canted them like a call girl. "So. You gonna go in there with me and make sweet love to me all night long? You up for that?"

He ran a hand through his hair, smoothed the other against his pants, unconsciously. "If you wish," he said, soft and sweet. He made his eyes change, so that they looked all at once like all he thought about was sex. But I'd seen how they looked before.

I shook my head. "I don't make love under duress. Either way, now or ever." I looked around the living room. "There's a spare blanket in the top of that closet. The bathroom's through there. You can sleep in here, if you prefer it to the streets. Otherwise..." I shrugged. "Do what you want."

He hadn't moved. He was still taken aback. I'd reached my bedroom door before he said anything. I looked back at him. He'd stiffened, like I'd insulted him or something. "You would enjoy it," he said, as I closed the door on him. Sometimes you could tell he was a demon, from his eyes.

I was really beat. Good thing it was Friday night. No work tomorrow, so I didn't set the alarm. I stripped and fell into bed with relief. I lay still, listening to him move around out there, clearing the table, running water to clean the dishes. I remembered how he'd looked when he came out of Thomas Fallahan's bedroom, all pink and sweet and finely made. John Dee must have given him exact specifications for the body he wanted him in. I wondered what Dee had wanted him for, and fell into wandering dreams on the thought.

In the morning, I pulled up from sleep as I heard the front door open and the guy go out. Oh well, I thought. That's it, then. He just wanted me to help him get his soul back. About an hour later, I came awake again when the door opened, and he returned. Hm. What next? I lay listening to the sounds of him quietly moving around out there. Somehow, I didn't resent him in my space, my den. The sounds were companionable. As though I had a pack again. Huh. That was making too much of it. Who knew how long he was going to stick around? He had a use for me; I understood that. All of his tricks and turns and strong assertions were designed to put me in a position where I stood between him and harm, whatever harm he thought was coming. If the World Snake was real, if it was really coming, maybe what he wanted was a ride to Colorado. But for the time being, he wasn't too objectionable. I smiled, as the vision of him emerging, sweet smelling, his body slightly flushed from the shower, from recent sex, from hope and desire and fear, rose in my mind. And he was doing everything in his power to make me think of him that way. I knew that too. I turned over, gave up thinking, and sank back into sleep.

I heard the shower run. Later, I heard the kettle boil. And some time after that, I smelled onions cooking. When I opened my eyes the sun was shining on my curtains. It was late. No wonder the smell of food got me up. I pulled on my robe and went into the bathroom and showered. I found a clean pair of jeans and a shirt, gave my hair a few licks and went out to see what the demon was up to. The living room smelled heavenly. The table was set. The kitchen smelled... different.

Barefoot, dressed in his jeans and his big new blue silk shirt, open at the throat and the baggy sleeves rolled up, and wearing an apron I'd never seen before covering him from chest to knees, he stood in my kitchen hovering over three pans on the stove. It seemed, too, that we now had a toaster. He'd washed his hair, and trimmed it as well. It looked neat and soft, curling a little just at the ends. He smelled really good.

Coffee was brewing in a brand new coffee brewing gizmo. His air of happy industry evaporated as I walked passed him without a word, opened cupboards, pulled open the fridge, looked in a larder I'd never used for the source of the new smells. He flattened himself against the cabinets, smiling a stupid, scared, fake smile. There was food everywhere. The fridge was full. There were green things in the bins.

"What have you done?" I asked him.

He straightened up a little. "I went grocery shopping. It's just down the street."

"I know where it is," I said. "With what money?"

"It's there on the table," he said, pointing with a brand shiny new cooking implement whose name I did not know. He followed me to the table. There was a pile of bills laid out, mostly hundreds, some twenties, a ten, some ones, and a little change. On top of them were some receipts. "I spent a hundred and seventy dollars and sixty-three cents," he said. "That's the rest of it."

"The rest of what?" I asked him.

"The money from Tommy's wallet," he reminded me. "Last night? There was eight hundred dollars in it."

"Eight hundred…?"

"It's all accounted for." He backed away to the stove, made things sizzle, made more heavenly smells.

He was distracting me. I said, "Is that breakfast?"

"If you wish."

I wandered back out to the table. "That money isn't mine," I told him. "You stole it fair and square."

He turned back to me. "It is yours. Everything I have is yours. I'm not allowed to have anything of my own."

"Is that another one of your rules?"

He gave another of his shrugs and turned away, got out plates, started dishing things onto them. I went and sat down, shoving the money and receipts into a pile at the end of the table. "I didn't make the rules," he said, with an edge. He put a brimming plate in front of me. "But I certainly know them." He set a mug of hot coffee by my hand. The food smelled really good.

I was torn between defending my Spartan and ascetic space, and the glorious smells that wafted from the plate in front of me. "You're just taking over here, aren't you?" I might have sounded more sincere if my mouth wasn't already full.

He smiled. "You'll get used to it."

It would certainly be easy to get used to him. The coffee was almost not bad. And gods, he could cook. "Where's yours?" I asked him.

He brought his plate then, stripped off the apron and sat down across from me in the place he had taken the previous night.

I sipped my coffee and dug in to the egg-and-shrimp thing with yellow sauce dripped over it, leaking mushrooms and tomatoes and peppers. There was crunchy buttered toast, and fried potatoes with onions and something else in there that he'd put on my plate, and slices of banana in a dish with a sugary brown sauce. I eyed him as he joined me. "What, you were going to eat in the kitchen?"

"It's usual," he told me, a little prickly, picking up his fork.

"On the floor? In the corner? With the rats?"

He put his fork down again. "If you wish."

"Don't be an idiot." I took another bite. "Oh gods, this is good."

He ducked his head and had some himself. "I wondered," he said with diffidence, "if you only ate meat... but last night... and the donuts..."

"Meat," I told him, "is what I know how to cook. And it doesn't take much, the way I do it."

"True," he agreed.

I shot him a look, but he was bent over his plate, wielding fork and knife like an epicure.

He must have eaten something earlier, because this time he

didn't go at the food like he was starving. He finished before I did and sat and watched me while I ate. At one point he got up and refilled my coffee cup. "I was wondering…"

"Hm?" I finished sopping the toast in the last drops of the yellow sauce and putting it in my mouth.

"What am I to call you?" He lifted his hands briefly. "What would you wish me to call you?"

Master of all masters? Your exalted greatness? I almost laughed aloud. "And you'll call me anything I want, right? It's another rule?"

"Yes."

"I'm called Amber, here," I told him.

He said, "But that isn't your name?" in a friendly, suggestive way.

I smiled, not my nice smile. "But you aren't going to know my name," I told him. "My kind know very well the power of such knowledge. Besides, you couldn't pronounce it."

"I could," he replied.

"But you won't," I said, still smiling. "You'll call me Amber. All right?"

"Yes, Amber," he said.

He might be in my service, I realized, but he certainly wasn't tame.

"All right," I said, when he had cleared my plate. "Let's see it."

He was so taken aback that for a moment he lacked the ingenuity even to pretend he didn't know what I meant. He stammered when he said, "Pardon me?"

I looked up at him, just looked, and waited to see what it would take to make him give in. I didn't have to do anything. In a short while his face crumpled. It was enough to make me start to think these rules he talked about really did bind him, as he said.

"It's mine," he said finally. He put a hand up to his chest, telling me where it was.

"Yeah? And what happened to 'everything I have is yours' from just a few moments ago?"

He looked utterly forlorn. "Please...," he said. "I have to have it... I need it."

"Well, I don't," I said. "I just want to look at it. I've never seen one before, at least not outside a person. Give it here."

He was wearing it inside his shirt. He'd bought a pair of shoelaces at the store and used one to knot a kind of basket tightly around the vial and the other as a cord to hang around his neck. He laid it in front of me like it was holy. Well, probably it was.

I couldn't see the vessel for all the string, so I pulled it away. He hovered in mute protest, but I gave him a look and he backed off to the end of the table.

It was in a small, thick glass vessel that fit in the palm of my hand. In it glowed something warm and luminous, with a pale white center, blue at the edges like an iris, entrancing to look at. The glass was rounded in the belly, tapered at the top, with a stopper of glass and wire that was welded to the opening and neck of the bottle.

"Where did you get this?" I glanced up at him, to watch him compose his answer. He might not be able to lie to me, but I was pretty sure he could equivocate till Hell froze. He answered readily, though, this time.

"I stole it."

"Who's missing this, then?" I held it up. It was difficult to put down, once I had it in my hand. He didn't take his eyes off it.

"No one. I mean, no one who is alive. I once met a sorcerer. He could extract that from a newborn child, as he killed it."

"Yuck!" I offered it back to him. He bent and gathered it gently in his hand.

"He collected these," Richard continued, his words still carefully light. "I was kept in his house a while. When I departed, I took this one with me. He was in no condition to miss it. No one else had a use for it. But I have."

"He was in no condition...?" I queried.

Richard met my eyes. "His house burned down. I was told he was dead."

"That's good," I said. I still had a feeling I was missing a trick somewhere. "He's long dead?"

"It was a long time ago," he conceded.

"Good," I repeated. I picked up the remnants of the shoelaces and tossed them towards him. "You don't want string for that."

"No."

"Why didn't you get wire?"

He sighed. "Because there are rules. I can buy boots for myself, and so I can buy bootlaces."

"You can buy thingies that I never heard of, but you can't buy yourself a piece of wire?"

"I can supply your kitchen, and your larder. I can clothe your servant."

"Fine. Buy some wire." I thought a moment. "Here." I pushed the cash on the table in front of him. "Take this. Buy whatever you need to make yourself comfortable."

"Thank you." He looked down at the thing in his hands. The white and blue light illumined his face. He looked like an angel in a candle flame.

I asked him, "If you have a soul, at least technically, why are you still a demon? I mean, shouldn't that make you—well, if not human, something like it?"

He shook his head. "I don't know how to bind it to me. And I don't know if it can be mine, even if I did. Those who have knowledge of the craft will not even speak to such as I am, without this. And without this, I cannot pass their wards. They usually know what I am on sight. My hope is, with this, I can learn what I need to know."

"To become human?"

"Good Lord, no," he said, the first honest exclamation I thought I'd heard from him. "To avert the Eater of Souls. Our common purpose," he reminded me. "The reason I entered your service."

"Yeah, right, I forgot." I tried another point I wasn't sure about. "I assumed, now you have a soul, you don't have to be in anyone's service anymore. You're free to go." He was shaking his head before I finished. I continued, "All right, what if I discharge you? What if I tell you you're not in my service anymore? You're fired?"

"After I cooked you that nice breakfast?" he said lightly, but his fear spiked again.

This did not add up. "Level with me, then," I said. "What do you want?"

"I want to defeat the Eater of Souls, as I told you. It's true, once I had this," he raised his soul gently in his hands, "I could duck service sometimes, if I wasn't properly bound in time. But the Eater of Souls is coming here. I need the most powerful master I can find, for all our sakes."

"And you chose me," I said. "Great."

He shook his head again. "I didn't choose you. In truth, I sought the sorceress. But I was truly bound to you by the events of that night, by the working, by her and by you. It's true by every sign I've learned to look for. I only hope it is enough."

❧❦❧

CHAPTER FIVE

Richard started on the dishes, and I let him. He was probably quicker at it anyway. And there were things to wash I'd never owned before, a colander, for instance. And if I had made breakfast, there wouldn't have been nearly so many dishes to wash, anyway, so I left him to it.

When he was finished he hung up his apron on a new hook he'd installed inside the larder door. He was just making himself right at home. He put his leather jacket back on, not because he was cold but because he'd put the soul in its inside zip pocket. He sat down across from me and took out the deck of tarot cards he'd shown me the first time he'd come to my house. He set them in front of me.

"Will you cut them?"

"What for?"

"I promised you the answers that you seek. Ask whatever you like, and I will ask the cards."

I had a lot of questions about my life. I had burning questions that I'd longed to know the answers to for years. Was my dad still alive? Was my older brother? But every hunter knows you follow one trail at a time. And everything I asked the demon would be one more thing he knew about me. I trusted him to the extent I did, in my house, and in—he said—my service because I knew I could kill him—in his human form, in any case. The Eater of Souls was coming. That came first. I pushed the cards back to him. He looked up at me, surprised.

"Not now," I said. "Later. Sometime. Maybe. Now we need to find some of those people you talked about, who can answer questions about what is going down here."

Another beautiful day in Southern California: cloudless and warm, and almost clear. As we headed down the freeway to Costa Mesa through the light Saturday morning traffic, I could actually make out the hills to the south and east that border Orange County. I can't say I didn't miss the sharp, cold air of the coast that I was used to, the long, empty beaches, the scent of the fog, the rain, the silence of the woods... but driving down the freeway, among thousands of cars, I was as free as I could be, while still very hard to find.

Richard directed me to a music shop just off one of the main downtown streets. We parked across the street and walked along the opposite sidewalk to World Music: Ethnic and Tribal Instruments. Under the sign was a large display window with masks and colorful draperies, guitars, and strange banjos made out of gourds. To the right of the door was a little brick courtyard with strange metal sculptures and a couple of benches. A group of black guys sat there, listening to the smallest of them drumming on a djembe. He was good. We were about to jay walk over to that side of the street when I caught a whiff of those guys. I stopped and put my hand out. I'll say this for the demon, he paid attention. He stopped when I did.

They were bears. Not the drummer, he was straight human. I thought about it, trying to remember what I knew of our larger cousins. I'd never met one before. I hadn't expected to find them in the city but, frankly I've never believed that myth about hibernation. And there were four of them. I decided they probably would not commit mayhem on a city street. Probably. Anyway, I could run. I wondered if the sage we had come to see was a bear as well, or if she just had powerful friends. I started across the street.

We were downwind. I saw them notice us, without turning. I knew to the second when they got a whiff of me. All four of them turned at once. They didn't get up, but they sure seemed awfully big all of a sudden. I stopped on the sidewalk so they could get a good look and smell of me.

"Hey," I said.

"How's it going?" one of them said after a moment.

"All right." I sure had their attention. The little guy left off drumming, not sure what was going on. The demon kept behind me. I made my intentions clear. "We're looking for Madam Tamara. This her place?"

The next-to-biggest guy answered me. He had a heavy face, and a scar over his brow across one eye. "Sure is. She's probably in back." He nodded to me, friendly, and turned back to the drummer, who was still smiling uncertainly. The others nodded in their turn. I nodded back and went on by. I didn't realize how keyed-up I'd been until I let go of my breath as we passed them.

"You meet those guys before?" I asked Richard. "Is that why you couldn't see Madam Tamara?"

He shook his head. "I never got that far. She has wards all around this block."

"I didn't feel any."

He smiled wryly. "Demon wards. For such as I am. I couldn't cross them, if I didn't have this." He touched the pocket of his jacket where he kept his soul. He stepped ahead and opened the door for me. "Are they her bodyguards?"

"Couldn't you tell?" I asked him. "They're bears."

His face changed. "Oh." He was still standing there staring back at them as I went inside.

I stopped just inside the door, taking in an intoxicating medley of scents as the hair rose on my arms. Wood, incense, cloth, paints and dyes, and a brush of traces of people from far away places, who ate differently, who had sweated and sometimes bled into the work of making the carvings, the weavings, the clothes, the instruments. It was like a hundred talking books all playing quite distinctly at the same time. As I took this all in, it was a moment before my other senses focused, and I heard the tap and whistle of the instruments being tried, the wind chimes gonging, muffled laughter and intense conversations, and saw the counters of beads and music, figurines and instruments, and the displays of clothes and bags, shawls and headdresses. But all that wasn't what was making the hair on my arms come up.

The air had a charge in it, a hum that can be sensed in any place that magic is frequently raised. Outside, the drummer keyed into it, helping to sustain it, and fed it into his own drumming at the same time, probably without knowing he was doing it. It made a pleasant buzz, a counterpoint to the symphony assaulting my senses. There were half a dozen customers. One tried on masks, taking them down one by one from the wall. A couple were experimenting with whistles, a pair of girls pranced in front of a narrow mirror, decked in colorful clothes, and one was in the corner examining every millimeter of one of the African drums. They were all caught in the buzz, I noted. I'd bet people hung around here all the time without knowing why.

Next to the corner with the drums was a doorway into the back, covered by a curtain. Richard followed me as I crossed the store toward the ward I felt there. It conveyed the impression that there was a wall beyond the curtain, though I could see it moving in the slight air current. There were layers to the ward that said, "Oh, look over there," and "There's nothing back here." She was strong, all right, and crafty. I called from the doorway, "Madam Tamara?"

A rich, melodious voice answered, "Yes? Come in." The wards parted as she spoke.

Well, she certainly wasn't expecting trouble. Or she was too tough to worry. I led the way through a narrow office, with desks on either side and shelves piled with papers, through another doorway and into a large workroom whose walls were lined with crowded counters, above which were crammed shelves. The center space was mostly taken up by an enormous long table, piled with half-unpacked boxes of ceramics, jewelry, shawls, carvings, and gourds, cluttered with instruments half-repaired, pieces of furniture awaiting another coat of paint, and lined with chairs that were also cluttered with piles of stuff. A tall, dark woman in a flowing dark blue cotton dress with an elaborate red and blue turban covering her hair was bent over what looked like a huge, hammered copper mirror. She looked up as I came in and started to smile in greeting, when her attention moved—and riveted—to Richard behind me.

She was quick. She spat a curse, leaped for the wall and lifted up a wooden crucifix. Her movements somehow set trembling a set of bells that hung in one corner of the room, and a free-standing gong on the counter opposite went off as though someone had smacked it but good. She held out the cross toward Richard, describing signs with her other hand, and speaking loudly and adamantly in a foreign language. I started for her, but stopped, because there was no point in scaring her. Richard walked on past me, went up to the woman, who held her ground, and fell on his knees. He leaned forward and kissed the crucifix, and then sat back on his heels. She fell silent.

"I went to mass twice a week for a hundred years," he told her. "I can recite by heart the entire Anglican Book of Common Prayer and the King James Bible."

"Be silent," she said. She laid the cross on his head. He didn't move, and nothing happened. Since Richard had started this, I waited to see how he'd resolve it, but that's when two of the bears came in the back door behind her, and the other two came in behind me. She wasted not a second, but stepped back, still holding the crucifix like a spear, and nodded at Richard. "Kill that thing."

The second-largest one, the one with the scar across his eye that had spoken to me outside, came forward from the back door. He changed as he went over to Richard, so when he picked Richard up without effort by the scruff of his neck, he wore his bear aspect and his man aspect at the same time. I could see them both plainly, superimposed one over the other. A neat trick. I'd have to try it some time.

I was already up on the table, the most direct route to both of them. I didn't change yet, as I wanted him to understand me, but my switch was thrown already and he knew it.

His arm swung back to swat Richard into oblivion.

"Put him down," I said.

"You know what that is?" Tamara asked me, calmer now that her friend had Richard in hand.

"I know what he says he is. I know that he is mine. Put him down and leave him alone." I waited another second and added, "Now."

"Do you claim to control him?" Tamara asked, with a good deal of skepticism in her voice.

That pissed me off. "He won't make a move without my permission. Now put him down."

The bear looked over at Tamara. She spread her hands toward Richard, as though trying to read his nature from the air. "Strange," she said. "He should never have been able to get this far."

"He is under my protection," I told them again.

Tamara gave me a quizzical look, and spared one more glance for Richard. "All right. Jacob, you can put him down."

The bear dropped him. I let that pass. After all, Richard had gotten us into this. Richard fell hard and didn't move. I jumped lightly off the table to stand over him. "You can get up," I told him.

"Did you raise that thing?" Tamara asked me.

I shook my head. "He was raised a long time ago."

Richard got to his feet, keeping his head bent and his arms crossed unobtrusively over the zippered inside pocket that held his soul.

"Are you a sorceress?" Tamara demanded. Her hand went out again, deep brown and long-fingered, feeling the air between us for some information I couldn't comprehend.

I laughed. "Not me."

"But this one obeys you?" She was studying us both intently.

"So he tells me." I turned to Richard, who nodded once, keeping his eyes down.

"You keep strange company, for one of the wolf kind."

I raised my brows. "So do you."

There was a shifting and a grunt of appreciative laughter from the four bears. Tamara glanced at them and cracked a smile. "A varied and interesting life brings varied and interesting company. True." She returned the crucifix to its place on the wall. "Very well. Now tell me, to what do I owe this visit? What has caused you to bring that thing into my presence?"

I looked at Richard. "Tell her."

Tamara interrupted. "I would rather that you tell me."

"All right. I hear you're one of the bunch that's up against the World Snake." They got still as I named the name. "Richard here tells me I'm in that fight, too. He tells me he has information that you need."

Tamara looked at me for a long moment. I was beginning not to like this bitch. "And you believed him?" she asked.

"He's not allowed to lie to me," I told her, though I was pretty sure he could find ways around that.

She smiled at my words. Obviously, she had the same reservations. "Let us hear this information. Reasonable people," she looked around, taking in the bears, "may then judge the value of the demon's words." She turned her cold glance on Richard. "You may speak."

"Hold on," I said, and asked Tamara, "First, tell me about the World Snake. Is it true that it's coming here? Do you know this? Because I heard it from him." I nodded at Richard.

Her face then looked as grave as it did strong. "Signs tell us she has turned. Many powerful adepts, whom I have learned to trust, have divined this, each in their own way. She has turned; she is moving this way." She cocked an eye at me. "You felt the earthquake?"

I nodded.

"Yes. This may well be her destination. That is what we fear. Do you know what comes of a visitation by the World Snake?"

I gestured to Richard. "He mentioned the names of some cities I never heard of. And one I do know that's gone, except I think it was an island: Atlantis."

"That's so." Her voice was strong and musical, despite the gravity of what she was telling me. "It is said that the Worm swallows cities, and no trace is left of their passing but human memory. We are taking what measures we can."

"Hah." One of the bears snorted, and she glared at him.

"The power raisers of this city are working together—" She shot a look at the bears, trying to figure out where the chortle had come from, but they were all looking up or down or away. She amended, raising her voice to make her point, "We are trying to work together in a meaningful way. Those who are able are raising barriers of deflection. Those who can do more are doing their utmost to send her away out to sea. According to legend, this was done successfully at least once before. Some are studying to find the means, or to make the means certain. Others are... doing what seems best to them." Another hard glance at the bears, but none of them had spoken. They might have been holding their breaths. She looked back at me. "Yes, to answer your question. The World Snake is coming here, unless something can be done to prevent it."

"All right," I said. "Then you need to hear this, too." I nodded to Richard.

Richard raised his head, and met her eyes as he spoke. "The Eater of Souls will come first," he told her. "Look for the signs. Look for the trail. Of the two of them, this one can cause the greater harm."

Tamara's expression gave nothing away. She continued to glare at him.

I said, "Is there a way of checking this out?"

"It would divert important resources but, yes, we can look into it."

Richard took a step toward her. His body radiated tension, and his voice was dead earnest when he spoke, but honestly, he was a pretty sight, with his fair hair just a little tangled at the ends, and his blue eyes darkly troubled in the face of her hostility. Part of me feasted on the sight of him, and part of me was pissed at the distraction.

"Whatever you think of me, Madam," he said, his voice low, "I am an enemy of the Eater of Souls. I know he is coming. I can feel it, and I know he is a herald of the World Snake. I can be useful in the fight against both of them. I have been, in the past. With these." He took out his tarot deck and laid it on the table.

She smiled then, in disbelief. "To help to save the city, you are going to read tarot for us?"

Before Richard could reply, there was a shifting around us. The bears caught each other's eyes and looked toward the back door. The really big one, that had a long face and huge hands, looked over at Tamara. "So... anything else you want us to stomp for you?"

She smiled at them and shook her head. "No. Thank you." She glanced at Richard and then said to me, rather pointedly, "I take it that my good friends may continue with their afternoon's leisure?"

I shrugged. The big one and two others were already on their way out. The scarred one called Jacob held his ground. His bear aspect had disappeared, but he was still awfully impressive as a

man. He was big, but there was a weight to him, a sense of con-
trolled power. He told me, "Out in the woods they are saying that
the wolf kind are missing a daughter."

My anger flamed. After all this time, and all my care, to face
betrayal now! I raised my head to look him in the eye. It was a
long way up. I thought of going with my sudden fury and growing larger, just to see what he'd do, but I realized it would take a
fair while to get as big as he was now. And anyway, he was a bear.
Bears get awfully big themselves. A wolf can take a bear, but it's
better not to try. So I said, "Oh? And will the wolf kind soon hear
of another place they should be looking?"

He smiled. "I don't think so. We bears know how to keep our
counsel. Not like some, who cry their business from the hilltops."

"It is said of the bears…" I began, stung.

"Yes?" His smile broadened, and he inclined forward to loom
over me.

"That they are graceful, courteous and brave," I finished.

"That is all true," he admitted gravely, straightening.

"And very vain."

He laughed, and the other bear in the doorway laughed, too.
Jacob lifted a hand to Tamara and went out.

Tamara motioned me to an empty chair and cleared a corner of
her huge table, piling a box of linen shawls on top of a stack of
catalogues on the counter behind her. She had dark brown skin
and an angular frame, and her every movement was precise, like
a dancer. She sat down in the chair on the other side of the table's
corner. She didn't offer a chair to Richard. He went to stand against
the counter behind my chair. Her face might have been a model for
one of the carved masks that hung in her store, with a heavy brow
and sculpted cheekbones. Her expressions were as precise as her
gestures. She was in her mid-thirties, but her eyes were older. She
looked me over now with professional thoroughness.

"This is a new occurrence, and full of omens: one of the wolf
kind with a demon in her service." She gave Richard another

long, hard look, and then asked me, "Where is he from? How did he come to you?"

I motioned to Richard to answer that question. He stepped up and began, "I was raised by the magician John Dee in 1583—"

Tamara head went back and she launched into a peel of laughter. "Dr. John Dee? Oh, no—"

"It is so," Richard replied stiffly.

"That amateur, that charlatan, that credulous old fool!" Tamara said when she could get out the words past her laughter. Finally she wiped her eyes. "So he did do it. He raised a demon."

"Or angel," Richard said, his chin lifting.

Her hand waved in the air at the detail. "Don't you know what you are?" She shook her head. "Oh, goodness. Wait till I tell my sisters. Oh dear. Wait till I tell my mother!" She looked at Richard a little more kindly. "And you've been stuck here ever since?" When he nodded in answer, she surmised, looking him over, "Then you came here to learn about yourself."

Now that made sense to me. I looked up at Richard. He stood still as a dog that's sighted game, so I could tell at once that he was interested, but he shook his head and answered her. "What I seek is protection from the Eater of Souls. Protection I will only gain if he is defeated."

She raised her brows at this, considering him. "And what you claim to offer us is what you may see in the cards?"

"It's more than that. These were given me by Dr. John Dee, who made them answer to me, so that I could answer to him. They will speak the truth to me of any question my master puts to me, present, past, and future. There are always questions that need answers, insights against the enemy it is useful to have."

Tamara lifted her hands, unbelieving. "But you are the Enemy!" she cried, pointing at him. "You are of the Enemy's get."

Richard flushed to his ears. He raised his eyes and met hers for once. "Then isn't it useful to know what the Enemy wants you to know?"

She considered for a moment, her head to one side. I said, "Isn't there a way to test what he's saying?"

Then she held out her hands for the cards. "Let me see your tarot deck."

He looked at me, and I nodded for him to hand them over. She glanced briefly at the pattern on the back, then she turned the cards over and spread them out on the table, now uncovering one, now covering another up again. She frowned at the medieval-looking paintings, their gaudy coloring, their seeming motion. She looked up at Richard. "What kind of deck is this?"

"It's based on one of the Lombardy copies," he answered.

She drew apart a couple of the face cards with two of her long fingers. "These were never in the Lombard deck."

"If I may?" Richard reached across the table, moved two cards aside to reveal one showing a bear holding a club, destroying some twisted creature on the ground. Strength, said the caption, in gothic lettering. Tamara stared at the bears, lifted the card from the table, stared at it again, then up at Richard.

"They change," Richard explained. "It's one of the ways they talk to me. Look." He drew out another. Against a background of stars, a dark-skinned woman in a blue robe, with cymbals in her hands, danced, eyes shut, above a precipice. The Priestess, the caption said. "I have never seen this aspect of the Priestess either, before today. And I have used this deck for four hundred years."

She took the card and gazed at it for a long moment. "Then by all means," she said at last, "you must do a reading." She let the card fall on the table.

Richard looked at me. "Sure," I said. "Go ahead."

He gathered up the cards while Tamara cleared a place at the table between us. When she finished, Richard rearranged the space for himself, making the clear place twice as large as she had. He shuffled the deck deftly despite the largeness of the cards, then handed the deck to Tamara.

"You must ask your question of the cards," he told her. "You may say it aloud or not, as you please. When you are ready, cut the cards and return them to me."

She cut the cards, turning them as she did so. She cut them again, pulled out a few cards, fed them into the deck in another place, her long fingers deft and precise. "How many times do I cut them?" she asked, smiling.

"You may cut them or shuffle them till Doomsday, if that is your wish."

Still smiling, she handed them back to him. Richard held them for a moment in both hands, and then began dealing them out, face down. He put one in the center of his space and crossed it with the other, then put one each up, down, right, left, saying, "In the name of the Father, and of the Son, and of the Holy Spirit—"

"Don't you blaspheme—" Tamara shot to her feet.

Richard stopped, the fourth card of the cross he was making on the table still in his hand. He said, in the same patient voice, "This is the way I was taught to do it."

She glared at him a long moment, then sat down again, lifting her hand for him to continue. He laid the fourth card, murmuring now under his breath, then laid two more to the right above the cross he had made, and two more to the left and below. When he finished he had three interlocking squares with a cross in the middle of it. He studied the pattern for a moment, then he said, "I'm sure you know how this works…"

She shook her head. "I've never seen the cards laid out that way before."

"It isn't very different. It's just the way I was taught." He lifted the center card and turned over the one under it, saying, "This represents the questioner—" He stopped, puzzled. It was not The Priestess, the dancer that he had showed her before, but a young woman with very dark skin, beautifully robed, her eyes downcast, pouring liquid from one jug to another in her hands. Temperance, said the inscription at the bottom of the card. Above her, there were bright stars in a dark blue sky.

Tamara was looking at the card with as much interest as Richard was. "Go on," she said. She then smoothed her face of all other expression.

Richard turned over the card that he had laid across the first. The Eight of Swords. "This is what crosses her. The card represents strife, a coming battle—"

"I know what the cards mean," Tamara interrupted. "Go on."

"I don't," I told them. I had a cousin who once experimented with tarot, so I'd seen a deck before, but I didn't know anything about interpreting them.

Richard answered obediently. "The first card is Temperance. It is supposed to represent the questioner. It means harmony, someone engaged in right action, in balance and what is good in the world." Tamara gave a little nod of agreement. "The second card is what is crossing the person, what is keeping them from what they want. The Eight of Swords represents strife, or war, or a battle to be fought." He turned over the card to the left. There was the dancing Priestess, finally. "This is what lies in the questioner's past, that is fueling the present question. The Priestess represents both knowledge attained and knowledge being sought." He hesitated a moment, looking at Tamara, then continued, turning over the bottom card of the first square. The Five of Swords. "This card represents a recent event that is propelling the problem asked by the questioner. The Five of Swords represents strife or a problem caused by an absence." He glanced at Tamara, but her face showed nothing, gave nothing away. He turned over the card to the right of the central card. It showed a pair of winged horses drawing a chariot across the sky. The Chariot, the gothic letters affirmed. Richard stood staring down at the card. "Difficulty and danger," he said. "Possibly during a journey. The position represents what lies in store for the questioner either in the present, or in the immediate future. This card—" he put his hand over the card at the top of the center square "—shows the outcome of the questioner's immediate problem." He turned over the card, revealing a picture of a tower being hit by lightning, its top exploding, and people falling out of it every which way. Cool! It was upside down. "The Falling Tower represents a cataclysm to the accustomed order, of a person, a government or an organization. Being reversed alters its meaning somewhat, so that it symbolizes an inability to effect positive change in a situation." He glanced over at Tamara, whose face was as expressionless as ever, but whose eyes showed she was caught up in the reading, full of thoughts. I could tell that this wasn't the sort of reading that was going to end with a journey over the water and a handsome stranger with a mind for love. I guess she could, too. "Should I continue?" Richard asked her.

She broke her concentration to glance up at him, lifting an impatient hand. "Yes. Please, go on."

Richard looked at me, and I nodded. He turned over the lowest card to the left. A smiling woman, crowned, sat on a medieval throne. In her right hand she held a staff. Her left hand was held out in just the gesture Tamara had made in trying to assess Richard's nature from the air. It may have been just because the cards were so old, but the woman seemed to have dark skin. "The Queen of Wands," Richard said. He glanced briefly at Tamara. "This is where the questioner stands at this time. A noble woman, gracious and good, powerful and kind." He turned over the card above and to the left of it. "This is the world the questioner dwells in at this time," he explained. It showed a sheaf of sticks, with a motto across the middle. It took me a moment to realize the letters were upside down. "The Nine of Wands, reversed. This card represents the expectation of adversity, soon to arrive. Reversed, the adversity becomes more difficult, or even impossible to overcome." He glanced at Tamara again, but continued without speaking. He reached to the upper right-hand card and turned it over. "This represents the hopes of the questioner, in the present situation." It was the Sun. Richard smiled at the card, and touched it with his fingertip. "The sun represents a victory. A glorious outcome." He reached up to the top card of the top right-hand square. "And this represents the outcome of the question taken as a whole." He turned over the card, and even I didn't need an explanation. It was a moment before Richard pronounced the word. "Death. Not necessarily the loss of life," he added quickly, "but failure, or a complete change of circumstances." He lifted one hand and made a gesture encompassing the whole layout of the cards. He said, with decision, "This is a clear and powerful reading, Madam, but it is not yours. For you to evoke such a strong reading on behalf of someone else, you must be deeply attached to her. This woman is strong in will, powerful in herself, young of heart, and closely allied to you, in craft and in blood. This is your mother, Madam, who is an ally of yours in a great battle soon to come. She hopes for a victory, through her wisdom, her strength, and that of her allies." He touched the final card again. "She will have a victory, one that she creates through her exertions, but not the one that she desires. Let us hope, for all our sakes, that it is not as bad as this." He touched the card representing Death, and then turned it over, out of our sight.

❧❦

CHAPTER SIX

Tamara gathered up the cards and folded them back into the deck. She sat shuffling the cards a moment, considering, then asked him, "Can you see so clearly into peoples' hearts without the cards? Can you see what card I am looking at now?" She turned the top card over and glanced down at it, shielding it with her long fingers. Richard looked quickly at me. I waited to hear what he would say. I wanted to hear this answer, too. Richard shook his head.

"I do what I am told," he said. "I was asked to read the cards, and I read them."

Tamara considered him for a moment, and then looked even more searchingly at me.

I said, "So, what can you tell us? About the World Snake, and the Eater of Souls? What should we do next?"

Tamara pushed the cards across the table toward Richard, who, when I nodded, put them away in his pocket. "I must have time," she said, "to meditate on the meaning of this new alliance. I must take council with my sisters as well." She said to Richard, "I will pass on your warning, and we will see what we can discover about the path of the Eater of Souls." She made a warding sign as she said the name. Then she rose, folding her arms. "Come back in a few days. I will have more to tell you then." When I started for the door, she stopped me. "One thing. You have not had him long, I think?" her gaze flicked to Richard, and back to me.

"That's right," I admitted.

She leaned forward, and I saw her grow, as I can grow when I'm angry, until her eyes seemed huge and commanding. "Be careful what you ask of him. Be very careful. And never, never give him a command that has no end to it."

I don't react well to other people chi-ing up on me. I was tasting her scent, musky and resonant, and for the first time I wondered if her blood was as sweet. Then she shook her head and sat back down. "Fools have wielded demons before."

I started walking back toward her, when she raised a conciliatory hand. "Sister, no offence. There is a demon, they say, that has been in a lake in Scotland for centuries, because his master told him to go fishing. He will be there to the world's end, I believe." She fixed me with her gaze again, but she didn't load it this time. "Be careful. You are dealing with more than you understand."

I shifted my weight. "All I know is, he makes a mean breakfast. Also…" I looked at Richard, waiting impassively by the door, his eyes lowered. "He doesn't like this Soul Eater thing, or the World Snake, either." Her fingers curled in a warding sign on each of the names. I almost smiled. "The first time he told me about them, I didn't believe a word he said, but now—"

She rose again, and for the first time took my hand in hers. "Believe. You may believe. I will discover all that I can for you. Come back in a few days, if you will. I will tell you then what I have learned."

She walked me to the door of her shop, and I lifted my hand to my nose and mouth surreptitiously and breathed in. She was being straight with me. I decided, for the most part, that I liked her all right.

Outside in the little courtyard, the four bears and their drummer friend were eating ice cream bars very tidily, and talking quietly together. Their heads came up and turned towards me as we emerged. They nodded to me. I nodded in return, and headed for the car. Richard hung back. He wasn't hard to read. This was not the outcome he'd been hoping for.

"What's wrong?" I asked him.

He shook his head, glancing again at the bears. "She will have more information for us in a few days. But we may not have days. We may not have hours. We don't know."

"All right. What do you want to do?"

"Talk to... others I couldn't talk to, when I didn't have my soul." His hand still lay protectively over his jacket pocket, where I knew the little bottle glowed safely. "There are scryers, diviners, wizards... " He looked me in the eyes. "Those who won't speak to me when I'm alone." He looked over at the bears again, who had resumed their seats on the patio. "They may know where I can..." He amended, "—where we can find someone called the Rag Man. He used to be on Wilshire, downtown, but he's been gone these many weeks."

"What's with the Rag Man?" I asked him.

"He's... he's under a curse. But he's the best scryer I've ever encountered."

Well, that sounded interesting. "All right," I agreed. "We'll go find the Rag Man."

I felt elation rise in me. We were on the hunt. It wasn't going to end in blood and fresh meat, but that was all right. Every hunt is practice for the next. I had hunted by myself for a long time, along crowded pavements that were the city's trails. This was better. I flashed Richard a smile, and caught his look of surprise.

The bears looked up politely when I walked over to them. Richard followed in my wake, close enough to hear, but far enough not to draw their full attention.

"Hey," I said. "Sorry to bother you again."

"No bother," the biggest one said, though he glanced askance back at Richard.

"I was wondering…" I realized then, I didn't know who the Rag Man was. I asked the first thing I thought of, instead. "Where are the lady bears?"

The four big men burst out laughing. The human looked up from his drum, smiling, but not quite sure what the joke was.

Jacob answered me, the laughter still in his voice. "This time of year, what with the cubs, and getting up so hungry, they really do not want us around."

The other bears shook their heads in agreement. "Mighty snappish, the ladies are, this time of year," the smallest of them added.

"Ah," I said, enlightened. I nodded back at Richard. "He wants to know where he can find a guy called the Rag Man."

"The Rag Man?" The human guy answered. "Oh, yeah." He tapped out a measure on his drum as he told us, "I know that guy. He reads the tea leaves, right?" He looked back at Richard, who nodded. "Yeah, they say he can read the stones in the gutter. Hell, I heard he can scry the wind."

"No one can scry the winds, Brother Ty," the biggest bear said gently.

"Well," said Brother Ty, "that's what I heard."

"Word is," Jacob said, "the Rag Man headed for the hills after the earthquake. You remember the earthquake?" He cocked an eye at me.

I nodded. Six point one on the Richter scale. No one forgets their first Los Angeles earthquake. "Nothing broke," I said, in the proper California style.

"Rag Man passed through here," the human guy said. "He was going on about something, you know how he gets. Wasn't till weeks later we realized, he was the first to figure it out." He looked up at me earnestly, and tapped his drum. "You know. What's coming?"

I nodded.

"He's out in the Valley," Jacob told Richard. "He hangs out at a little park near a car wash, over on Mission. You'll find him there most days."

Richard smile was true and sweet. That was new. He must really like the Rag Man, I thought. For a moment, I felt a little bereft.

Richard said, "There's a taqueria nearby?"

Jacob nodded, smiling back. "I see you know the man. There's one right across the street."

"Whereabouts on Mission?" I asked.

Jacob gestured northeast. "It's in Pomona."

"In Pomona?" Richard said.

"Yeah. You been there?" asked the bear.

"No," said Richard. The way he said it made me think he was lying.

We caught the 55 to the 57 and headed up to Pomona. You can't live happily ever after in L.A. if you don't like to drive. If the traffic is moving, it takes forty-five minutes to get just about anywhere in the city. If it's not, well, there's no point in thinking about it.

"So tell me more about this Rag Man," I said to Richard. He was staring out the window, looking away from me, but his attention came back at once.

"He's a scryer, as the little bear said."

"That wasn't a bear!" I told him. "The four big guys, they were bears."

"Pardon me," he said politely, but there were teeth in the words. I showed him mine.

"Where did you meet this guy?"

Richard's glance slid away from me. There were things he didn't want me to know about him. I wondered why. "I was on the streets now and then, in the last year. Before I lost my soul, he was kind to me." He shook his head. "He has dreams. He sees visions. Sometimes one can read some sense into them. He is the one who told me that to find help, I had to climb the hill. He described it well enough so that, in time—I hope, in time—I found the right hill."

"He sent you to the Wiccans?"

"He sent me to the sorceress."

"Who gave you to me."

"Just so."

"And I'm supposed to help."

He smiled wryly. "So I must hope."

"Me too," I said, sincerely. "What do you want him to scry now?"

He paused a moment. I tried to decide if he was prevaricating, or thinking about my question. "He may be able to tell us where the greatest danger lies, what to do, what especially not to do."

"Can he tell us when the W—" I glanced over as he started to wince, "—the Worm is coming?"

He shook his head. "Time is all one thing, from a certain perspective. One can as easily map a single wave in the sea." He paused, and added, "Unless it's now. He could tell if it is imminent."

"And that's what you want him to scry?"

He shrugged. "He can sense the shifting of forces. He may give us questions, and the answers may lead us where we would not otherwise have gone. He was helpful in the past. After I lost my soul—" Again, he made that protective gesture over his jacket pocket. "I went to see him, and he, well, he sounded crazy. He looked right through me. He saw what I was."

"What did he say you were?" I asked, curious.

Richard answered unwillingly. "He said I was darkness."

I had a visceral moment of remembering his scent when the sword touched his head, and the sight of the swirling, unknowable form. He'd been a lot more than just darkness. I tended to forget that, when he was just sitting next to me. His scent, in his human form, had a pleasant tang. I was getting used to it.

Then it occurred to me that he had not given me a straight answer about why he wanted to talk to the Rag Man. That made the meeting we were going to that much more interesting. I decided to leave it at that, and asked him, "Why does Tamara think you're dangerous?" We fled along the fast lane with the flow of traffic at eight miles over the speed limit. "Why did she want to kill you out of hand? And the sorceress the other night, she thought she should kill you, too."

He took a moment before he answered, his voice light. "Many of my kind are said to have been able to do great works."

"Great works like...?"

"Setting the world on fire."

I took my eyes off the road for a moment. "Literally?"

He nodded, jerking his chin towards the road ahead at the same time. I swerved back between the white lines. Then I said, "And you? Done any great works in your time?"

He stared straight ahead. "I think shoveling shit for a century could qualify as a minor great work. I could probably qualify for the *Guinness Book of World Records*."

"She was afraid of you," I said, thinking aloud. "And there were moments when she was afraid of me, and I hadn't given her reason." I glanced again at Richard. "When I was leaving, she gave me a warning. Should I be afraid of you?"

He shrank just perceptibly in his seat. "No," he said. "I've told you—"

"Was John Dee?"

"John Dee was so afraid of me he kept me suspended in a cage in his cellar for the first two years of my existence in this world, with bars that he blessed twice a day with holy water."

I thought about that for a second. "And did that keep you in the cage?"

"No!" his eyes glinted. "What kept me in that cage was that he had told me not to leave it."

I slowed briefly as an idiot passed me on the right, and cut in front of me. "But he let you out, eventually."

"Yes. He let me out when he found I couldn't tell him the formula for turning base metals into gold. He got me those cards, and I did readings for him. But readings were common in those days. When he tired of that trick, he gave me to his daughter. As I told you."

I'd thought of a more important question. "Can you be killed? Can I kill you?"

He shrugged. "It doesn't change anything."

"What do you mean?" Did the car swerve just then? Did it seem to be heading straight for the truck that shouldn't have been in the second lane next to us? He didn't tense. I straightened us out again.

After a moment, he said with precision, "If you hit that truck, or if that ass in the SUV behind us that's riding your tail crawls over this car and sends it into the median wall, and I'm killed, I'll wake up again a little ways down the road a few moments later, with my body as fresh and new as the day John Dee first called me up." He gave me another glance. "All scars and wear gone."

"Have you been killed before?" I let the car slow down gradually, until the SUV jerk behind me went nuts, and passed me on the right with a roar and a few rude gestures. He almost didn't make the gap ahead to pull in front of me.

Richard answered me when the little drama was over, letting his breath out. "I've been killed four times that I remember. And I've died twice."

"That you remember?"

"I think," he said, his voice low, "that I don't always remember."

"How did you die?"

"Once of hunger," he answered. "Once of the plague. That wasn't bad. It stops hurting as soon as you fall unconscious. Hunger's worse. It takes forever."

"And how were you killed?"

"The drayer I worked for beat me over the head with an iron bar one day when he was drunk and things weren't going well for him. That was the first time I died. I thought, when it happened, that that would set me free. But then I woke up again, in the same stable. He got rid of me quick, after that. He remembered what he'd done, and he couldn't find the mark. He didn't like that."

"And the other times?"

There was a little silence before he answered. When I glanced over at him, he was studying me. I raised an enquiring brow.

"I told one of my masters that killing me made me whole again. He did it twice. He knifed me the first time just to find out. He gave me poison the second time."

When he didn't finish, I prompted, "Why?"

His voice was low. "I'd gotten a skin disease. He'd given it to me, but he didn't like it. So he cured me."

"Ah." I thought for a moment. "That would be the earl?"

"That's right."

"I hope he died hard," I said.

"No such luck," Richard said, but his voice was lighter. "In his bed, at a ripe old age, with me at his feet."

"Damn. Makes you want to believe in Hell."

"Oh, I do," said Richard fervently.

I counted. "And the fourth time you were killed? What was that?"

There was a long silence. I looked over at him, and he was staring straight ahead, his jaw working. He looked pale. "Richard?" I said.

He looked at me, and his eyes looked so weary that for a second I felt sorry I'd asked. But he was already answering. "The fourth time… that was the Eater of Souls."

He looked out the window, and I decided not to ask him anymore just then.

We got off on Mission to look for the car wash, and almost at once I felt a surge of energy. "Whoa!" I said, as we crossed it. "Did you feel that?"

I looked over at him. He'd gone white. "That… was a very strong ward."

"Someone around here is sure scared of something."

"Someone who knows what they're doing," he agreed. His hand was over his jacket pocket. "I couldn't cross that ward, before I had this."

I glanced at him. "Someone worth talking to?"

"If you please."

"We'll look around, later," I said. The idea of someone that strong marking territory anywhere near mine got my hackles up. I had to know who it was. I had to see what they were made of.

We trolled along until we found the dollar car wash with the little park next to it. There was an eye-searingly colorful play structure in one corner. Next to the car wash some old trees leaned heavily over a couple of picnic tables. I passed it up, turned down the next street, and parked. I opened my mouth slightly as we walked through the heavy grass toward the picnic tables. I itched to change and get a better sense of what I was smelling. An old lady was walking her two little pugs along the edge of the park, where a hedge divided it from the dilapidated front of a tire store. The dogs stopped to snuffle deeply along the ground. I shook my head.

"Is something wrong?" Richard asked me.

"If those little dogs start digging," I told him, "we're going to have half a dozen police cars here in no time."

He looked across the park. Fortunately, the old lady was dragging her little darlings away. "What is it?"

"There's a body down there," I told him. "A human."

"What should we do?" Richard asked.

"Let it rest," I told him. "It's old. Maybe as old as this park. Where's your guy?"

When the lady and her pugs had trotted off, there was no one but us in the park. I sat on the bench while Richard crossed the street and went in to the little twenty-four-hour grocery and taqueria on the corner. He came back a short while later with two bags of food and half a dozen bottles of water. He opened one bag and laid out napkins and a big burrito for each of us, and I was suddenly hungry.

I was halfway through my beef burrito when I noticed the guy hovering behind us. I stiffened, and glanced over at Richard. I hadn't felt the guy coming up to us. And that was really annoying. It wasn't like the burrito was that good. I'm not usually an easy stalk. I wondered if the guy was just that hard to sense.

Richard was slowly unpacking the second bag, piling wrapped-up burritos and a couple of tacos on a napkin. The guy smelled gritty, and fearful. He was hesitant, poised for flight. He was not a predator. I finished my burrito. As I was wiping my fingers the Rag Man came around and slipped onto the bench across the table and a little ways down, smiling and nodding. Richard gently pushed the napkin with the food toward him, and the guy lit into it.

He was lean and weathered, with lank stringy hair under a knit cap, a long face, and a straggly beard. I couldn't tell how old he was. He wore layers of clothes from which rose a fascinating array of odors. I looked at him in appreciation while he fitted food into his mouth in efficient bites and chewed quickly. His hands were stiffly wrapped in rags, leaving only the fingers protruding. Then I noticed the traces of smells coming from his hands. Burned flesh, oozing sores, old and new blood. I opened my mouth slightly and breathed in.

"He's hurt," I said to Richard quietly.

Richard lifted his hand slightly, glancing over with a look that asked me to let this meeting play out. All right, I thought. I sat back and waited to see why we were talking to the Rag Man.

"So Stan, hey Stan, long time," the Rag Man said to Richard. He picked at the bits of lettuce and cheese left on his burrito wrapper. He slid a glance at me, and stopped. He stared, frowning hard. "Uh…" He moved his head closer, then raised a hand over one eye. "Uh, ma'am. No offense. Do you have two heads?"

Well, that was one way to put it. "Yes."

"Yeah. All right."

He kept staring at me, shifting from side to side. I damped down my passion. I closed off my senses. I drew in my spirit, the way we learned to when they bussed us over the hill to middle school, where people didn't know what we were. "Better?"

He stopped moving, and just stared, just above my head. "I saw them, right?"

"You saw them," I agreed.

"Okay. Okay. So, Stan, you found her, then. I told you—" He leaned forward. "I told you danger would walk by your side." He nodded, sat back, and his eyes slid to me again. "No offense, ma'am."

I nodded. I do like respect.

Richard looked startled. That was fun. "You told me—"

"You were running to danger, and would walk by its side. There you go." He picked up the wrapper from one of his tacos and began to shred it into narrow strips.

"Then she's the right one?" Richard sounded relieved.

"Just don't let her take you home to her folks." The Rag Man was still, staring at his fingers. They twitched. I was possessed of a brief vision of me walking in the door with Richard in tow, and all the heads turning to look at him, and scent him. Yes, that would be a problem. I almost laughed. The Rag Man shook himself, glanced at me. "Just don't do it."

"Okay." I looked quizzically at Richard. He didn't get it either.

The Rag Man pointed at Richard with both hands. "The last time I saw you…"

"It was on Wilshire. I looked for you later, but you had gone."

"Oh, yeah, I am so out of there. That place is history, man, I told you. I saw you there. I saw…" The Rag Man's eyes changed, and for a moment he seemed to stare into another world. "Darkness," he breathed. He looked up at Richard again. "You… I saw…"

Richard, his hand over his jacket pocket, smiled at the Rag Man, and seemed to be trying to look as harmless, as normal, as human, as he possibly could. "I'm fine now," he told the guy gently. "I was sick."

"I know what I saw," the Rag Man said.

"Look at me," Richard insisted. "I'm better now. I'm just the same."

The Rag Man didn't look at him. He gathered up the strips he'd made and began meticulously to shred them into tiny squares. "What do you want, Stan?"

Richard said quietly, "You left after the earthquake. I just wanted to know why."

The Rag Man looked up, surprised. "You know why! The Worm, she's coming. Man, I had to get out of there, that's like, prime target uno, that's where she's heading for."

"Will it be soon?"

"I don't know. Time..." He tried to make a shape with his hands, as though to illustrate his point. "Time isn't real. It moves. You can't nail that down." He stirred the little squares he'd made. "But where she's coming, I seen that."

Richard said to me, "He can scry anything. He scryed a handful of glass once, on the sidewalk."

"No, no, not like that. I'll show you. I can show you. You can see it. Anyone can see it." He got up, brushing a handful of his little paper squares into a pocket of his coat. He pointed to a shallow hill rising to the east. "Up there."

Richard let the Rag Man into the backseat of my car, which annoyed me. I don't like someone I don't know hanging out that close behind me. He rode leaning right up between us, pointing the way. Good thing I like a lot of strong smells.

As we drove toward the ridge, heading north, we passed through that surge of energy again. "Wow!" the Rag Man said, like he'd hit a blast of cold water on a hot day. Richard leaned back hard in his seat.

"What was that?" I asked the Rag Man.

"Comes from the church back over there. I don't know how they do it. They got them all around."

"The church?" Richard said. "What church?" He turned around to the Rag Man, his voice sharp. I looked at him, and he subsided.

"I don't know," the Rag Man said. "You know, the one with the tower."

"It may be the parish boundaries," Richard told me. "They used to ward the parish against evil, back in the day. I didn't know anyone was still doing that." I heard the suggestion in his voice.

"We'll go talk to them," I said.

We headed uphill on a road that wound up to a reservoir through a county park. I stopped when we got to a tollgate.

"No, no, not that way," the Rag Man said. "Turn right, up there."

Further up the hill on the right we came to another gate. As we drove up to it, the Rag Man was unrolling the backseat window on my side. A big, heavy-set guy in sunglasses came out of the booth, but before he could speak, the Rag Man leaned out his window.

"Hey, man, it's just me, I want to show these guys something." And darned if the big guy didn't wave us through.

There was a tingling of energy up there on the hill. The grass was green and manicured, and everywhere, in neatly marked spaces, divided by perfect green lawns, were parked big, handsome, clean, new RVs. "Someone's been doing a working," I said, tasting the air.

"Oh, yeah," the Rag Man said. "They've been up here for months, these guys. Heilige Arbeiters, they call themselves. The Holy Workers. There's been a gathering every night."

We passed a few heavy-set, slow-moving men and women grouped beside barbecues or stretched out in deck chairs. They were dressed like people on vacation from somewhere else. They looked up when we drove by, but then lost interest when the Rag Man waved and called out a greeting. Some of them waved back. A few of them smiled.

We got out on the far side of the park and stood on the verge where the hill dropped away, and we could see across the great bowl that held greater Los Angeles. And if the air weren't so hazy, we could have seen all the way to the ocean.

"There," the Rag Man said. "I saw it in my dreams. I saw it in the fire. I saw it in my goddamn oatmeal, for God's sake. This hill. This view. So finally I found this place, and this is what I saw." He pointed down to the foot of the hill. "Waves crashing right down there. And out there..." His arm swept across the greater Los Angeles basin. "The ocean. No city. Nothing left. The bottom of this hill—that's going to be her bite mark."

Richard and I took in the view. That was going to be a lot of missing city. That Worm had one enormous bite.

"You saw it more than once?" Richard asked.

"Over and over. I came up here, I recognized the view. Check it out, man. From here, down that way, all along that ridge down to Diamond Bar and the Chino Hills, this is going to be the new coast line." He held up his hands. "Why do you think I stayed out here, hanging out in old Pomona? Come on!"

I looked across at the farther ridgeline and realized, "There've been workings up there as well."

"Oh, yeah," the Rag Man said. "The Holy Workers here, the Air Dragons up along there, and Eddie Mack's tai chi group down that way. All along the high points, they're all doing their thing."

"Can they deflect her?" Richard asked.

"They might. Sure, they could. But there's folks up north along the coast working for the Worm to swallow L.A. and leave their cities alone. The Buddhists up on Mt. Baldy are chanting all the time these days, but no one can figure out what they're trying to do. Maybe they just don't know. And the folks here aren't working stop her. They're just trying to keep the Worm from going any further inland than here. And guess who they're drawing some of their power from? Guess!"

I sensed the air, the remnants of currents, and the patterns that lay on the currents, still in motion from recent workings. "These people are drawing some of their power from the magic users in

L.A."

"Not just them," the Rag Man added.

"Huh," I said. "No wonder the bears were laughing."

"Power wielders working together," Richard said. "That would be a miracle."

I stared out over the city that was my home. The city I had chosen. I could, after all, just start driving. I've heard Colorado is really nice. But here, in this city, I was still in my family's greater territory. Once I left California, if I staked out territory on some other pack's mountain, I wasn't going to be anonymous anymore. Also, my chances of survival might not be very high. Besides. I'd claimed territory here, in this city, and it's not in my nature to give that up without a fight. Not without doing whatever it takes. Not, in fact, at all.

"So what do we do to save her?" I asked. "How do we beat the World Snake?"

The Rag Man shook his head. "That's what they keep asking me. And I look and I look, and all I see is darkness. Deep, strange darkness." He turned and looked at Richard. "Like I saw in you."

"Look again," Richard asked him earnestly. "Please. Not for the Worm," he added, as the Rag Man shook his head. He stepped closer to the man and dropped his voice. "Look for the Eater of Souls."

"Oh," said the Rag Man. "That."

"I must know if it is coming. I must know... if I am to be taken."

He gave a side-long glance at me, and I had the answer to my question. This is why we were consulting the Rag Man. The city was on the verge of being annihilated, but what Richard wanted to know about was his own personal fate. The Eater of Souls must have done quite a number on Richard. Besides killing him, at least once.

"All right, yeah. I'll do it."

The Rag Man walked to the very edge of the hill and sat down.

Richard sat down next to him. The cards said my fate was bound up with that of the city, and Richard's was bound to me, so I followed them and sat down on the Rag Man's other side, to learn what the Rag Man would discover.

A little ways down the hill, the green, watered, manicured grass of the RV park gave way to the brown of the California hillside, shaved down already for the fire season. The Rag Man sat with one knee up, plucked the seed heads of some dead grass blades, and gathered them in his hand. Richard and I watched as he reached into his pocket and added a pinch of the little paper squares from his lunch. He didn't seem to be doing a working. He wasn't raising any energy. I looked over at Richard, and he met my look briefly, meaning for me to be patient, wait, watch. Well. That's one thing my kind can do, no problem.

The Rag Man felt in his various pockets and added another pinch of something small and green. Rosemary leaves, I knew at once from the smell. The Rag Man reached out to Richard with a smiling query, and Richard bent his head for the Rag Man to pluck a single short yellow hair. He turned the little concoction over and over in his hands, stirred it with his fingers, shook it in both hands, and then opened them.

The wind picked up a few of the papers and blew them away. Some of the rosemary dropped between his fingers. It took me a moment to realize the Rag Man had stiffened, and sat glassy eyed, staring into his hands.

"Oh," he said, "oh oh oh shit, oh shit oh shit," and his handful of telltales burst into flames between his palms. I leaped back and started to change, to land on four feet, but stopped myself. The burst of flame was gone. The Rag Man was yelling, "Ow ow ow," and patting the rags that covered his hands, which stank of new ooze and new charred flesh and cloth. He unwrapped the ragged bandages.

I landed on two feet and one hand, the other one held out as though to ward something off. I said, "What the fuck was that?"

"You tell me!" the Rag Man wailed. "You tell me! It happens all the time. Sometimes I wake up and it's happened. Sometimes I'm not even looking." He peeled off the inner layer of bandages, wincing as he revealed fresh pink oozing burns on the palms of his hands. "Ow!" he said, with emphasis. He looked at Richard accusingly as he pulled a couple new fairly clean cloths from various pockets, and began to wrap his hands up again.

Richard picked up the discarded cloths, unperturbed. "What did you see? The Eater of Souls, is he coming?"

"Don't go looking," the Rag Man said. "It's here."

∞

CHAPTER SEVEN

Some of the Holy Workers stopped us on our way out and asked the Rag Man to stay with them that night. We left him popping a tall beer and choosing between barbecues, and drove on back down the hill. We were looking for the church with the tower that sat at the center of these wards.

I drove back the way we had come until we crossed that ward again, which made Richard sit up. I turned right at the next major intersection, intending to hone in on the source of the wards.

"I've heard of this parish," Richard said, bracing himself against the seat.

"Oh, yeah?"

"There's a story. A priest from this parish, a long time ago, made a pact with one of my kind, thinking to use the power to do good. They found him out, and he was sent away."

"The demon?"

"No, the priest."

"You think it's true?"

Richard shrugged. "Someone has set—" He tensed as we passed over another one. I made another turn. "Someone knows enough

84

to set very powerful wards. It may be the priest, or it may be someone else who has studied the disciplines."

"So we should ask him how you can get yourself free." I felt his surge of hope. I wondered why the fear was rising in him as well.

I pulled into the parking lot of St. Joseph's Church. It wasn't hard to spot. The tiered white bell tower stood three stories high. The church was held up by big square pillars on either side, with a high round window at the top.

I parked the car and turned to Richard. "What's wrong?"

"He may be a very powerful magician."

"Isn't that the point? To find out what they know?" He said nothing, but he didn't look happy. "You think he's going to hurt me?" I meant it as a joke.

"He could, if he's that strong."

"Oh, yeah?" Then I figured it out. "You think he could get a hold on you?"

Richard said lightly, "It is possible he may know more of me than I know of myself. It's how I came to grief the last time, seeking help from a magician. I was caught in one of his demon traps."

"I thought what we were looking for is people who can tell us more about you. Isn't that why you wanted to speak to Madam Tamara?"

He shook his head. "Madam Tamara is well-known as a woman who is wise and good. This ward-maker could be anyone of power, but without wisdom or virtue."

"That's possible."

"Don't let them take me from you."

Ah, I thought. There it is. I smiled at him. "Don't worry. I won't." We got out, and he followed me across the grass to where the steps led up to the big church doors. I didn't think for a second that I was the one who might be in any danger. They say you learn something new every day. If you live.

"So you think this old priest is the one doing the wards?" I asked.

"If he was able to deal with a demon, he must be a powerful magician."

"Has anyone asked him how to deal with the—" I shot a glance at Richard, and refrained from saying the names. "The problems that we're looking at?"

Richard shrugged. "I don't know. But if the Eater of Souls is here, any powerful magician must know of it. He may know how to fight it, and how to turn the World Snake." He met my glare. "This is holy ground. Evil is already being turned aside. The names may be named here."

I did not bite him. But I gave him a look so he knew I'd thought about it. He dropped his eyes.

There were three sets of huge arched double doors into the church. I pushed open the first one we came to and stepped in to a big stone-paved lobby. Richard reached for the bowl of holy water and crossed himself, as a cheerful voice called to us from one of the inner doorways.

"Hi! Can I help you?" A girl with long black hair fastened back with a couple of barrettes, wearing jeans and a little white shirt, was staring at Richard. She had a bucket and a rag, and had been wiping down the glass windows in the doors between the lobby and the nave.

I watched Richard switch on the charm as he walked up to her, smiling a delicious smile. "We're looking for Father Joseph. Can you tell us where we can find him?"

"Father Joseph?" Her smile switched off like a light, and she looked around, as though seeking back-up. "Uh… I'm not sure…"

"Perhaps," Richard suggested gently, "there is someone who can tell us where Father Joseph may be found?"

"Can I help you?" The girl turned with relief as another woman came into the lobby through the door the girl had been polishing.

"Oh, Sister Catherine, please. These people are asking after Father Joseph."

"Father Joseph?" Sister Catherine turned bright eyes and a

beatific smile on the both of us. She had short fair hair and wore a high-necked sweater and a gray pleated skirt. "Why do you want to see Father Joseph? He's retired, you know." Her manner was gentle and welcoming, but there was a watchful core of steel in her. She wore a filigreed silver crucifix around her neck.

Richard opened his mouth, probably to lie, I thought, so I stepped in. It's much better to go on the offensive.

"He's not allowed visitors?" I suggested.

"Well, of course…" Sister Catherine glanced at her little helper, who caught the hint and went back to wiping the glass.

"Do you think he wouldn't want to see us?" I pressed.

Sister Catherine's smile reasserted itself. "Of course he'll be happy to see you." She looked over at the girl now industriously wiping away at the glass window, and decided to be cooperative. "Come with me. I'll show you where he is."

She took us back outside and around the side of the church, walking with small steps in her sensible shoes. There was a guy clipping the grass around a statue of the Virgin Mary, where offerings and flowers had been piling up for weeks, it seemed. She greeted him graciously but without pausing.

Behind the church was a heavy rectangular building, with curtains in the second story windows. A locked gate led into a short, dark passageway hung with shovels and brooms and other gardening paraphernalia. She took us through into a walled garden that hugged the side and back of the residence. Ancient rose beds were pruned to the quick all along the walls. In the middle of the garden, framed by a square of lawn, an old man dozed in a big straw chair on a sunlit patio. Beside him was a table holding a teapot, and some plates. He's been eating scones. With butter. Sister Catherine signed us to wait, walked quietly up to him, and bent to speak in his ear.

He started awake, and turned to look at us. He was dressed in traditional black robes, and a wide-rimmed black hat shaded his face. His eyes widened when he saw us, and he rose hastily from his chair, grasping the back for support, seeming to grow as he stood up. He reached out with one hand, groping for his stick with the other, and started toward us.

"Boy!" he said. "You, boy! Come here!"

Richard glanced at me, and then walked over to the priest, who grabbed him by the shoulder and thrust him behind him, and pointed his stick at me. "Avaunt ye! Thing of evil! Hence from this holy place!" His voice was growing stronger as he gathered his power.

"Father Joseph? Father Joseph!" Sister Catherine admonished him ineffectually.

The priest brandished his staff, standing between Richard and me. "Thou monster of darkness! I say ye depart, or I will call down upon you such forces—"

Sister Catherine hurried back to me apologetically. "I'm so sorry, I don't think this is a good time—"

"Sister, step away! Creature of darkness! Be gone!" He pushed Richard back again as he made to come forward, and pointed his staff at me again. He was raising a lot of power. This church had stood for a long time, and the daily rituals, woven into the very air day after day for what felt like a hundred years, was a well that he was drawing on to increase his power. The hair on the back of my neck rose as he began slowly to walk toward me.

That's when I realized that the wards we had crossed were raised against me. Well, not exactly against me, but that I was included in the things he'd raised the wards against. The rage rose in me. What an idiot! What was it he was seeing when he looked at me that made him think I was one of the bad guys? I'd put on a clean shirt, after all. I'd combed my hair. I felt myself grow larger and I advanced to straighten him out about a thing or two concerning me, and evil, and which was which, and that's when Sister Catherine whacked me from behind with a shovel.

All right, I hadn't seen it coming. And I'd let her get behind me.

But I felt the wind of it as it came and leaped forward as it struck. I landed and turned and leaped on her, grabbed the shovel and bore her back until she ran into the wall, and if she saw me change from the time I turned to the time I grabbed the shovel, well, it was her job to rationalize it. I didn't have to explain anything.

"What the fuck?" I exclaimed, in righteous anger. "What the fuck was that?"

Sister Catherine's mouth was opening and closing, "I...."

I smiled at her. It was not one of my nice smiles. It was, in fact, one with teeth in it. There are times when I look like I have a lot more teeth than I ought to. This was one of those times.

Sister Catherine had been praying and moldering over evil probably for her entire life. Well, if I was what she thought evil was, then she was going to get a bellyful. Her eyes grew very wide, staring in to mine, and then she dragged them away and shrieked, "Father!"

"Let her go!" The priest roared, advancing, his staff raised against me, shaping the power he held to pinion me. I was shaping to change, twist out of it, and bite his leg. Maybe his thigh. Hell, maybe his groin. Then Richard was between us.

"Father Joseph, please. She's with me, it's all right. She's with me."

"Then make her get back! Make her let the Sister go!"

I turned yellow eyes on the priest. Richard was holding the father's shoulder, keeping him away from me. The priest probably thought Richard was protecting me from his righteous wrath, or his staff, or his magic, or all three, but I knew Richard was holding the priest back so that his blood would not be spraying the floor in another moment. Richard moved to block my gaze and meet it with his own.

"Lady," he said, "Amber, please."

I became aware that Sister Catherine was mewling beside me. I lowered the shovel, whose blade I happened to have pointing at her throat.

"Father Joseph," Richard said earnestly, and I was aware at once that he was going to lie his head off. "We have come to consult you regarding the mysteries that we have heard you are wise in. This is Amber, and we have—private, personal matters to discuss with you. She's not dangerous—"

Hah!

"She came here with me, and I promise you, we aren't going to do any harm."

I noted with interest that he hadn't said I was promising anybody anything.

The priest's power was leaking away. He faltered, and Richard held him steady. He looked Richard in the face. "My son?"

Richard looked up at him, beautiful as an angel. "Father, please help us. We need your counsel."

"I haven't done anything," I put in judiciously. I made sure my voice was a little outraged, which wasn't hard. "She hit me with a shovel!" And, out of the eye line of the priest, I smiled at Sister Catherine really hard, because, you know, I could.

The priest turned back to me. I saw his certainty falter. He grasped his staff convulsively, and then it was only a cane to help an old man to walk without stumbling.

"We just want to talk," Richard continued, using his voice to weave a kind of spell of his own. "We heard that you might be able to help us."

"Father Joseph—" Sister Catherine began.

He held up a hand. "I will help you if I can, my son," he said. "Sister Catherine, thank you. You may go."

"But Father—"

I stayed on the offensive. "We came to ask Father Joseph a few questions. Is that some kind of crime?"

"Please," Father Joseph held out his hand. "Forgive me. I acted hastily. And Sister Catherine is very sorry for what she did. Aren't you, Sister?"

Sister Catherine was still staring at me. "But—she—I saw—"

I looked at her and let my eyes go gold. My head didn't hurt yet, but I could feel where it was going to. Sister Catherine choked and stopped talking. Then I looked away and very kindly stopped smiling.

"It's all right," Father Joseph said. "You may go, Sister. I'll be a few minutes with these young people."

"Perhaps I should stay and—"

He said to us, "Please come and sit down, and we will talk. You won't be assaulted again." He waved Sister Catherine out of the garden. We heard her shoes clicking on the stones as she hurried away. By then my eyes were mostly green again. Father Joseph looked right at me, and right through me, and I was pretty sure he knew exactly what he'd seen. He moved toward his chair and stumbled a little, and Richard took his arm. The priest said, "Thank you, my son." He opened his hand. "Will you come and sit?"

Father Joseph resumed his chair. Richard brought another chair from near the wall and set it across from the priest's. He was going to stand there holding it for me until I pointed, and made him get another one for himself.

Father Joseph looked at me warily. "Have you come to me for help? Are you under a curse?"

Oh, those myths! I shook my head. "No, thanks, I'm fine."

"I know what I saw," he said. "You cannot deceive me. And yet…" He lifted his hand toward me, with that gesture Tamara had made when trying to suss out Richard. "Who are you?"

He meant, what was I? I told him, "I'm called Amber. He's called Richard, and he's the one who wants to ask you some things."

Reluctantly, Father Joseph turned his attention to Richard. He was shrunken with exhaustion, now that the power had left him. He sank back in his chair. His face was long, and his features stood out beneath his wizened skin. His brows were heavy, his nose long and bent partway. His mouth was habitually tight, habitually turned down, but his eyes were knowing and unafraid.

His large hands gripped the arms of his chair. "What do you wish to ask me?"

Richard shot a quick glance at me, and then said to him, "A hundred years ago there was a priest who, it is said, was a great student of the ancient arts. He studied so deeply that he thought he could make a pact with a demon, and bind its power to use against evil, against itself."

Father Joseph's head went back in his chair as Richard spoke. "Oh," he said, "oh, is that story still told?" He put his hand on his brow.

"It is said," Richard continued, "that the demon turned tables on the priest, so it was the priest who was bound, never to leave this world, until the demon should release him." Richard waited a moment until Father Joseph lowered his hand again. "Is it true?"

"No," the priest said. His voice became firm, admonishing. Funny to hear him sound so certain when, of course, he was lying. "Of course not. Devils are simply a metaphor for the evil Man finds on this Earth. But the greatest battle each of us must fight is against the evil within ourselves." He shot me a look then, which I did not appreciate.

Richard shook his head impatiently. "There are worlds that exist beyond our own, as numerous as the bubbles in the sea. And some of the denizens of these worlds can cross over from one to another, especially when a way is made for them, especially when they are called by name."

Father Joseph laughed. "Oh, my son, you've been reading too much."

I said, "Then what did you think you saw when you looked at me?"

The priest stopped smiling. I met his gaze, but he didn't look away.

Richard said, "There have been those who have called demons into their service. Many great scholars in the past—"

"No," the priest interrupted him, waving his hand. "Vanity!

Pride! Those who traffic with the demon kind learn to their cost: all the studies of a lifetime cannot stand between them and the darkness, the power of the darkness." He shook his head, banishing inner visions of his own, and looked over at Richard. "Do you know why you do not find demon wielders on this Earth? Because the evil they call forth consumes them."

"But you survived."

"Oh, my son…" He closed his eyes, and pressed his head back against his chair. "It did not eat me because it was too busy laughing at me."

"I need to know," Richard told him, "not how to call a demon, but how to dismiss one."

That got the priest's attention. "How's that?" he asked sharply.

Richard leaned forward toward the priest. "There is a demon trapped on this Earth. It has no powers to speak of, but because it was ineptly raised, it is bound here until the world ends, and perhaps beyond."

"Oh, that," the priest said. He leaned back again. "I've heard of it. The one in Loch Ness."

"No," said Richard, reaching to touch his jacket pocket.

The priest continued, "That was a bad business. But as long as the demon is held harmless, it doesn't matter how long it is here, does it? We needn't worry about it."

"It matters to him," Richard said darkly.

"Do not meddle with such matters," the priest's voice sharpened. He looked at me. "You have meddled in the dark arts enough already. Abjure it! For your soul's sake." He glared again at Richard. "Leave the demon kind to their own devices."

"I only wish to know—" Richard tried.

"You do not know what you're asking. You don't know what could happen. Do you know how long it was before they let me out of that monastery? Before they let me speak again? Before I was allowed to return to this parish that I swore to defend?"

"Against what?" I asked. I was wondering if the World Snake

had been on its way for a long time.

His eyes shot to me again, and his voice dropped. "I was a fool. I thought the devil was coming here in his legions from China. The Chinese, you see, there were so many of them. Raise a devil to fight a devil, I thought! They were so different. They had such strange magic..." He shook his head. "Now, of course, one realizes..." He gave a ghost of a smile. "I was a fool. Don't you be one."

"Father Joseph!" Sister Catherine's voice called across the garden. She had opened the double doors to the house and was advancing upon us with half a dozen others. Four were nuns in traditional habits, one was the gardener we'd passed earlier, and one was a security guard. "Father Joseph, it's time for you to come in." She led her little platoon to stand next to Father Joseph's chair, and put her hand on it protectively. She smiled at us, her professional smile, but she avoided meeting my eyes. "Father Joseph needs to rest now. Thank you so much for coming to see him." The sisters helped the priest up and ushered him back to the house. He stopped them, and turned back to Richard.

"Leave such matters alone. For your soul's sake!" Then he glared at me. "And you. Pray!"

Then Sister Catherine interposed herself between us and told us that the gardener would show us the way out.

I gritted my teeth as we crossed the ward on our way out of town.

"Are you hurt?" Richard asked me quietly.

"What?"

"Your head," he reminded me.

"Oh. No. My head is pretty hard." My wolf head is hard. And I'd been moving when she struck. The spot was tender, but not what I'd call hurt. "Do you want to go back and pin the priest to the wall, and ask him again?"

"If you wish," he said.

I thought about it. The only way we'd get information from the priest was if we got him alone, away from the church and all his minders. "We'd have to get him alone," I said aloud.

Richard was shaking his head. "He is too well warded."

"All right," I said. "We'll leave him." For now, I thought.

Since I got to L.A., on the weekends I get out my maps and look for the open spaces in the city, and go and explore them. Alone. It wasn't that late in the afternoon. We were on the 57, going south, but I didn't take the cutover on the 60 back to Whittier. The freeway was moving well, and I just kept going.

I saw Richard notice that I missed the exit. After a moment he said, "Can I ask where we are going?"

"Someplace where I can think."

I like to move while I think. I like long, open spaces, preferably along the ocean. I've found a couple places I like, and I headed for the nearest one now, jogging down the 405 to Long Beach.

What was I doing? I'd come to Los Angeles to keep my head down, to make no noise, to stay out of sight, until I gained enough strength to fight the battle I knew would one day come. But now I was involved in something much more imminent, that might be just as dire. And I was teamed with this creature, who looked like a man, a very beautiful man, and smelled just as good, who followed wherever I went, and what was I doing with him?

And I had to admit, he was a delight to the eye. Probably John Dee had specifically designed him that way, from his blond hair, his high cheekbones, his sweet body, slight and smooth, his eyes that were bleak with ancient longing and remembered pain, and warm and questioning when he looked at me.

I made the choice to leave home, leave family, to be alone. But I confess, having even a bit of a pack again comforted a part of me I hadn't realized was aching. And that was what I needed to think about.

It wasn't hard to find parking since it was March, and not a lot of people came to the beach this time of year. The surfers and dog walkers were out, some couples, and a few families with kids digging in the sand. There's a long, black beach at home, cold and mist-shrouded and empty most of the time. I like to run there. Here, there are no rocks, and the sand is blindingly white, but there is plenty of space, and no end in sight. That's why I like the place.

I walked out to where the sand was packed hard, close by the water line, and started southeastward at a good pace. Richard kept up easily. After awhile I said reflectively, "So John Dee got a dud. Demons are generally powerful and dangerous, but—" I said his real name, just to see him start at it, "is not?"

He didn't answer for so long I thought I hadn't worded it sufficiently strongly as a question. At last he said quietly, "I beg you not to say that name aloud."

I stopped and faced him. I was about to tell him that I could say what I want, that I'd understood him the first time, and anyway there was no one near enough to hear, but when I turned I saw there was a couple behind him running toward us after their dogs. I'd been paying attention to the dogs and missed the humans, which I didn't care to admit. So I only said, "All right. Point taken. Now answer the question."

The fairness of his skin was even more obvious in the merciless late afternoon sunlight on the beach. His arms were folded loosely as though guarding a wound, but I knew he was just keeping a wary hand over the important jacket pocket. He met my eyes to answer my question.

"I don't know. I don't know exactly what I am. John Dee scored over my understanding with so many commands and admonitions, decrees and geases that I barely remember that anything came before the moment I appeared in the midst of his pentagram. I was hoping..." His eyes drifted out to sea for a moment. "...that the priest could tell me. Or the sorceress."

"I thought we went to Tamara to tell her—and ask her—about the Eater of Souls."

His eyes fell. "Yes, of course. That, too." He shrugged. "I didn't try and ask more. It was obvious that she thinks me hateful."

"True." I cocked my head at him. "The priest didn't think you were hateful. He was pretty sure I was, though."

Richard smiled. It was a really sweet smile. I looked away. "When I have my soul, I avoid no end of troubles," he said. When I looked back, he was waiting to meet my eyes. "Thank you." He looked out over the sea. There were clouds over the water on the horizon, so you couldn't see clearly the line between the sea and the air. He said, "It is my hope that if I help them—you and them—with the coming cataclysm, some one among the sorcerers will, in return, tell me…" He glanced at me sideways. "With your permission, of course."

"Tell you what?"

He shrugged, lowered his eyes again. "Who I am, what I am…"

"How to get home," I said.

He nodded, looking down at the water rushing almost to our toes.

"All the things that John Dee thought it would be better if you didn't remember."

"He was an ignoramus."

"In these matters, don't forget, so am I."

His eyes were troubled. The wind had come up, ruffling his hair. Beneath one of his eyes was a tiny scar. I wondered when and where in his travels he'd gotten that one. I wondered about the ones I couldn't see, and the ones I'd never see, because his body had been new made, what, more than six times? The noise of the waves beside us, the distant roar of traffic, the smell of salt and the sea, and the scent of him, and all these questions, raised a tide in me that a stiff walk was not going to satisfy.

"Wait here," I said. "I'm going to run." I took two steps away and stopped in my tracks. When I turned back he was standing there, and I knew he would stand there until I came back and told him to move. And the tide would finish coming in, and…hm. No commands without an ending. I came back to him, looking around. There was a barbecue area up the beach, deserted now, but with places to sit. I pointed. "Wait over there."

He gave a brief nod and started off. I watched him go, moving easily despite the weight of the sand on his boots. Not a dud, really. I turned suddenly and ran.

One thing I've found about the beach is there are dogs that run there, as well as people, and down near the waves people can never be absolutely sure what they see. I changed as I reached a group of people walking along the surf, and leaped on four legs into the ocean. I ran along its edge, leaping the fingers of foam, then widened my stride. Down along the beach a couple of people were walking with their dogs, who leaped in and out of the surf wearing big dumb grins. I charged through the dogs and watched them scramble away, howling and yelping, and then at my clamorous challenge they ran to join me again for the joy of the chase, any chase, their owners calling uselessly behind them. I let them keep up for a while, and then left them in the sand.

I kept clear of people for the most part, because it's not worth the trouble, but I did run right through the elaborate castle being perfected for the high tide, and ran on, grinning, to the music of the various yells and howls of the builders behind me.

Further down the beach a couple of guys were throwing frisbees into the sea for their dogs, so I joined them, making catches with leaps into the air that left my limbs flailing and their eyes starting out of their heads. They walked softly toward me, speaking kindly, and I let them think for moments that they might take home a new dog, a big one, before I kicked my heels in their faces and left them behind.

All right, I wasn't thinking. I was just charging around making fun where I found it. But I needed to blow off some steam before I gave serious consideration to what I had found myself involved in. And anyway, I felt like it.

I ran along the surf until I was panting so hard my tongue kept tasting sand, and the scent of the water was driving me crazy. Then I walked up to human country where a kiosk sold cold drinks and coffee, and I bought a large bottle of water and made my way back at a walk.

All right. Was I committed to this adventure, or not? If I was not, I needed to leave Los Angeles, which wasn't as simple as just driving out of town. I would need to form a whole new set of plans about where to hide next, and how to get there without leaving a trail.

If I stayed, it meant I was committed to the side of the power raisers who wanted to stop the World Snake from devouring the city. That was only right, because Whittier was well within the bite mark that the Rag Man pointed out to us.

Everyone said I was important in this fight. I couldn't just hide anymore, biding my time, inhabiting a little space, putting food on the table and paying the bills. I liked the idea of being a player, a power in the land, someone who mattered. And if I wasn't in this fight, why had I driven all these miles already, to ask questions and find things out?

Well, because of Richard. Richard needed my help. I was involved in two quests, not just one. I'd helped the demon recover his soul. We'd found a sorceress who might be able to help him get himself free. We were bound together in the battle against the World Snake, but before the World Snake would come the Eater of Souls, and defeating him, Richard said, came first. I was already involved. If Richard needed saving, I would save him. I walked faster. If he was going to face the monster, I would face it with him. We would fight together. I wasn't alone anymore. I was committed. I turned and started back down the beach to where Richard would be waiting.

We needed information. We needed to know how to kill these critters, if they could be killed, and how to get rid of them if they couldn't. Tamara might come up with something. We'd found the priest. He might tell us more on another day. In this big city, there might be others. I'd get Richard to tell me who else we could ask.

The shadows were growing long. The air was chilly. Walkers

along the surf huddled now in coats and sweaters. The patient surfers were paddling in. My hair was ragged and damp from the sun and wind and water. I was sweaty and sticky from the salt, still exhilarated by the air and exercise. I started thinking about dinner.

Bonfires blazed up ahead on the beach. People claimed picnic areas in groups or extended families, and brought out the hot-dogs, s'mores, and beer. The smells were tantalizing. I quickened my pace.

I smelled the fire first, up where I'd told Richard to wait. Then I smelled the pack—or gang, rather, for these guys were quite de-pressingly human. Most of their heads were shaved, and all they'd brought to the party were bottles of beer and bottles of harder stuff in paper bags. And a bunch of them were holding Richard down on the sand while some stood over him, pouring something onto his face.

Rage roared up in me, and happy anticipation sang. I glanced up and down the beach—no one to interfere as far as I could see. Oh, this was going to be fun.

❧◌◑

CHAPTER EIGHT

There were about a dozen guys, and three or four girls on the sidelines preparing food. The girls were staying well away from the ones tormenting Richard. As I came up closer, I caught a whiff of Richard's blood, and then I wasn't happy anymore. But I didn't change. I sashayed right into their group, all five feet of me, in my dark blue sweatshirt, and black jeans, and tennis shoes. I tagged the leader, the danger-man, standing back a little while his lieutenants vied for his favors by thinking up new things to do to the blond intruder.

"Hi!" I said cheerfully, when I got close.

The danger-man turned. He was in his late twenties, one of the oldest of the bunch, with a clean-shaven head, wearing an ironed white t-shirt like most of the other guys. He held a bottle of beer close to his face, as though for comfort. His eyes were dead. One of the handful of guys next to him, younger, this one with a stubble growth of hair, said to me, "This is a private party."

"Yeah?" I sashayed some more and smiled at them. "What about him?" I pointed to Richard, still lying on the ground, three guys on top of him, five more standing over him.

"What, him?" the biggest of the tormenters laughed, and hauled back his leg to kick Richard in the ribs.

I told you I'm fast. With a leap I landed with my paws on the ground and his leg between them, took a huge, satisfying chomp out of his calf, and twisted for good measure as I stood up, spitting denim and blood and hair as I rose and faced him very close on two feet, and said, "Yes. Him." And I smiled. I could still taste the blood on my lips as he fell down, shouting. The others were paralyzed, not sure what they had seen, but pretty sure they saw me now, bigger than I looked, with yellow eyes, and with blood dripping from my mouth.

Then the leader said, "Get her," and the guys around him charged.

I backed away, laughing. I was still having fun, then. The rest of them were circling and I started to think about retreat and escape—but there was Richard, still held down, and he couldn't run as fast as I could.

I edged to the left, so that one of them got between me and the other two. That one swung at me, and I ducked and kicked him hard in the side of the knee. He cried out and went down. The other two lunged and I went down as well—onto four legs, my blood up. One little hop and I'd have a throat in my teeth, and I cannot tell you how satisfying that feels, how soft the flesh is, how it collapses as you press your teeth together. You can do it slowly, and hear the scream drown in a gurgle, or you can do it quick and hear the intoxicating crunches as the blood comes up on your tongue… but I couldn't kill them. Come on, it wouldn't be fair. So this would be a leg fest. But I struck high at the next one, and caught his thigh at the groin and, oh, did he leap away, the baby. The next one, I went for the knee, but he was already dodging as I leaped, and he fell. I charged back to the fire, where the women were screaming and running, and several of the guys had retreated behind the fire. One guy was on a cell phone shouting to the police about a crazy lady and a crazy dog, no, a wolf, really! Come quick, half in Spanish and half in English. And the dead-eyed guy stood steady as I came on, with a gun he lifted from his waistband cool as can be, and aimed straight at my head.

License to kill. Just as I can grow large, I can grow small to the eye. I shrank on the bound and then leaped in the air. He fired twice, once into the sand and once over my head, and then I was on him, both paws on his shoulders and he went down backwards and the gun flew into the air, and he was flat on his back, and I was above him and he stared up at me, and his eyes weren't dead any longer. They were like a helpless child's, staring up into the face of a nightmare come to life. He closed his eyes and tried to get his hands between me and his throat.

Yeah, okay, I didn't kill him. The first scream was when I took off the end of his nose. That hurts a lot, you know. I took a delicate chomp on his lip—that was the second scream—then I reached out and grabbed his gun hand and chewed three or four times, working my way up his forearm. Felt the bones crack, but it was the tendons I was after. He wasn't going to shoot a gun again with that hand, not without a lot of major rehab first. Then a couple of his boys came up to tackle me, but I heard them and I was gone while they were still in the air. They fell on their boss hard, and that was the third scream, and then they were crying out because there was quite a lot of blood.

I stood up and looked around. "Richard?"

"Here."

He was sitting up, giving a shove to the gangbanger who hurried to get off his legs and back away with the other two as I came up. There was blood in his hair, but it wasn't running hard.

"Can you get up?"

In answer he did so, stiffly but quickly.

Four or five of them were regrouping, starting toward us again. Behind them people were clustered around their leader, trying to stop the bleeding. People were calling to one another in Spanish and English, some of them hysterically. One of the women walked toward us holding up a little silver cross from the end of a rosary and screaming prayers. I backed away from the guys coming at us as Richard limped to my side.

I looked him over quickly. He'd taken some damage, but it looked like mostly bruising. "You all right?" It was hard to see in the twilight.

He nodded, his eyes wide. We backed away from the five of them now making a wide circle, pushing us toward the sea.

"How's your fighting?" I asked breathlessly. "You been in scraps before?"

I saw him smile then, and it did wonders for me. "I've been in the wars," he said.

I grinned back at him. "All right, then. They're toast. Come on, this way—follow me!"

I charged the nearest two who were closing in on us. I changed as I leaped for his body, and almost stopped in the air as a gray form streaked by me, and a second wolf leaped on the other man. There were more screams, and the others turned and ran. I caught a whiff of the wolf. Gods damn. It was Richard. I charged past him at the next gangster, but they were all running now, and we chased them down the beach in a wild flight, their screams, their scent and Richard's all urging me on, and Richard only a little behind me. I caught up easily and passed through the midst of them, enjoying the howls, the falls and the floundering as they found me among them, and the second wave of howls and dodges as Richard came up behind me, and we passed them by, and they turned and ran the other way. We let them run for a while, and then we went after them again. That time as we passed through them we heard the sirens, and we kept going, running in the deepening twilight along the surf at an easy lope.

When we were out of sight of the gangsters' bonfire, I changed, and turned. The gray wolf was favoring his left side. He looked ragged and unsure, and his tail hung down as I looked at him. I waited, to see what he would do, if he would change back right away. I wondered if he could, or if I'd be breaking my lease's "no pets" policy from now on. He let out a whine, turned one way and another, and then he changed and fell to the sand as a man.

I dropped down near him, staring down at him. He was breathing hard. He reached out to me, and I grabbed his hands and held them. After a moment, he turned over on his back, and I let him go. His eyes were wide, astonished.

I said, "Have you ever...?"

He shook his head.

I said, because I knew it, "You're not..."

He shook his head again. Then he sat up, put his hands to his face, took them away, stared down at them. He touched his lips, found blood there, and wiped at it hard. Then he got on his hands and knees and retched. I knelt down next to him. I reached out and laid my hand on his head for a moment. He crawled to the sea and got himself a handful of water. He cleaned his lips. When the next wave came in, he gathered a handful, soaking himself to the knees, and washed his face, took a sip, and spat. Then he came back and sat near me.

"Better?" I asked.

He nodded.

"Tell me what happened," I said. "You changed. How did you do that?"

He looked at me, eyes wide, his face lit by the faint last evening glow of orange twilight. He said, as though I should have known, "You told me to."

❧❦

CHAPTER NINE

Richard reached out and touched his fingers to my side. I let him. When he brought them away, wet and dark, I felt the pain for the first time.

"Hey!" I exclaimed, touching my ribs myself. Son of a bitch! If I'd known the bullet came that close, by the Lady, that maggot-eyed muscle-driven piece of work would have been dead. I snarled. I could still taste his blood. I became aware of other bruises and aches as I got to my feet.

Richard started to get up, and I gave him a hand as he got to his feet pretty slowly too. But when he spoke, he asked about me. "Is it bad?"

I was still swearing. "No." I pressed my sweatshirt against my side to staunch the bleeding. "What's bad is having regrets. Come on."

I was still holding his hand. We went up the beach a ways further before we headed up to the streets. We could still hear sirens and babble and see a dark crowd of people gathering down the beach. Richard gently drew me close and put his arm around me. We wandered back to the car, keeping to the unlighted side of the street, but no one spoke to us, and there were no cops by the car. It was a long drive back to Whittier. I turned the heat on full. Richard was shivering.

"You all right?"

"Yeah." He flashed me a grin. "That was…" He shook his head, wide-eyed. "Amazing."

There's a great Chinese restaurant down the street from my house on Philadelphia. I went in and ordered take-out. The waiter pretended he didn't notice the state of my clothes. Or me. Richard hobbled down to the drug store while I waited for the food, and then we drove up the hill.

When we were full up of House Special Lo Mein, tangerine beef, and shrimp fried rice, I went into the bathroom to clean up and have a look at my wounds. I had some bruises and abrasions, most of which I had no idea where they'd come from. The bullet had split the skin in one place along my side. When I pulled off my sweatshirt, it opened up again. I took a quick and not very effective shower because everything had started to hurt. I used one towel to staunch the blood while I dried myself with the other one. That's when Richard knocked on the door.

"What?" I couldn't hear him. I pulled on my sweats and opened the door. "What."

In the light, he looked pretty trashed himself. They must have kicked him a few times before I'd shown up. A rage rose in me, and once again I felt regret for things I hadn't done. His face was clouded with bruises. His hair was matted with salt. His new shirt was torn and stained. Tomorrow he'd have to get some new clothes.

Richard said, "I bought some bandages and salve, and some disinfectant. Want me to look at your…" He nodded to where I was holding the towel against my side.

I said, "Why don't you get cleaned up first?" I went to my room, leaving him the bathroom.

I lay down on my bed and fell asleep without even thinking

about getting under the covers. I woke up a long time after the water stopped, when Richard came into the room. He paused by the bed for a moment, and then sat down beside me.

"'Turn over," he said softly. I did so. He lifted my sweatshirt and I felt him gently pry off the towel I still held wadded to my side. That pricked me awake, but I didn't move or open my eyes. He cleaned off the blood, and then he said, "This is going to hurt," and it did, as he patted on some ferocious disinfectant. My eyes were open then. He made a neat bandage and taped it to my side.

"You've done this before," I commented.

"Many times."

My eyes had closed again. I heard him open a small jar and a pungent scent arose. I felt his fingers lightly exploring one of my bruises, rubbing in the salve. After a moment, a pleasant, warm tingling began.

"What's that?" I asked, without opening my eyes.

"Comfrey. Helps you heal faster."

"Mm."

He slipped off my sweatshirt without my having to move, and his fingers sought out other bruises. It wasn't long before I realized there was nothing businesslike about what he was doing. Still, it was pleasant, and I let him go on for a while before I asked, "You trying to seduce me?"

One warm hand continued to move slowly down my flank. "Of course."

I opened my eyes and regarded him, bent intently on what he was doing. "Think you can?"

He only smiled.

I sat up. He wore only a towel wrapped around his waist. His body was smooth and very white, almost without hair. As I looked him over, a pale pink flush rose from his belly all the way to his neck and into his cheeks. I smiled. There were bruises on his arms, a couple on his face, and some really spectacular ones, in layers, over his ribs. "Boy, they really got you. Lie down. Your turn." I took the jar of comfrey cream.

He lay down warily on the edge of the bed, and closed his eyes as I traced the bruises on his face. I brushed his hair back, dripped some of the antiseptic into the scrape above his temple, and then onto the one beside his lip. He was tense, and that bothered me. He rolled over onto his stomach when I told him. I took my time then, rubbing the scented paste into the darkest bruises on his ribs before I started on the paler, deeper ones. I moved on to the bruises on his arms, and the shallow ones on his back and shoulder. His skin was soft and pleasant to the touch, and as my fingers traced the marks along his ribs, his scent changed. It was clean and sweet from the bath, but some new tang was rising. Beneath that, deep in my throat, I still held another scent, a wolf scent I could not forget. And anyway, I love a challenge. His tension changed, and I smiled. I could feel his his awareness of my every move. I wormed the tag end of the towel out from where it fastened at his waist, and I told him to turn over.

I couldn't say, after the fact, who had seduced whom. He fell asleep before I did, but I lay there beside him, elated, every nerve wrung, with a whole new outlook on the activity. I had never done this with someone whose object was to ravish me unmercifully into a state of blissful exaltation. The way my stepbrothers and their buddies played, if you found yourself pinned to the floor, you lost. Nothing memorable in that, except repulsion, and the impulse to bite.

Richard was different; that was clear. I lay on my side and with my fingers gently traced the line of light that fell across his body from the streetlamp outside the window. He sighed in his sleep. Maybe he had won. In the morning I woke him up early to try for best two out of three.

I gave him full points for getting up after that to make breakfast. He did something with eggs, and bacon, and cheese, and bits of bread, that had me practically licking the plate. He brought me strawberries with little hats of whipped cream.

"What shall we do today?" I asked him, as I licked the last of the cream from my fingers.

"Whatever you wish," he replied. His stare was sultry, and he was thinking that what I was thinking was that we should go back to bed and stay there all day. And that we should bring the whipped cream, and the rest of the strawberries, and improvise until we laughed so much that it ached. Which wouldn't take long, after all. We were both stiff and sore from our various hurts.

But we had a city to save, and I wanted to see his eyes change. So I said, "We should go talk to the Buddhists up on Mount Baldy, don't you think? If they're up to something particular, maybe they have some answers for us."

And his eyes lightened with relief, and hope, and that's when I learned about kissing.

The first time we took the wrong exit, off the 210 to Mt. Baldy Road, I thought we'd misread the map. The second time, we took a wrong turn and ended up back down on Baseline. The third time, I was certain we were on the right road, but then I had a sudden conviction that my gas gauge was wrong, and that we'd better go back and fill up while we could. This resulted in our winding around the streets all lined with river rock and the remnants of orchards, heading away from the mountains again.

When I found a gas station and put six gallons in my car, I decided I was ravenous. We went back to the grocery and deli that we'd seen on Foothill and got sandwiches. As we sat on the porch outside eating them, I listened to myself saying that going up the mountain was probably not a good idea after all, and then I grew angry.

"What is going on? We are going up that mountain! What is getting in the way?"

"It may be," Richard suggested, "that someone has laid down a spell of misdirection."

"A spell? Are you kidding me?"

He shook his head at my anger. "It works the same as a ward, except it's a deflection rather than a barrier."

"Well, we are not going to be deflected. And whoever is trying to deflect me is going to enjoy an interesting afternoon." We got back into the car. I turned onto Foothill, turned left at the first significant road I came to, and pointed my car at the mountain. "That's where we're going. Pay no attention to anything else."

Just past the dam I was momentarily distracted and almost turned off again, but I recognized the turnoff I'd taken before, and this time we held the course.

I was a little annoyed that after the intense intimacy of last night—and this morning, I remembered with a smile—to have in the car the dutiful, attentive servant again. I glanced at him with a trace of that smile still lingering. He caught my glance and his eyes ignited, and it was a second before I could look back at the road again, my breath high in my throat. It was all right.

We continued up the mountain, crossing into the Angeles National Forest which, in this area, had a surprising number of trees. The peaks on either side of us were topped with snow, and there were grimy patches wearing away in the shadows. The rocks grew larger, and a crashing stream ran parallel down below the road. I felt a sudden urge to stop, to go fishing in the stream—in March, come on!—and then that urge passed.

"Did you feel that?" I asked him. "Another ward—or misdirection?" He nodded. After I thought about that for a moment, I asked him, "Can you feel the wards before I do?"

He turned to me with a surprised look.

Well, that was interesting. "John Dee really did get a dud," I observed, watching him. His eyes flared. That was interesting too.

He replied tightly, "John Dee took two years to think of every possible consequence of having a demon on the loose, and lay every possible binding upon me to prevent them." He shook his head. "I don't know what I am." I heard the bleakness in his voice. But honestly, I wasn't sure I wanted to find out exactly what the rest of him might be, after what I'd seen on the first night, when that sword touched his head.

We reached Mount Baldy Village and crept through. The traffic going up the mountain to the ski resort, and from the Snow Lodge in town, allowed us to watch carefully for the turnoff to the Buddhist priory that was on this road. The Rag Man had told us it was just outside of town. We kept going up the road, back and forth on the hairpin turns, until we dead-ended at the ski resort parking lot. I uttered a curse and threaded our way through the lot until I was able to turn around. We drove back down, against the traffic this time, until we were in the village again. There we considered every building as we passed it, and every access road, until we were through the town as far as the turnoff to Cedar Creek Canyon.

I pulled off on a side road and found a place to turn around. "You know, these people are really starting to bug me. Why don't they want people coming to this place? What are they hiding?" I thought about the problem for a moment and asked, "Richard, do you have your cards?" He produced them from a pocket in his jacket "All right. Can your cards be misdirected?"

"No," he said and smiled at me, his blue eyes bright. "They cannot."

"Good!" I decided not to be distracted in yet another way, so I did not lean forward and kiss him. "We are going to find the priory. First question: right or left?"

He cut the cards. "Left," he replied, and we drove back up the road into the village.

We played "hotter or colder" with the cards, and after one more pass found the access road—and also why we had missed it so many times. There appeared to be a fence across the road until we were right beside it.

"I don't believe it," I said, eyeing the fence. "Ask the cards again: right or left?"

The cards said to go right. I turned the car into a collision course for the fence, and just before we might have struck, it turned out that the fence was just suggested to our eyes by the way the tree shadows fell. There was no fence there at all. Huh. Good one. Ahead of us was a rocky, deeply pitted dirt road partly covered with snow. I pulled over and parked, and we walked along the road to the house, trying to keep from slogging through the deeper puddles. A chill breeze blew lightly down from the mountain. I lifted my head and scented the air.

"There have been a lot of workings around here," I noted.

Richard, walking half a step behind, at my shoulder, added, "For a long time."

"But not right here," I said, as the road stopped at the only house. It was boarded up, decrepit, and abandoned. A living dwelling has laid upon it a tangled web of comings and goings, laced with intention, with excitement, frustration, happiness, or pain. You can sense the ambience that this energy creates. A long time ago, an old man lived in this house. He had walked up and down one side of the steps, beside the rail, with an old, sick dog. But they were both gone.

"No," Richard agreed. "Not here."

"Your cards said this is the priory."

Richard held out the deck and turned up one card, and then another. "This was the priory, the place originally used as the priory. A long time ago."

I don't like being fooled. I liked these Buddhists less and less. "What is going on here?" I looked around. Behind the house, a dip led down to the distant roaring creek. Beyond the creek the slope rose steeply, the scree partly covered with snow and occasional stands of weathered trees. "Let's go hunting," I said to Richard. "Let's hike around until we find all the workings these folks have been doing and see what they're up to."

Richard looked at me as though he wanted to suggest that in leather boots, with me in tennis shoes and a sweatshirt, we were about as prepared to go hiking in the rocks, and the water and the snow as we were to fly.

I grinned at him. "Not on two feet. On four." Already, in the back of my throat, the memory of a marvelous scent was rising. Richard smiled back at me, and I had to turn away before he saw the heat in my eyes. But he probably knew.

We consulted the cards once more, drove out of the village, and parked at a popular trailhead. The lot only held a few cars. The canyon had patches of snow on the steep slopes on both sides. It was too cold and wet for casual hikers at this season. The well-worn trail along the swollen creek was empty, though there were myriad traces of the people—and dogs, and other critters—who had traversed it over the years A few people had gone up along it in the last couple of days. There were cabins up the canyon. A trace of wood smoke along the creek gave away which ones were presently inhabited.

We hiked up the trail, and the noise of the creek, the brushing of the wind in the trees, our muffled footsteps, were a counter-point to the mountain's soundlessness. There was no one in sight. There was no one around. I said to Richard, "This way, follow me!" and I changed and leaped up the trail.

The gray wolf bounded after me. I turned and touched his snout and he slathered my jaw and I slathered his head, and my head was full of his scent again and I charged up the trail with him after me.

I felt the abrasion on my side and slowed down until I found a pace where I could run without noticing it. The trail was snow-covered this far up the canyon. The gray wolf ran in my tracks. I could taste the scent of deer, of raccoon, of human, of coyote who'd used this trail recently. The intoxicating presence behind me galvanized thoughts of the hunt we could make, the two of us, against anything on this mountain, the stalk, the two-sided attack, neck and heel, the gorgeous kill, the taste of blood, the bloody excess of meat, the joy that would come after, the two of us—oh shit shit shit shit shit—

I changed so suddenly I stumbled and fell down. I pulled myself up from the rocks, my knees banged, my pants wet, my tennis shoes beginning to be soaked by freezing snow, and I stood there, dancing from one foot to the other, staring at the big old cedar tree ahead, its bows protecting its trunk from the snow. Oh shit shit shit shit shit!

A whine from behind me, a struggle, an awkward shake, and Richard stood with one hand on a rock, and then straightened up. "What's the matter?"

Wordlessly I turned and began picking my way down the trail, back the way we had come.

"What's wrong?" he asked. "What happened?"

"Scent marker," I said quietly, as though the sound of my voice would change anything. As though the trail I had left wouldn't be a banner proclaiming to anyone around where I was, where I had come from. Oh stupid stupid stupid stupid—

Gray Fox has been allied with our family for time out of mind. The fox kind are our heralds, our emissaries and, when needed, our scouts. And one of the fox kind, one that I knew, had left a scent marker on the trunk of the cedar tree not five days ago. I knew they would start their search for me in the wild country. I'd done everything I could think of to make that happen, and I'd gone to live in the city because there I would be harder to track. In the wild, once you've left a trail, it can be scented for months or even years in certain conditions. It's useful to let your enemies think that you're stupid. But now I had been stupid. Running up into wild country, where I was easily tagged—that had been stupid. Going back down our trail wasn't going to help. He would know where I was today. It wouldn't take them long to lay a net. And I knew they would come after me, they had to come after me. I'd always known that. I'm the daughter of the Moon Wolf. I carry the line in my blood.

∞CR

CHAPTER TEN

"A mber?" Richard asked, stumbling again behind me. "What's wrong? Can I do anything?"

I stopped and turned. "I'm being sought. By my family. One of their—one of the folks they sent to find me has been here."

"The gray fox?" he asked.

I'd forgotten that he, too, had been scenting as a wolf. I nodded. "Let's get down off this trail. Then… I'll figure something out," I said numbly.

I sensed the people before I saw them, and because of the state I was in, I changed at once and turned to confront them. There were two figures standing on a ridge across the creek, watching us. I lifted my lip to them, even angrier at myself for having been caught out, for having changed without thinking, for having assumed they were foes. They were a couple of older women, and they were here a lot. There had been traces of them on the trail, in layers, going back a long time. And there were more traces of them here. I stared up at them. Harmless. Fine. Who cares what they thought they saw? I was about to head on down the trail when the taller, older woman squatted down, holding out her arms. Then the other woman did it as well. Then they both stood up.

"Come up here," the first one called. "It's all right."

Okay. Crossing the creek, crossing their paths, would obscure my trail. I'd be offering something besides a straight line back to my car. I stood one more moment because I don't come when I'm called. Then I trotted back down the path, until I found the branch to where they crossed the creek. There was a boulder there, with its flat side facing the trail. I'd passed it, running joyously up the trail, without noticing.

Three signs were carved in the granite in a triangle, connected by a painted design of Celtic knotwork. I stood up so I could look at them properly. I'd seen them before. Welcome. Friendship. Safety. A tangle of energy hung about the stone, the trace of small workings going back a long time. I looked up at the women, still waiting patiently. I changed again, took the cut-off down to the creek, and crossed it in a bound.

I trotted up the trail to the ridge. I heard Richard making his way up slowly behind me. I hadn't told him to change, so he was picking his way over the slippery rocks, across the board these women used to cross the creek, and up the path behind me.

I changed again as I reached the ridge. The women's eyes were startled, almost awed. Yeah, I like that. But they were smiling, and their hands were open.

"Ladies," I said evenly. I stood just outside their wards that said, "There's nothing here, you don't see anything, there's no cabin, nobody lives here," tendrils of which wound down the creek, and up and down the trail. Here, I could see the snug little cabin set back from the ridge in a little clearing near a stand of cedars. A flattened, rock-lined space created a little yard overlooking the stream, and an impressive stack of firewood lay under the cabin's eaves beside the back door. Smoke rose from a stovepipe in the roof.

Richard climbed up and stood beside me. He bowed slightly, his eyes wary.

The older woman had curls of sandy gray hair spilling down from her dark green wool cap. Her long, green coat fell to her soft leather boots. She was holding out her green-gloved hands, but did not try to take mine. "Welcome. Will you come in? I'm Marge. This is my friend Andy."

Andy was smiling broadly. "Hi!" She was a little taller than me but heavy-set. She wore a red knit cap, probably from the same set of knitting needles, and a dark blue ski jacket over her jeans and hiking boots. She was practically hugging herself with excitement and astonishment. "Come right this way. We were about to serve the soup."

"Will you eat with us?" Marge asked.

"Thank you," I said formally. "We will be happy to. I'm called Amber. This is Richard."

Marge nodded, indicated the way, but did not offer to touch us. Someone had taught her good manners.

The warmth of the cabin was imbued with smells of beef, of wine, and of baking bread. I started to salivate. It seemed like a long time since those sandwiches.

We stepped in to a large main room lined with bookshelves filled with dusty old books. Beside the door was a stand for hiking sticks and ski poles, and another for coats. Marge took off her coat, and Andy hung them both up. I didn't take off my sweatshirt, Richard had his hands in his jacket pockets, and they didn't ask for them.

The stove in the corner was burning nicely, and Marge laid in a few more logs to keep it going. A narrow staircase off the kitchen led to the rooms upstairs. Under it was a bathroom with a compost toilet.

One thing was out of place. I opened my mouth a little. "Who's missing?" Another woman, young and active, had slept over on the couch the last several nights, and, yes, hers was the knitting basket by the smallest chair.

Marge and Andy glanced at each other. "My daughter," Marge said, "Hannah. She went to gather kindling. She should be back soon."

"She has the little dog?"

Marge nodded and Andy laughed. The dog's scent was everywhere, and the size of it was evident from the small basket next to the stove. "Do you mind?" Marge asked.

"I don't," I told her. "She will." I saw the thought dawn in Andy's eyes, and said, "I won't eat her."

"Of course not!" Marge said, and Andy bustled off to the kitchen to dish up soup, while Marge offered us seats by the fire. I stood looking at her, waiting until she answered the question that was between us. She said, "My mother, Candace Wilmot, was a friend to one of the raven kind. We lived next door to a pair of them while I was growing up. She was able to be helpful sometimes." She smiled. "So, the first thing I thought, when I saw two wolves running up the trail was, I'm seeing a pair of the legendary wolf kind."

All right. That would do. I nodded and sat down, and Richard took a seat next to me. "That's why you have the signs on the rock."

"That's right." Marge handed each of us a mug of steaming coffee. Richard cupped his hands around his and bent to take in the aroma as he sipped. Marge sipped hers. I tried mine. It was not as bad as usual.

"We lived down the road in the village when I was young," Marge said. "When my mother built this cabin, she made those signs on the rocks."

"Did she teach you magic?"

Andy laughed as she came in from the kitchen with four bowls on a tray. "Magic? What do you mean?"

"There are a lot of workings on this mountain," I said. "You've put some good wards around your cabin, and there've been workings by that stone."

"Oh, that!" Andy handed me a deep bowl with a handle to hold it by, and a plate with a wedge of fresh bread and butter. "Is that magic? Chanting and singing and waving joss sticks?" I waited until Marge started on hers before I took a bite.

Until I left home, it never occurred to me that there were people who didn't know how to lay wards or raise whatever power they could. In Los Angeles, not only did most people not know how to do it, a lot of them were oblivious to power once it was raised, even when they reacted to it. Everyone I knew, growing up, knew about these things. The wards on our valley, on the roads in and out, and the bridge to the east, were renewed at each solstice, and had been for over a century. I didn't set any wards on my apartment. I'm all the ward the place needs, after all. And a ward is a beacon to those who know how to look for them; I was supposed to be lying low.

"When chanting and singing is done with intention and with power, it can be shaped into a ward, or even a spell, if there is power enough," I explained. "Fire is a focus, in any form."

"You're kidding!" Andy looked over at Marge, smiling in delight.

"We came up here," I told them, "because we heard down in the city that the Buddhists up here are chanting aversion and protection against the World Snake. It's said the World Snake is coming and will take the city when she arrives."

Andy stared at us, but Marge nodded. "I've heard that, yes."

"The priory people aren't working on saving the city," Andy burst out. "They don't care about the city. All they care about is their precious cave."

I looked over at Richard. "We've been running up and down this mountain fended off by misdirection everywhere we go. We've ended up at the ski resort, on the wrong road, at a broken down house—"

Andy was laughing again. She stopped when I looked at her. "Yeah, that's Roscoe. He's paranoid."

Marge explained. "Some years ago, the Buddhist Center for Peace got a new leader."

"And that's when it all went to hell," Andy interposed.

"It's because of the cave," Marge explained, but Andy burst in again.

"There were these stories, about miners going into the cave and getting lost. It's only about eighty feet long, so how can you get lost? But a couple of people from the priory spent the night in there, and after that—"

"Nothing happened," Marge said. "I was there. Nothing happened." I looked into her eyes and wondered why she was lying. Andy took up the story.

"One of them told some kind of story to Roscoe, and now he's the leader. And now you're allowed to join them for prayers, at certain times, but if you want higher knowledge, you have to pay, and there's a hierarchy, and steps to the inner circle, and you have to swear oaths of secrecy, and the Roscoe-worshippers spend a lot of time sneaking around."

"They've been laying the misdirection wards?" I asked.

"They don't want anyone finding the cave," Andy said. "Though there's nothing there. Honestly."

She wasn't lying. She didn't think there was. "They don't want people finding the priory either," I commented. "We never did."

"You have to have an invitation, now," Marge said. "It's all very sad. Andy and I quit the group a couple of years ago."

"So what is this World Snake?" Andy asked. "Some kind of monster?"

I looked at Richard, Richard looked at me, and Marge was the one who answered her. "It's a mythical being, isn't it? One of Loki's sons, the serpent who spans the whole world?"

Richard asked, "Did you feel the earthquake in November?"

Marge and Andy grinned at each other. "One of the perks of living on a mountain," Marge said. "We don't get earthquakes up here."

"The Worm is one of the original denizens of the Earth, Creator and Destroyer," Richard said. "When she moves, the Earth trembles. When she feeds, cities are devoured. Or so they say."

"So, why's it coming here?" Andy asked.

Richard shrugged. "She doesn't need a reason. She is a god."

"And you and I are supposed to stop it?" I said. "We need to talk."

Someone was coming, and the dog outside started up a tremendous racket. I grinned. I couldn't help it. There's nothing like a little dog screaming, "Oh my god, there's a wolf in there!" at the top of her lungs, and nobody believing her.

"Mom! What's wrong?" Hannah burst into the cabin in a swirl of freezing air and a flying brown poncho, carrying a big basket of kindling over her arm, while the little dog bounced up and down outside, barking and carrying on. "Oh," said Hannah, when she saw the two of us. "Rose! Shut up! It's all right."

Richard stood up.

Marge said, "Honey, this is Amber and Richard. They got this far up the trail and got cold, and we asked them in for soup. This is my daughter Hannah."

Hannah glanced at me, but she couldn't seem to help staring at Richard. "Oh!" she said. She came over to Richard and held out her hand, smiling. "Hi! Rose, shut up! I'm sorry…"

They finally got the dog to come inside, and she went straight for me. I looked at her, and she went straight back again, so hard she fell over backwards. She bounced back and forth, barking all the time, and then dashed behind the couch where Marge was sitting. From there, she kept a close guard on me and uttered occasional growls.

"She's never like this," Hannah apologized. "I don't know what's come over her."

The two women looked at either other, but neither offered to tell her what was going on.

Andy dished up soup for Hannah, and we got our bowls refilled and our bread replenished as well. The soup had beef, barley, to-mato sauce, and carrots. It was really good, and the bread was warm and crusty. I wondered if Richard was taking notes. He certainly did justice to his share.

"We were telling Amber and Richard about the priory," Marge said.

"Oh, uck," was Hannah's comment. "Those people! You'd think they'd invented religion. You know they wear their robes into the grocery store now? And they're just visitors."

When she finished eating, Hannah collected the dishes and took them into the kitchen. I asked Marge, "Are you working to deflect the World Snake? Allies are being sought, in the city."

"I don't give a damn what happens to the city," Andy said.

Marge looked at her and shook her head. "There are a lot of people down there."

"My ex, for one," Andy replied darkly. "That's probably why the Snake is coming. He needs to be devoured."

"My son lives down there, too," Marge reminded her. She said to me, "I don't know what I would do to be of any help or how to do it. My mother showed me how to, what you call, ward this place, and what to do about the stone. I don't think we'd be much of an ally."

"But you know about my kind," I reminded her.

She smiled. "I know a few things. Things my mother told me. Like, 'Tell one Raven, tell them all.'"

I grinned. I knew this list. "'Tell a Crow, tell the world.'"

"'The Bobcat is a great and mighty hunter. Just ask her.'"

"'Be kind to Bears, for they have long arms,'" I added.

"'Do not cross the Wolf," Marge held my gaze. "'She will remember.'"

"Yes," I said.

"Oh, I know those!" Hannah announced, coming in from the kitchen, wiping her hands on her jeans. "Mom used to make up a ton of them. What was it—'The only one who sees the Cougar is her prey.' And what's the one about the deer, Mom?"

"'Deer are sweet,'" I told her.

"No," said Hannah, "there's something else." She gathered up her knitting. She was making a blue hat this time.

"No," I said. "They're just sweet."

Andy looked over at Richard. "You're awfully quiet," she said. "Are you two related?"

"Not at all," Richard answered politely. "I am a demon out of hell, but I take the form my mistress commands." There was a short silence, and then they all laughed. It was so funny.

"Okay," I said, standing up. "Thank you so much. The soup was great. Time for us to head back down."

Marge said, getting up, "Is there anything we can do for you? What was it that was bothering you, up the trail?"

I held her gaze a moment. I remembered her awe and the absence of fear. I remembered the stone and her welcome. I'd been stupid. I didn't want to be caught. Not yet, not now, not before I was a lot stronger. And older. So I told her, "I'm being sought by my family. There's a scent marker on that big old cedar. The one who made it is looking for me."

"Ah," said Marge. "And you've left a trail right to his mark."

I nodded. "He'll be back. He'll cross that trail again, and he'll be able to backtrack me. I am not ready to be found."

"Well," Marge said, "I can obscure a trail."

She went and got an old Indian blanket, worn and ragged, but clean. She produced scissors, cut off a strip off, and handed it to me. "You'll need this." Then she laid the rest of it on the floor. "Here. Roll on that."

I looked at the three of them. Marge was calm and certain. Andy was suppressing excitement. Hannah looked confused. No one would believe them anyway, if they told. I love the Age of Science. I changed.

I was aware of the dog going nuts under the couch and Hannah collapsing onto it, her mother holding her hand. I rolled on the blanket, over and over, making sure it was imbued with my scent, and then I stood up again.

"You said, you said—" Hannah was gasping, "You said they were stories!"

I grinned. Marge murmured, "I never said they weren't true."

Andy was still staring at me. "But—what about your clothes?"

I almost smiled. Every pup spends long afternoons changing and changing and changing, trying for speed, or for slow motion, or the illusion of invisibility. We all experimented in what we could carry with us as we changed, punctuated by screams from the adults of, "Hey! That's my shovel!" and "Not the good silver!" And often we were successful. But Aunt Dora never got her shovel back. There is a story about my great-grandmother, who grabbed her enemy as she changed, and was able to yank him with her around the twist as she turned from human to wolf, and when she turned back to human, he was gone. We don't know where the things go that we lose there. We never find them again. But things worn close to our bodies, or caught firmly in our hands or teeth, can often be brought back again. Our clothes go with us when we change and come back again. Things in tight pockets or, even better, zipped pockets, almost always come back with us. But sometimes they don't. And we learn not to change wearing scarves, or backpacks. Finding yourself all twisted up in what you were wearing is just embarrassing.

A couple of Dad's cousins got everyone to believe they could change clothes when they shifted shape. One in a black t-shirt, the other in a red, they'd change together, and when they changed back, they'd switched shirts. The whole valley was astonished into thinking the old days were back again, when it's said we were much more powerful. A lot of my relatives lost their shirts trying the same trick before Dad figured it out. His cousins were wearing one tee shirt over the other, and the top one was cut and ready to tear off, so they'd each shift back in the shirt they wore under it. Everyone had a good laugh. Dad and Aunt Dora went to the cousins' house, grabbed up every stitch of clothes they owned, then changed, dropped all the clothes, and changed back. And everyone had a good laugh about that as well. Trying to figure out where things go when we change is like trying to look at the back of your own head while you're still wearing it. It is said that in the old days, our human natures could wear weapons and armor into the change and emerge on the battlefield armed and at the ready. Mom says that's only a story. I lost a whole lot of kitchen knives trying it. Dad did the stitches for me so Mom never found out.

Andy repeated, "Where do your clothes go, when you change? Why don't you have to take them off?"

I shrugged. "It's magic."

They cut the blanket into strips, and Marge and Andy wound two of them around the outside of their boots.

"I'll hike on up the trail," Marge said. "I'll go up to the ski resort, march around the lodge a few times, and then I'll take the chair lift back down, so your trail will go all the way up there, and just disappear."

"I'll go with you as far as the cut-off," Andy said, "and then I'll take the trail through the pass and over to the cave. If I walk around the cave entrance a few times, and then back down to the village and into a few more of the inner circle's misdirection spells, that'll confuse anybody."

"And then we'll burn the rags," Marge finished.

Hannah sat forward. "I can help," she offered. "I have to drive back to Redlands tonight. After I walk down to the parking lot, I'll rub your scent on my car tires. When I get to Redlands, I'll wash the tires, and the trail will disappear."

"Thank you, Hannah," Marge said. "That is an excellent idea."

I smiled at them. Turns out I do have a nice smile. "Thank you." I nodded to them. "The Wolf does remember."

The little dog never did come out from under the couch. I don't have to be friends with everyone.

We drove back down the mountain and headed home. Traffic

was light. I didn't talk, though the thought of that little dog almost made me laugh. The scent of the gray wolf was in my throat, and a tide in me was already rising. When I glanced at him, Richard's eyes had darkened.

We stopped for pizza at a place on Whittier. We waited, sitting side by side on the bench inside the door, until they handed us our box, and Richard paid. When we got to my apartment, we put the box down on the table and went straight to the bedroom, peeling shoes and dropping clothes on the way.

When Richard had left me panting and oblivious, helpless and replete, when he brought me slices of cold pizza and fed them to me, looking smug, when I had done my best to even the score until at last he fell asleep, I lay looking at him. I ran my hand gently down his neck, along his shoulders, down his spine. He smiled in his sleep.

My days that had so long been empty were suddenly crowded with incident and adventure, with things to do, and with people. I had more to think about than I had in months, which is why I wasn't thinking at all about some of the things I should have been.

❧❧❧

CHAPTER ELEVEN

I went to work the next day at the proper time, despite the temptations of Richard, French toast, and maple syrup. I ate my last piece in the car on the way to work folded in half around the slatherings of butter and syrup. We moved the scaffold over to the next section of the upstairs lobby. Yvette brought some donuts, and she and the guys sang most of the day, once the sugar high kicked in. I found myself singing along now and again, when I wasn't just staring at the wall and smiling. I took some ribbing, which I normally don't tolerate, but that day I hardly noticed.

I resisted calling Richard from work at the noon break. He wasn't supposed to be home anyway, since he planned to take the bus to the mall and buy himself some clothes. That night we were going back to see the sorceress Tamara, to see if she'd come up with anything in the meantime, and I was going to be sure we asked some questions about Richard.

When I got home from work, dinner was hot on the table, some kind of lamb stew with all kinds of unidentifiable succulent lumps in it. I love lamb. It's in my nature to do so. After we ate, he had to show me all his new clothes, and this turned into a fashion show, which turned into a ritual of a completely different kind, and by the time I'd inspected everything he'd bought, including socks and underwear, we were both exhausted and, quite frankly, unfit to be seen in public. So we decided we'd hit Tamara's the next night, and went properly to bed instead.

When I got home the next night, Richard was gone.

I didn't think, even for a moment, that I'd been taken for a chump. Why would he have bothered to do the breakfast dishes if he was doing a bunk? Why was there dough rising on the stove, overflowing the bowl and all over the stove top? And, conclusively, why had he left all his new clothes, except the ones he'd been wearing that morning? He hadn't even taken his snazzy new tennis shoes, but had gone out wearing his old boots. He had taken his jacket. His soul was gone.

His scent was faint on the steps—he'd gone out hours ago. Nonetheless, I had little trouble tracking him down Philadelphia, smiling at the tiny remaining scents on his new jeans, which he hadn't washed since last night. On Greenleaf he'd turned right, toward the grocery store, which is what I expected. I'd already heard a couple of Richard's riffs on food having to be fresh, not frozen, not prepackaged. He'd gone out to buy whatever was to go with the biscuits for dinner, and it wasn't supposed to take long. Not longer than it takes bread to rise, anyway. Near one of the sidewalk coffee shops, the trace of Richard ended, and I picked up another scent, which sent me trotting back up the hill to get my car. I knew that one. And I knew where he lived. This wasn't going to be hard after all.

When I pulled up in front the bungalow in Laguna Beach, I was tingling with pleased anticipation. After all, I'd played this scene before, and I'd come out the big hero, rescued the beautiful guy and taken him home to my bed—eventually. I scented Richard's recent trace on the path, and this time I hopped the front gate, insinuating myself over the top of it and under the rose-tangled archway above in a suave undulation, graceful and with no loss of motion. I hoped Richard was watching. I trotted up the steps and knocked on Thomas Fallahan's front door.

His friend Chris opened it. I saw him recognize me and, in the same instant, try to close the door in my face, but my foot was already there. I was hyped up enough that when I put out my hand and pushed open the door, he backed up fast and I breezed in right past him.

The elegant leather-and-wood living room was the same, except the candles were gone. The couch was right-side up and back in its place before the fire. I looked around curiously. There had been one distinct addition to the décor: garlic wreathes. In all the windows. Hanging over the door. With silver crosses hanging from them. Some of them were big. I had to laugh.

"That's a myth, you know," I said, pointing at a particularly heavily decorated window. I wandered over to it, grabbed the garlic skin and made it crackle, dangled the cross in my fingers. Old. Kind of pretty, in fact.

"Oh," said Chris, and swallowed. He still stood near the open door.

I wandered over to the bedroom, glanced in. It was dark and there was no one in there. I looked at him quizzically.

"He's not here," he told me warily.

"Who's not here?" I asked. "Tommy?"

"He's not here either."

"That's okay," I told him cheerfully. "I'm not here for him. I came for..." What had these guys called him?

"Stan's not here." Chris supplied the name for me. "They left."

I wandered around the living room, thinking. "They left. They were here, but they left. What was—Stan—doing here in the first place?" I turned and faced him, not trying anymore to seem friendly. Not trying anymore to pretend I wasn't right out of his worst nightmare.

Chris had his back practically against the wall. He shook his head. "It wasn't my idea. Honestly."

"Why don't you tell me—right now—what Tommy was doing in my town, and what he's doing with—Stan."

"A guy came here—friend of Tommy's, I'd never seen him before. He wanted to know where Stan was. Tommy's—he's pissed about the other night. You scared him or something."

Or something. I smiled my not-nice smile, remembering. "Yeah." I remembered, too, Richard coming out of the shower, smelling of sweet unguents, his fine body flushed, and his eyes troubled. "And so?" I prompted.

"This guy, this friend of Tommy's, he said if Tommy brought Stan to him, he'd..." Chris's eyes left my face. That keyed me up even more.

"Oh yeah?" I asked him. "He'd what?" I walked casually over to Chris until I stood just within reach. "He'd what?" I asked him, softly.

He put his hands out in front of him, as though to ward off what was coming. And I hadn't done a thing yet! "Look," he said, "this has nothing to do with me. If I tell you—everything—could you just go away and..."

My eyes dripped sympathy; I'm sure they did. "And not hurt you?" I took another step forward. "Why don't you tell me every little thing you know, and then hope that puts me in a really nice mood. How about that?" I took another little step forward and ran my finger down his arm. His biceps were taut. He watched what I was doing with an expression bordering on horror, as though my finger had grown tentacles. God, I enjoy respect! "Go ahead." I gave him a little poke. "Start talking."

"Listen," he said, "this was all Tommy's idea. He's been ranting and raving ever since you were here last time. He was really upset. I've never seen him like that."

"No?" I asked. "'Cause usually he's just a sweet, gentle nice guy, is Tommy. Wouldn't hurt a fly, right?"

Chris shifted. "Okay. He wanted to get back at Stan. And then Marlin came over and said if Tommy brought him Stan..." I looked up, letting my finger dig into his arm. He winced. "He said he'd take care of him."

"'Take care of him?'"

Chris gave in. "He said he'd see to it that Stan regretted ever leaving this house. He said Stan would regret ever being born, and for a long time."

I thought about that. I wondered if those guys knew what Stan was. If they didn't, then this didn't sound so very bad. But if they did... I felt myself growing. Funny, I didn't feel more than ordinarily angry. This was new. This was about... lying in bed beside Richard while he fed me bits of pizza from his fingers and said things that made me laugh. It was about straining against his strength for my joy and his, all thoughts dissipated, all desires known. And the long night I'd spent, his head on my breast, his breathing slow, his scents and mine mingled into a new one, intoxicating, that I could still taste at the back of my throat. It was about love. I felt very strong.

"Where are they now?" I asked. Even my voice sounded different. There was a level of menace in it I had felt before but never managed to convey.

Chris was white. He leaned away from me. "I don't know." He looked sideways at me and added, "I could call his cell but he said something happened to it."

That's right. Something had. I was smiling now, the smile with a whole lot of teeth in it. I said, "All right. I will deal with him in good time. Right now, you can tell me, who is this Marlin person, and where do I find him?"

He didn't even hesitate. A short time later I was charging up the freeway as fast as one ever goes on the 405 at six at night, heading north past the airport. That is to say, I was going very slowly indeed. And cussing a lot. I distracted myself from road rage by remembering the scene as I'd left it in Tommy's living room. I'd given Chris' arm a sisterly pat and told him that if I ever saw him again, he'd be very, very sorry. Likewise, he should tell Tommy that he'd better pack his stuff and go, because he had messed with something of mine, and I knew where he lived. And then I'd taken a run around the room over the furniture. My, how the stuffing had flown! Like snow, with bits of leather and shreds of draperies, and over all, the smell of crushed garlic, everywhere. Sometimes I think I'm just a puppy at heart. With very strong teeth.

It took me an hour and a half to get up to West Hollywood. When I finally found the place Chris told me Marlin lived, I parked down the street and walked back along the two sides of the building I could get to. I got no sense of Richard anywhere. I didn't see Tommy's bike. The apartment on the second floor was dark. The glass door in front was locked, and when I knocked, no one came to open it. I found the carport behind the building that corresponded to the apartment number, but it was empty. No luck.

I'm a good hunter, but there has to be something to hunt. I walked up the street, keeping an eye on the place, willing Marlin to arrive with Richard in tow, and Tommy, conveniently for me, riding shotgun. Nothing. A couple of guys walked their dogs along the street, bringing home the shopping. When they passed me, and a glance showed me the coast was clear, I changed, just long enough to let the pets get a whiff of me, and turn, shrieking and howling, tangling their leads and yanking their owners into the street. I changed back the same second, before the guys saw me, and had a good laugh watching them try to get untangled and recover their bags. I don't usually do things like that. Just when I'm annoyed.

The next building up was a bookstore. A tall, thin, bearded man stood in the doorway, watching the guys finish comforting their pooches and walk away. I stepped past him into the bookstore, consciously waiting for his comment, since he might, after all, have seen something. He gave me a long steady look through deep-set, humorous eyes, and then followed me back inside. I was close enough to him to scent that it had been a long time since he'd eaten meat, which explained his hollow look. He went behind the counter and asked absently if he could help me find anything, and at the same time sat back down to his radio and his stack of open books.

"Nope," I said, avoiding another of his long, steady glances. "Just looking." I positioned myself behind a shelf, which gave me a good view of the building and the front window of what Chris had told me was Marlin's apartment. The bookstore guy put on a pair of glasses but watched me over the top of them, so I stopped checking out the window and looked at the books in front of me. New Age Psychology, the shelf in front of me said. Gods, what a lot of books. I picked one up at random and rifled the pages.

The storefront bookstore had a wall of windows on the street side. I wandered along, peering over the four-foot row of bookshelves to see which vantage point gave me the best view of the apartment across the street. I worked my way along past Mysticism and Healing to Self-Help, pretending some intensive browsing as I went. The bookstore guy must have thought I was a basket case.

The rows of bookshelves marched in lines all the way to the back walls, where the shelves went from the floor to the ceiling. There, a ladder ran on a track along the walls, so you could climb up and browse the top shelves. The counter stood to the right of the entrance, lined in front with cardboard boxes full of books. I wandered over there and looked down at them, while trying to glance out of the front door. The bookstore guy took off his glasses and looked up at me.

"Those aren't for sale yet. I just got those in."

I nodded and turned away.

"Anything I can help you with?" he asked. I thought he sounded sarcastic. I mean, I'd been in there almost half an hour already. I turned around, but he'd already put his glasses back on and was gazing down at his stack of open books. There sure were a lot of them.

I went back along the shelf on its other side, this time with my back to the windows, but turning every time I picked out a book, opened it, flipped a few pages and put it back, stifling equally the dust that threatened to make me sneeze and the sense impressions of the people who had previously handled the book, or stood where I was standing. I was about to peruse the whole front shelf over again from its other side, when the bookstore guy called out, "I generally close at nine. Can I help you find anything particular?"

I thought, what the hell. "Do you know Marlin? He lives in that building there, second floor?"

"Yes," he said, surprising me so much I turned to face him for the first time. "He's in here a couple of times a week. Not on a Tuesday, though. He gets together with his group on Tuesdays."

"Oh yeah?" I asked, starting for the door. "What group is that? Where do they meet?"

He smiled at me. He was older than I'd thought at first, probably in his fifties. His cavernous face and eyes lit up now he was smiling. He wore faded jeans and a dark green flannel shirt, and short, old boots that had walked up a lot of distant roads. "The Thunder Mountain Boys? It isn't a group you'd want to drop in on, believe me."

"Yeah?" I said, challenged. I canted my weight onto one leg and folded my arms. "You think they would offer a threat to a girl like me?"

He stood up, looking serious now. "I think they would eat you for breakfast, puppy dog."

I was so taken aback I didn't move while he lowered the blinds over the front door, turned the sign around that said they were Open to Sorry We're Closed. He came towards me, holding out his hand like you would to a dog to sniff and make friends. When I didn't move, he changed it into a gesture inviting me to the back of the store. "I knew you were coming," he explained.

All right, that intrigued me, but it wasn't what I had come for.

"When will Marlin get home?" I asked.

He stopped by a door at the back marked Office—Private. "I don't know. He's a ritualist. Lately, he and his group have been meeting more often, and for longer. We all have work to do. We are all doing everything we can to defeat the same enemy." He opened the door behind him and motioned to me. This time I followed him. In the back of the store, if I had to kill him or anything, no one would see anyway.

Behind the door a curtain covered the entrance. Both the doorway and the curtain were loaded with wards. The ones on the doorway gave out a strong impression that the door was locked, and never opened. These parted as he passed through the door. The wards on the curtains were more complex, but before I could tease the sense out of them, the guy swept the curtain and the wards aside together and pronounced, "Come in."

He loaded the phrase with a weight of meaning, but as soon as I stepped past him, I was too distracted to try and analyze it. I walked into a square, windowless room filled with a low sweet ringing sound that I almost couldn't hear, and smelling of dust and books and—strangely—water. I looked around quickly. The walls were lined with bookshelves, only three feet high in here, but filled with books, mostly thick and brown with age. There was a futon in one corner, neatly made up and, against the wall in the corner opposite, well-lit by an antique standing lamp, was a desk on which stood a big silver bowl half-full of water—but that wasn't what I smelled. I was distracted again by the sound, the low mellifluous ringing, and then I saw them: small golden bowls spinning where they balanced on slender wands. These were full of water, too, water that was swirling as the bowls swirled, and filling the room with that scent. Spinning, balanced where they spun, and not stopping. Impossible—unless... I turned to him as he walked past me into the room. He took a stance in the middle on an ancient Persian rug from which wafted scents so curious and appealing I wanted to bury my nose in it. I slapped away that distraction as he lifted his hands and stood there, quite still, his eyes closed. The little bowls slowly ceased spinning. One by one they dropped off the sticks that had held them and fell, ringing, onto the bookshelf or onto the floor. The sticks fell after them. Nine of them, one after the other, and the ringing stopped.

He opened his eyes, turned to look at me. "I'm Darius," he said. "I am a geomancer. That's how I knew you were coming."

The scent of water changed. I picked up the nearest bowl, which wasn't gold anymore, but brass, and smelled it. Nothing. And it was quite dry.

I held out the brass bowl. "How did you...?"

He took it from me and laid it gently on the shelf. "Trade secrets, and a lot of practice. Sit down?"

There was only one chair, the one at the desk, a heavy ancient wooden armchair. He pulled that out for me and when I sat down he folded himself up on the floor on the rug.

"How did you know...?" I didn't want to spell it out in case he'd only made an inspired guess, but people almost never spot me. Even if they see me, they make themselves believe they didn't see anything out of the ordinary. It's one of my favorite human traits. He'd shocked me with that "puppy dog" remark.

"I saw you in the water," Darius leaned back on his hands, looking up at me. "Sometimes, when I see things, I know things too. So I knew you would be coming to my shop. And then of course, you pulled that stunt outside. I wouldn't have believed it if I didn't already know."

I looked past him, embarrassed for a second. Honestly, sometimes I think I should do something to control these mad impulses of mine. What the hell.

He went on. "I knew what you were—are. And I know you are in the fight against the World Snake. We are required to meet because I have information for you, and through me you will learn something that you don't yet know you need to know." He grinned at me suddenly, which put unexpected crinkles in his long face.

"All right," I said, sitting back. "Tell me."

"Ah," he replied, "but it doesn't work that way. Would that it did."

"All right then. How does it work?"

He shook his head. "Try this. You ask me questions, and I'll see if I can answer you."

That was easy. "Where's Richard?"

He looked at me blankly.

I tried again. "Marlin has him. I want to know where he is."

He got to his feet like one of those stick men refolding itself and went to the desk. He bent over the large bowl for a moment in silence, then stirred it with one hand, once, twice. He stared into the water again. After a moment he stood up and shook his head. "Richard? I can't see anything. Maybe you could tell me about him?"

What could I say about Richard? A glint of his eyes in the half-light came into my mind, together with the memory of what his hands had been doing at that moment, and the gentle, quizzical smile on his face while he did it, and I felt myself blushing. Damn. I got up from the chair, walked over and looked at the bookshelf opposite. More books. "Well," I said, "he's a demon."

Darius let out a snort, lifting his hands. "Well, no wonder. I'm not going to see a demon in the water. They don't show up like that."

"He's human—I mean, he has a human form."

"Yeah, nevertheless. You'll have to ask me something else."

I folded my arms. Was he trying not to be helpful? I said, "Tell me what you know about demons. All I know is what Richard told me, and hey, you never can tell."

He sat on the edge of the desk. He looked at me intently, like this teacher I once had used to look when I'd failed to live up to his unreasonable expectations. "Did you summon this demon?"

He was beginning to piss me off. "No, but he's mine now. He

says. Then this guy, Tommy, that he used to go with, he came and picked him up—I think he was on the way to the store—and his friend Chris said Marlin wanted him, and that he would make Richard sorry that he was ever born. Except, he wasn't born."

Darius listened to this without expression. When I finished he asked, "What do you want this Richard for?"

"What do you mean?" I said. "I mean, he's mine, and anyway, I don't think he wanted to go with that guy—Marlin."

"Did it ever occur to you," Darius interrupted, "that the demon was sent to distract you from your true mission?"

"Huh? I mean, come on."

"Our fight is with the World Snake, isn't it?"

I shrugged. "I only heard about that last week, I'm still not sure what I'm supposed to do about it."

"The demon told you of it," he said, as though he knew already. "Did he tell you how to fight it?"

"He told me," I said, remembering, "He said that before the World Snake, the Eater of Souls will come. And he says that may be the greater danger of the two."

"Right," Darius said, disgusted. "And why is that?"

I thought back. I was starting to not like this guy. "I don't know."

"You do know," he insisted.

I shrugged. "Richard's scared of it."

"Is he?" His voice was growing milder with every question. It made him sound sarcastic. "And does he have a soul to be eaten?"

I felt the color rise in my face as I realized several facts weren't adding up, which made me feel stupid, which made me feel embarrassed, which made me feel angry, but I said, without missing a beat, "Yes, he does."

"Does he?" Darius said, in honest wonder. "Well, that changes everything." He thought a moment, and then nodded to himself. "I'll have to find out more about demons. The only ones I've known so far are treacherous, lying bastards."

"Have you had one?" I asked, curious. "One that was yours?"

He shook his head. "No. Thank the Spirits that be, I have not."

"Then you don't know much about it, do you?" I said.

He laughed at that. "All right. You'll have to find your Richard on your own. I don't think that's my province. I seem to be the clearinghouse for information on our prime enemy. I put groups in touch with one another, I take questions, and if I can't find the answers myself, I find those who can. I marshal our resources. I know already that you're going to be one of our most important ones." He added in a murmur, "Maybe the most important one."

"Yeah?" I was still thinking about how to find Richard. "What can I do against the World Snake that all you power-raisers can't do?"

He looked surprised. "Well, for one thing, you'll be able to sense where it is. Won't you?"

I thought about that. He was right. If it was nearby, if it was that big and that powerful, I'd know. So I nodded.

He nodded back. "That's useful to all of us. You'll begin at once, of course."

Huh? "Begin what?" I asked.

"Seeking the Snake. We don't know where it is. We need that information. We need you to do this for us."

"Do what?"

"Quarter the city. I'll give you some numbers you can call in to, to tell where you are and what ground you've covered, and some other numbers in case you sense the enemy. You can't begin too soon."

"Now just a minute," I protested. "I never said—"

"You are with us?" he asked, sounding as reasonable as any adult sane person can who has just said something totally unbelievable.

"Look, I may be with you but—"

"Good," he said. "I'll get you those numbers."

I followed him across the room. "Now hold on just a minute!" He turned back to me with mild, enquiring eyes. I stood my ground, not letting his quietude disarm me. "I am in this fight. But I am in on my own terms, and I will do it my own way."

"But you just said—"

"I'm not finished! This is my city. But I am not your hunting dog. I am not running around this whole stupid basin sniffing for your stupid Snake. At least not until I find Richard. Now tell me what Marlin is doing with him."

Darius smiled. "Well, we know it's not a virgin sacrifice, don't we?"

❧❧

CHAPTER TWELVE

I left a little later with a brand new Thomas Guide turned to the right page, an address clearly marked, and my ears still ringing from the sound of the chiming golden bowls. It had taken precious minutes of waiting while Darius carefully and deliberately set each brass bowl spinning on its slender wand, one after another until he had all nine going again, with me sitting stock-still in the chair, admonished not to move or even think too loud while he did his casting.

Once the first bowl was spinning I heard, so faintly it was almost like a miniscule buzzing in my ears, the slight ringing sound they had been making when I came in, and I smelled water. When all nine were going again, Darius took a stand in the middle of the room with his arms out and his eyes closed. The ringing grew louder as the bowls seemed to spin faster and faster. I wondered if I was being hypnotized, enjoying a hallucination or a carnival trick. The bowls spun on and on. They changed tone. One turned onto its side. No way should it have been able to do that. Darius's head was thrown back. The expression on his face was distant and intense. Sweat had gathered on his brow.

All at once two of the bowls exploded from their perches and shot across the room with a whiz and a splash. For an instant I felt water on my face, but when I touched my cheek, it was gone. Darius wavered a little and opened his eyes. He studied me gravely.

"I asked if it is imperative that you go to work for us now." He frowned as he thought about what he was saying. "They said you are already working for us." He shrugged. "So be it. You should ask me, not where your Richard is, but where you can find Marlin."

With the address and the Thomas Guide, in about fifteen minutes I pulled up at a three-story building in Beverly Hills. The front door to the glass office building was open and I caught one of the elevators to the third floor. I stepped out and was brought up short: it was faint, and it was hours old, but I smelled Richard. Richard had been there.

Only one of the four offices was currently lit and occupied. Fortunately, it was the one Richard's trail led to, or I would have had to do some breaking of glass doors. I was tempted to anyway. I hit the door to the Lemmon and Frazier Dance Studio hard, but it was heavy and did not give me the satisfaction of crashing open in front of me. Darn. I resisted the temptation to go out and slam it open again as a bunch of guys were already looking at me.

They had been doing a working. I could feel it in the air, the power swirling like a strong current, only beginning to dissipate at the edges. But it was over, and groups of men were standing around on the brightly lit hardwood floor, reflected on three sides by mirrors set over exercise bars, and on the fourth by a wall of windows looking out onto a view of the city. Some were still dressed in their workout clothes, tank tops dark with sweat stains, and tight spandex pants. Some had showered and changed into clean, dry shirts and sweats, or back into the suits or slacks that were their day wear. They stared at me as I walked a third of the way into the room, my head lifted and casting around for scent. Great gods, what had gone on in there was complicated!

There were ancient layers of heavy sweat as a backdrop to the day's events, both men's and women's; this place had been in business for years. I caught Richard's familiar, sweet tang, overlaid by the scents of more recent exertions. Clearly and sharply, I smelled sex. My hackles rose. For a moment I felt I was wearing two skins at once, wolf and woman, and I took a moment to think that this was how Jacob the bear had done his dual-aspect trick. But I was mad, and I wasn't giving anything away.

The guys had stopped what they were saying or doing to watch me. I walked on into the room until I stood over the place where Richard had been about three hours earlier. The buzz of magic raised, a wild magic, powerful and rough and a little crazy, was strongest here, at its vortex. I looked around at the dancers, beautiful and fit, their faces open and their movements graceful with strength, satiety, and release. I knew what they'd done with Richard.

One of them, a lithe, olive-skinned man with close-cropped black hair and a small mustache asked, "Can we help you, honey? I'm afraid this is men's night. The girls—"

I turned on him with a snarl, and I got large. There was an instant response from the group, a connection, an alertness, but I was too angry to pay attention. "Where's Richard?" I asked. I headed toward the showers calling, "Richard?"

Another of them, smooth and heavy-set, answered me, as four or five converged to bar my way to the door of the men's showers. "We don't have anyone here called Richard. I'm sorry." He smiled apologetically, but he wasn't afraid.

I stopped. Richard's scent petered out near the men's room door. He hadn't been in there. I explained, "You had a guy here. Young looking. Blond. Maybe you called him Stan?"

There was a tightening of tension in the room. Some of the men looked at one another, and others made some effort to *not* look at each other. The first one who'd spoken to me said, "He's not here now—"

"I know that," I said, and I could feel the anger coursing through my body like blood, adding to my power. I felt myself growing larger; I felt their collective energy falter as they took in the change. I almost felt like laughing as I looked around over the tops of their heads. My anger was feeding on the magic buzz in the room. Soon there would be action. Soon, there would be blood. "He came here with Marlin. Where's Marlin?"

The energy in the room diminished, like air leaking out of a balloon. Now they looked around at each other, trying to get a consensus, trying to get an answer. Another guy spoke for them, this one tall and lanky, with a neat beard. "Sure. You can talk to Marlin. He's right over there."

The man sitting on the bench in front of the piano was older than most of the other dancers. He was hard to notice, because in this room full of men buzzing with vitality, he seemed empty. He was dressed in brown corduroys and a loud, red, button-down shirt. I could smell Richard on him faintly, and the fact that he'd showered recently, but overlaying those traces was a bubble of raw fear that I didn't understand. It had nothing to do with me; it was older, and he wasn't looking at me. Five or six of the men surrounded him, offering drinks, massaging his shoulders, chafing his hands, but he sat there as detached as a homeless guy in a crowded train station. When I came over to him, he looked up and smiled. He had a thinning head of dark hair and a fine mustache.

"Hi, guys," said Marlin. He looked down again immediately, and the smile vanished.

"He isn't like this," the guy rubbing his hand protested. He had a neat, square beard and was dressed in purple spandex shorts but had put a dry blue sweatshirt on. "He's—" He looked around at the others for concurrence. "He's *Marlin*," he said, as though that would say it all.

"Where is Stan?" I asked the group at large, and Marlin in particular.

The men around him looked at each other. "We don't know," purple spandex shorts replied. "Marlin had to drop him off somewhere. He left early. He was supposed to come back here—"

A guy in a suit, who was on one knee offering Marlin spring water from a fresh bottle said, "I came late. I saw Marlin walking down Sunset Avenue on my way here. I knew he was supposed to be here, so I stopped." He looked up at the others, as though they alone could understand his pain. "He didn't recognize me."

Another of the men bent over Marlin gently, his hand on his shoulders. "Marlin? Marlin?"

Marlin looked up again, smiled cheerfully, and said, "Hi, guys." Then once again all expression drained out of his face.

"Where did he take Richard?" I asked.

They looked at one another again in silent conference. "We don't know," a slender young man beside me answered. He stretched his arms behind him unconsciously till his shoulders cracked.

"Look," I said, putting it simply for them. "Richard is mine. Marlin's friend Tommy took him, gave him to Marlin—" I snarled at the hint of laughter in the air.

The little one said apologetically, as the laughter abruptly ceased, "We didn't know he was—anyone else's. He had a little chain around his wrist. Marlin said, while that was there, Stan would do anything we said." He shook his head, wonderingly. "And he did. He never said a word. Marlin said we could use him, and then—"

That was all I could take. I changed and lunged for Marlin's throat in the same instant. His head came up and that same smile had started on his face as my paws passed his ears and my jaws closed round his throat and the first sweet taste of salt and flesh and blood melded with the feeling of cartilage ready to snap between my teeth.

Gods, those guys were fast. I didn't see it start, I didn't see what happened, but the next moment I was ass over backwards and a mirror smashed against my back. I slid down the wall and twisted to my feet. They stood across from me, holding one another, every hand grasping arm, wrist, or shoulder, feet set wide and strong. Connected like that, they radiated a wall of power that they had raised and focused and used to knock me away. Two of them had Marlin by the shoulder. They hadn't, in that moment, even started to staunch the punctures I'd made in his throat. I could tell by the small amount of blood that either I hadn't managed to do much damage, or they'd stopped that too, when they threw me across the room. I lowered my head as though I were sorry. I wagged my tail like a dog—a gesture I was sure they'd recognize. Then I trotted forward slowly, like a sorry puppy finally answering to her name. They let me come; they didn't do anything. Two steps away I gathered my strength and my fury and leaped again at Marlin, and once again I felt the air tighten around me like a fist. I twisted and smashed, sideways this time, into the mirror adjacent to the one I'd hit the last time. I heard an angry protest, and at least I had the satisfaction of having broken another of their mirrors as I hit the ground again. I got up. Looked at them, still interlocked, still sustaining their power. Hey, wolves never hunt the whole herd. Wolves cut out the losers. Wolves wait until they know they will win. I sat down, licked blood off my paw. My blood, damn it. Wolves are patient. Wolves are patient hunters. Right. That's what my dad always said. All right. Since I didn't have a choice, I'd be patient.

I changed. They didn't move. They stood, holding one another, focused and braced against me.

I could smell the blood running down my back as much as feel it. There were places on my shoulders and side that stung, but this wasn't the time to think about them. The olive-skinned man relaxed his hold on the two men beside him and stepped forward. "Listen, honey, we don't want to hurt you—"

I stepped forward. "No? You up for breaking another mirror? You think the bad luck cancels out after two?"

One of the older men said, "We didn't ask you to come here—"

I said, "You took Richard. That's like sending me an engraved invitation, don't you think?" And I stepped forward again. Wolves are patient. But that's not what my blood was saying right then.

The olive-skinned man took another turn. "Honey, please. We didn't know he was yours. Marlin brought him—"

"We thought he was a volunteer," another voice concurred.

"He never said a word," another insisted.

"You always treat people like that when they come here?" I remembered, which made my anger surge. "And you *knew* he was under constraint, with that bracelet—"

Their glances swept one another once again. The olive-skinned guy tried again, "Honey, Stan—Richard—whatever you call him, he wasn't people. Didn't you know?"

The air grew thick with my anger. I felt it differently that time, cold, not hot, steel, not blood. Certain. Enormous. Patient. Maybe I was growing up.

"I don't give a flying empty shit if you think of him as *people* or not. He was people to me." They grabbed one another as I took another step forward, my rage carried with me like a giant wave. My voice dropped again to that malevolent resonance. The air, still organized with their working, thrummed to its sound. "Do you know the wolf kind?" I asked them. "Do you know what you have done? To touch one of us is to touch us all. You may be strong together." I stared down the lot of them. "But you are not always together. And we wolves are patient hunters. You owe me blood for this, and blood will be paid." Great exit line. I turned to go.

"Whoa, whoa, wait a minute, honey."

I knew who it was before I turned back. The olive-skinned guy had come forward, together with the slender guy, and the suit guy who had brought Marlin here. The older guy said, "Listen. We don't have time for this now—"

I laughed at that.

He continued right on. "In case you haven't heard, we're in a war here. We're raising power every day and every way we can to use against a common enemy. A lot of people are helping us. We thought your Richard was just another one."

"Under constraint," I spat back. "Did he *look* like he was having a good time?" There was a long pause after that question. I laughed again, but tears were pricking my eyes. Damn! I don't cry—and never in public. But the thought of Richard, and how expressive his face could be, in this room, with these guys... I stared down the lot of them, furious once more. But underneath this new surge of anger, the huge, cold anger swelled, strong and long-lived as a glacier. It gave me comfort. All accounts would one day balance, from every one of these guys.

"Listen," the older guy said again. "We'll help you find—Richard—in any way we can. When Marlin gets better—" His voice thickened as his throat tightened on the thought. "We'll find out where he took Richard, all right? And we'll tell you. How's that? Fair enough?"

"Ask yourselves," I said coldly, "if it were one of you, or yours, if that would be enough." And I walked out.

When I had cooled down enough to think, I turned my car around from where I had been heading toward the freeway and went back to Darius's place. If Darius knew everyone, as he said, he might know where I needed to go to look for Richard now, where Marlin might have dropped him off.

Darius's shop was still dark; all right, I expected that. I went down the narrow passageway between two buildings that led to the door that he had let me out of, when I left his back room. I knocked there. No answer. No sign of any movement inside. No noise, no scent. I walked around to the back of the building, hopped up on a wall, dropped into the adjoining yard where someone was storing shelves of potted plants, backed up to find the narrow window that looked into Darius's room. It was dark, too.

The yard dogs came on me silently, in a rush, a pair of German shepherds, trained not to bark. I changed, grew large the same instant out of annoyance at the inconvenience, and stood there on four feet looking down at them while they stopped, stared wide-eyed, whined, and then their tails began to wag in apology. I should hope so! I advanced on them, lowering my head, and they scrammed, which gave me time to change back and hop back over the wall before they smelled naked meat and got brave again.

I checked Darius's door one more time. Hey, the great sorcerer, shouldn't he be spinning his bowls and keeping watch over the world? Shouldn't he be paying attention to me in case I needed him? Damn! I banged on his door quite a lot, until I saw a cop car cruising the street, slowing down to look for undesirable elements. That's the trouble with hanging out in good neighborhoods when you're not, exactly, a good neighbor.

I'd get back to him. I'd get back to Tamara as well.

I drove home. When I opened my apartment door, I almost expected to find the odors of food waiting for me and Richard there to tell me it was all a mistake, Marlin dropped him off back at home when he was finished with him, and he'd showered already, and hadn't quite gotten dressed again. But my apartment was dark, and Richard's scent was fading, overpowered by the yeast-based bread dough still expanding in my trash can. I went to my room, fell down on my bed without bothering to undress, and went to sleep.

The scent of the sheets gave me strong dreams. I saw Richard hanging in a cage. I saw him dressed in a filthy smock, shoveling shit in a barnyard. I saw him come into my room, bend down and whisper in my ear, but I was so engrossed in his touch, in feeling him against me again, that I didn't hear what he said.

When the alarm jerked me alert in the morning I went automatically to the shower and got ready for work. I hesitated when I picked up my keys and then thought, why not? The city may be about to be swallowed into the sea, but I still wanted my paycheck.

At Arches Auditorium, I got out the linseed oil and stood under the platform applying the first coat to this part of the lobby while the others worked above me. When break time came, I went on working. Yvette joined me after that and worked in silence, while the guys chattered above us about some movie they'd seen.

Yvette said, "You're not so cheerful today."

"No," I said.

"Right. Yesterday, you were like a real person, all smiling and laughing, and today… you act like your man left you for his boyfriend."

I cracked a smile. "He did. Just about."

"No kidding?"

"That's what I'm told."

"Well," Yvette said, instantly pissed on my behalf. "Fuck him. That's what I say. Fuck 'em all."

"Yeah. Right."

We painted for a while in silence, rubbing off the excess oil with a rag when it had dried to the point of tackiness. Then she said, "What are you going to do to him?"

"To who?" I asked, dropping to my knees to polish the wood I'd already oiled.

"To that guy, who left you."

I rubbed fiercely. "I'm going to get him back, that's what."

Yvette laughed, egging me on. "You do that, girl. You show him."

"Yeah," I said. "I will."

We worked in silence after that until lunchtime, when Yvette offered to take me to the place where they made the best enchiladas in town. That's when I realized that I'd missed a lot of meals since walking into my apartment the previous night expecting dinner to be on the table. I have no idea if they were the best enchiladas in town. I scarfed down six of them without stopping to taste them. Getting food into me also brought me to my senses. Painting Arches was not accomplishing anything. If the world ended (or the greater L.A. basin, whatever), I wasn't going to need rent money at the end of the month anyway. When we got back to the auditorium, I told Yvette to tell Pete, our boss, that I was feeling sick and going home. Yvette raised her brows at this and replied, deadpan, "Yeah, you got the wicked hunger fever, I know that. Six enchiladas is a definite symptom." She went into the auditorium laughing at her own joke and shaking her head, and I drove away smiling.

I drove fast. My little Honda Civic shook at the way I pushed her, but I pushed her anyway. The cold raw anger that had risen within me the night before swelled in me now, coloring my every thought and passion stronger and more certain. It felt good.

I found my way back to the music store in Costa Mesa without any trouble. I can generally find my way back to somewhere I've been, even if I wasn't on foot and didn't leave a trail. I parked my car down the street and made my way to Tamara's shop. There were no bears outside today, and when I went in, the shop was empty of customers. Jacob, the bear with the scar across his eye, was sitting behind the counter. I went over to him. I don't let bears scare me.

"Tamara?" I asked.

He gazed at me coldly. "She waited for you. She was here yesterday, and the day before. You don't have a phone?"

I shook my head. I hadn't gotten a phone. I didn't want any calls.

"She was looking for you."

Unbelievably, I felt myself blushing. I suppressed it hard. "I was busy," I said, and it sounded more belligerent than I meant it to, but what the hell. No one tells me where to be, or when. That's a promise I made myself.

His brows arched like he was getting mad. "You were busy? What are you talking about?"

I changed the subject. "Where is Tamara? When can I see her?"

He settled back on the stool he was using, and it creaked under his weight. "She's in the desert scrying the stars. You were lucky to find her here once. She doesn't stand still often."

"I have a few questions for her."

"They'll have to wait," he pointed out. He looked past me to the door of the shop. "She left a message for you."

That was more like it. "Yeah?"

"Where's the other? You know. The demon."

It surprised me to see the great bear so diffident. So, bears didn't like demons. I looked around behind me in all innocence. "Richard?" I called, as though he had come in behind me. "I don't know," I said, turning back to him. "He'll be here in a minute."

He leaned forward to tell me quietly, "Lady Tamara says, you beware of that demon."

I stiffened, and I didn't bother to lower my voice. "Oh yeah? Why?"

He looked around sharply before he answered me. "Something the demon said, when he was here. You remember he spoke of the Eater of Souls?"

"Sure I do. That's what we came here for."

"Yeah, well." Jacob leaned forward farther over the counter, and the stool creaked again under him. "Tamara looked into it, asked questions, and the Eater of Souls is real, that's sure."

Strangely, what I felt was relief. Not what I would expect on hearing that a second terrible enemy was coming to town. Then I realized it meant Richard had been telling the truth. I smiled. "So, my demon wasn't lying after all. Well, then."

Jacob raised one hand. "Ah, but he was. If you remember, he referred to the Eater of Souls as a male. He said, *he*."

I frowned, trying to remember. "Yeah, so?"

"And the demon said he'd run into the Eater of Souls before, so he should know—the Eater of Souls manifests as a female. An old woman, an ancient one, bowed down by the weight of her years, which number the centuries like days." Jacob pointed his finger at me. "Your demon is lying. He lies about one thing, he could be lying about many another. You be careful. The Lady Tamara says, you check with her before you believe any more of your demon's information."

I felt my back go all hard and straight and my mouth tighten. I do not like being told what to do. I started thinking of open spaces, of being on my own again, and away from the stupid troubles of this stupid city.

Jacob shook his head sadly. "You can't."

I brought back my gaze to him sharply. "Can't what?"

"Run off, like you did before."

"What are you talking about?" I demanded.

He chuckled at that, and for a moment I saw the bear in him again. "You think I don't know you? We who have two natures, we're more alike than you know. And one thing that makes us is wise to each other's tricks. In any case, we know you won't be going. You're bound here like the rest of us. Lady Tamara read it in the fire."

I thought about this for a moment, and then asked, "And did Lady Tamara see the demon in her reading?"

He said with disgust, "You can't scry a demon. You know that."

Actually, I only knew what Darius had told me, and he didn't have to be right. "So she didn't know Richard's gone. He was taken from me."

He frowned at this, looking past me around the store. "I thought you said...?" Bears can be slow sometimes. Then he shook his head. "Well, maybe that's for the best, if he's a trickster."

It was my turn to lean on the counter. "All right, but think about this. If there are those of us on one side of this battle, there are sure to be those on the other. And one of them may now have my demon. Is that good?"

He sat arrested by that thought for a moment, then said slowly, "Maybe the demon will work just as contrary for the one who has him now. He left you, did he?"

"He was *taken*," I emphasized again.

"Lady Tamara said, it can't be a good thing, a wolf with a demon." He was totally under her spell all right, if spell it was. I said, just to see what he'd say, "And what about a bear with a demon? Would that be all right?"

He shook his head. "I wouldn't have anything to do with one of those. Even if," he smiled at me slyly, "you could find a demon anywhere who could comprehend the ways of the bear kind."

Well. At least he was consistent. Bears are, though. It's one of their weaknesses.

"When does Tamara get back from the desert?"

But he didn't know. Scrying the stars could take a night, or a week of nights, now that the moon was full. "She'll send for you," was all he'd say.

I was back on the freeway before I realized she didn't know where I lived. I thought about turning around, but I didn't. She's a sorceress, after all. If she found me, I'd know a little more about how strong she was. I took the 5 north, then dog-legged over on the 101 and then caught Santa Monica to West Hollywood.

It took me over two hours to get to Darius' bookstore as I hit rush-hour traffic almost as soon as I got on the freeway, half the time gazing into the blazing sunset. But what got me actually cussing was trying to find a place to park. I finally took a spot around the corner this time in a bank parking lot—Bank Parking Only, We Will Tow, but it was after business hours, so who would know? Bunches of other people seemed to have the same idea, anyway.

I wanted to side-track Marlin's group of guys. I wanted to know who Marlin's contacts were, where he might deliver Richard, since he knew he was a demon. And Darius said he knew everyone. And he might. I went blazing into the store looking for him. The little bell hanging from the door handle tinkled as I went into the shop. A dozen people were rooting around through the books, one of them up on a ladder. One was hunkered down in a corner, surrounded by half a dozen open books like he was in for the duration. Darius sat behind the counter. He didn't have any books open in front of him this time, his radio was off, and he wasn't wearing his glasses. He smiled at me as I came up to him. "Hi," he said. "What can I do for you?"

He didn't look right. He didn't feel right. He smelled the same, but... no, he didn't smell the same. The Darius I had scented yesterday lay on him like a coat. What was emanating from him now was pitiful, like last year's scent. Like an empty bottle that once held something pungent.

"Darius?" I said. His gaze had wandered into the middle distance while I studied him, but now it came back to me. He smiled.

"Hi," he said brightly. "What can I do for you?"

"Darius?" I leaned over the counter. "Do you remember me?"

The smile faded from his face and he looked up at me blankly. I wondered for a moment if it would remind him if I changed suddenly, right now, with my front feet—my hands—on the counter. Just as I thought I'd try that, a guy sidled up with a stack of books in his arms. Darius turned to him with his smile renewed. "Hi," he said again. "What can I do for you?"

"I'd like to get these," the man said, and got out his wallet. I backed away while Darius slowly, methodically, re-piled the books, then slowly, methodically, looked up each price, and slowly, methodically, wrote down each book and its price on a receipt. The customer waited patiently.

This was not the Darius I had met the previous night. I turned and made my way as unobtrusively as I knew how to the back of the shop, trailing my fingers along the spines of the rows of books, pretending to browse as I went. I stood by the ladder in front of the wall of books right next to his back door. I waited until the woman pulling out cookbooks from the shelf on the other side of the door made a considered selection and turned away. A quick look around. When I was sure no one was paying any attention to me, I tried the door. It opened under my hand. With another quick glance, I slipped into the back room.

The wards on the curtain that separated his room from the shop were in shreds. I went inside, my senses taut at the smell of some searing conflagration that had not been there when I was last in that room the night before. I eased the door closed behind me and found myself standing in darkness. I reached for the light switch and turned it on.

The walls and ceiling, and the backs of the books, were blackened as though by a swift, hot fire or explosion. The futon had been thrown against the wall, the bedding scattered, and it too bore marks of scorching. The bronze bowls were strewn everywhere, and several had melted. The silver bowl of water had turned over. There was blood on the carpet in the middle of the room. I changed in order to be sure, but I knew already that it was Darius's blood—not much, but his. The conflagration seemed to have obliterated all other scents in the room. Something violent had happened, had happened fast, and what remained of Darius was sitting outside, smiling a happy smile, slowly and methodically keeping his accounts. Who didn't remember me at all, one he had called a player in the game.

Like Marlin, there didn't seem to be much left to him. And it seemed to me, the Eater of Souls had come to town.

❧❦

CHAPTER THIRTEEN

I don't remember getting back in my car. I don't remember starting up and heading off. I came to myself when some idiot tried to pass me on the right on a single-lane two-way street and almost hit me. I realized I was heading back to Marlin's dance studio. I realized also that I was so furious and so upset that I was on the verge of changing involuntarily, something I grew out of a long time ago. The first time you change, you have no idea what's happening. Your brain changes too, you see, so you generally go right on with your life looking at things from several feet lower to the ground, and with a whole new set of strengths and senses and emotions, and you don't even realize that you're different until you try to talk or use a hand. As you get older, you learn to control your changes. I sat crouched over the wheel, holding on to my human nature for all I was worth while my thoughts roiled over the mess I was in, and my body wanted Richard, and my blood wanted to kill something *now*. I passed the turn to Marlin's studio with both hands clutching the wheel, turned up Beverly, and headed for the hills.

It's better to run these moods out than try and live your wolf nature in your human form. The two sometimes are not compatible, and you're liable to do something that for a human isn't forgivable, though it's passable in a wolf. So what I say is, better to be a wolf when you do it.

I stopped the car on the roadside, fell out already changed, and headed up the verge.

I ran straight uphill so the running would take all my strength and I'd spend this excess passion all the sooner so I could think. I needed to think. Up on the top of the slope I could see the lights of the city spread out all around me, like jewels in the darkness. There's no illusion of being in the country when you're up in the Hollywood Hills. The roar of traffic is loud and ceaseless. You can even hear voices from the streets below. I paced the ridge like a rooftop, still feeling confined. I startled a pair of picnickers sitting on their blanket, holding glasses of wine. They sat frozen while I passed them by and then started arguing as soon as my back was turned, as if I couldn't hear them.

"That's a wolf!"

"No, it isn't."

"It is! Look at it!"

"Darling, it can't be a wolf, we don't have wolves in Hollywood...."

Ha. I ran down the slope and up the next, around the side of the hill out of sight of any people. I sat down there, looking down at the red lights and the white lights of the freeway below. The cold, strong fury I first felt in Marlin's dance studio swelled up in me again, comforting me with its power. While that passion was in me, I wouldn't stop, I wouldn't change course, and I wouldn't lose my way. I felt its dimensions, glorying in the strength of it. This was going to be fun.

What was I doing?

Three different magic users said I had a part to play in the coming battle to preserve the city from the World Snake. Fair enough. I was here, I'm important; of course they would want me to be involved. And on their side. The thing was, I would take part the way I chose, or not at all. It would be entirely up to me. If that was good enough, then fine. If not, the city could go under, for all I cared. I looked around, taking in the extent of the lights, all the way to the horizon and beyond. I knew: to the north up to Calabasas, to the south as far as Orange County and down into Irvine, to the east along the basin, to the little ridges of hills—that was going to be the new coastline. I thought of the ocean lapping its way up Baseline Avenue, and grinned.

How did someone like me take part against the World Snake?

By being able to tell where she was, Darius said. I sniffed. No World Snake here.

But that wasn't why I was up here, was it? That wasn't why I had run all this way, why I had fled in my car, holding onto my nature like a pup unable to control herself.

The Eater of Souls was here, and I was the only one that believed in it. Besides Richard, who had been left somewhere by Marlin, who had then, or so it seemed, lost his own soul. And Darius, another powerful user of magic in the neighborhood, had gone the same way, or so it seemed.

I would rather not become a vacuous idiot, thank you very much. That isn't really in my life plan. So leaving town right now really did seem like the best option. Except there was Richard. Who had gotten himself into my service in order to have some protection from the Eater of Souls that he feared. Who appeared as an old woman, according to Tamara, but Richard had mistaken for a man.

Could Richard be made into a vacuous idiot, if he didn't have a soul inside him to be eaten? What could the Eater of Souls do to him? I didn't want to know. I whined a little, softly, remembering the scent of him. Remembering how it felt to be stretched out along his length. Remembering some of the things he had done. I lay down on the grass, still green up here from last month's rains, damp from the night's dew, and rolled, enjoying the raw scent of grass and dirt and dust—and other critters that had passed that way tonight, today, this week, since the last full moon—that launched into the air around me as I rolled. I lay still then, looking up at the sky. The moon had risen bright and full in the east. Only a few stars made it through the haze to stand out against its brightness. The traffic roared below me. A plane tore the air overhead. I sat up. It was a crowded city, and a busy one, but it was mine.

To hell with the World Snake, anyway. Who knew if she was going to come here at all? But the Eater of Souls was here already. I had evidence of that. And more than that, I wanted my demon back. That was it. I wanted my demon back. Whatever fight anyone else was in—the power raisers, the magic users, the sorcerers, the wise ones, the dual-natured like me—I was going after Richard, and to hell with anyone who got in my way.

I took my car back down to the town in my human nature, but the cold still fury that had taken hold of me was so strong that I went without thought, without distraction, as though I was still in my wolf nature. It felt good. I knew where I was going. I was going hunting.

The building that held Marlin's dance studio was open and the lights upstairs were on, but the scents leading to the elevator were children, pubescent and prepubescent, mostly girls, spiking with excitement and joy, and their tired, overworked parent, escorting them to dance class. I looked at the schedule on the poster. Thunder Mountain Boys Dance Rehearsals on Tuesday, ballet class tonight, women's jazz tomorrow. No boys around tonight, but no matter. Of all the boys that had been there last night, one at least must live in walking distance.

I changed and crossed the lobby, nose to the ground. I found a faint trace of Richard's scent from the day before, coming or going, I couldn't tell, but I followed it out to the sidewalk and down the street to where Marlin must have parked his car. It ended there. I shivered in the dark and made myself small. There were voices coming from across the street. If they glanced my way I wanted them to take me for a stray dog, not a wild animal.

I went back to the lobby and cast around again for the scent trail of another of the Thunder Mountain Boys, coming or going from their weekly meeting. It took me dozens of casts, but I had time, and I was patient. I found one at last that led down the street, turned the corner, up the hill, and turned another corner into a street of apartment buildings. Two of them walking together. I could even put a face to one of them; it was the olive-skinned man, Honey. The two of them had gone in to a three-story building together, one that Honey had gone in and out of dozens and dozens of times as far back as I could tell. The companion had left this morning. Honey had left later... and unless there was another entrance, he hadn't yet come back. A narrow driveway led to a tiny set of carports in the back. The building's fire escape was near a back entrance that smelled of laundry, but Honey hadn't been through there in days. Good. All I had to do was wait.

I checked the front door again. This was fun; there were wards there telling dogs to go away. Honey and his friend had spent some time last night putting them in place. The woman on the second floor who owned the sheltie must have had one hell of a time getting her little friend back into the building after his walk that day. Even if the ward worked on my wolf nature, which I doubted strongly, it wasn't going to matter. I wasn't planning on going into the building. I was going to meet Honey somewhere in the surrounding streets, and we were going to have a little talk.

I followed the scent that was most current; he'd gone out in the afternoon. There was nothing more recent than that, which is how I knew he wasn't home. I tracked it onto a major street and then wended my way along, holding my tail high and pretending to be afraid of people till I got to the bus stop where Honey had spent half an hour or so. Then I lay down there for a few minutes right near where Honey had stood. I let myself be petted by a tough old woman in a uniform that smelled astringently of detergent; off to work, I suppose. Honey was letting off a little trace of fear. I put my nose right near that where I lay on the ground and took it in. He was nervous too, and, after a few minutes, he'd lit up a cigarette, bad boy. Too late to enjoy it completely; his bus must have come in the middle of it. He'd thrown it in the gutter, and there it lay. I trotted back up the street to Honey's apartment, keeping myself small, dodging the legs of people who took any notice of me and wagging my tail like a good dog.

I didn't have long to wait after all. As I was trotting back to Honey's door a car double parked in the street and Honey got out. He looked around. The driver got out of the car. He was the young guy from the night before. He looked around carefully, too. They were using magic-enhanced senses, but whatever they were looking for must not have looked like me, where I sat between two parked cars waiting quietly to see whether I'd be taking both of them out, or just the one. But after looking around carefully, the two of them exchanged a few words, and the young guy got back in the car and pulled away just in time to avoid the wrath of the guy in the truck coming up behind him. Honey headed for the front door of his apartment building, his key ready in his hand.

Honey never knew what hit him.

I sprang from where I was, and I felt myself grow huge as I went. I get big when I'm angry, but never before had I grown so monstrously, my cold fury tinged with red and gold unleashed at last. It must have something to do with being flung into a mirror a couple of times. Or because I wanted Richard back. Now.

I knocked him flat and picked him up in my teeth without breaking the skin, as though he were a blind puppy, light as a feather. I crossed the street in a bound with my prey in my jaws, leaped on a car roof parked by a dumpster, onto the dumpster, one leg on the fence, another hop, and I was on the roof of the two-story building opposite Honey's. I was really huge. I cast around, made two roof-top jumps to a taller building, then one long one to a building around the corner that was empty, and high enough that it was out of sight of any building around us. A quiet place to talk. I dropped Honey sort of gently on the rubble-strewn roof, and prepared to wait.

I was exhilarated. I was enormous. I was powerful in ways I'd never felt before. I should go home and tear up every guy that ever looked sideways at me. I should go home and kill my step-brothers, rip my stepdad apart and strew his limbs at my mom's feet and say...

Honey uttered a groan and sat up. I came and sat very near him. He had to look up and up to look in my face. He was terrified. I could smell it all over him. But he reached out with his mind and tried to connect with his fellows. I nosed him flat, and changed.

"None of that."

He got up and came at me fast. I changed, picked him up in my jaws by the head and upper body and shook him. I put him down, scraped him over a few times, nosed him once, stared down at him. He lay quite still, staring up at me in horror. He was covered with drool. I resisted the urge to give him another lick for good measure. It's just too damn bad wolves can't talk. It was obvious he had much less respect for me in my human nature. Oh, well. I could go on teaching him to respect me for hours, if need be. I had time. I wasn't going anywhere.

I changed, and told him as much. This time he just lay there and heard me out. "Now, listen. I'm not planning to kill you to-night. I want information." I leaned closer to him and smiled. "If you give it to me, then we can both go home, all right?"

He nodded, but added, "I don't know that I can tell you any-thing—"

I put a hand on him, and he shut up. "Just answer the ques-tions. What time did Richard get to the dance studio yesterday with Marlin?"

His eyes flickered as he registered the question and tried to think of the answer. "I don't know," he said at last. When I moved in protest, his voice rose, as though a higher register would convince me he was telling the truth. "I don't—I got there after Marlin did. Richard was already there."

I liked it so much better when he didn't call me "honey." I told him so.

He sat up in fury. "Is that what this is about, because if it is—"

I knocked him flat. I didn't even bother to change to do it. "What time did you get to the studio yesterday?"

A pause while he thought. "About four-fifteen. We're supposed to meet at four, but my bus was late."

"All right. What time did Marlin take Richard away?"

He thought again. "About seven. He said..." He stopped, as though he suddenly wasn't sure he wanted to tell me something.

"Yes?" I asked sweetly.

He continued, "He said Stan—Richard—was only on loan, and there was somewhere else he had to be."

Honey had the most enormously long lashes. They were dark, like his hair and eyes. His eyes were large and expressive, especially now that he was so scared.

I thought about what he had said. "So Marlin took Richard away at about seven. What time did Marlin come back?"

"Arthur brought him back—"

"Yes. What time?"

"That would be..." He thought about it. "About eight-thirty? I think? Look, I'm not sure. We finished—what we were doing—at eight, and Arthur brought Marlin back after that."

I thought about that. Between seven and eight-thirty Marlin had had time to go to whatever place he had dropped Richard off, have whatever it was happen to him, get lost and get found on the street by their guy Arthur. So probably Richard was within half an hour's drive of the dance studio. Maybe forty minutes at the outside.

What kind of power did it take to contain a demon that didn't want to be there? I thought about the chain Richard had had on his wrist, which Marlin said made him do whatever they wanted.

Honey had sat up while I thought. I looked at him and he lay back down again. Finally, some respect! I said, "That bracelet Marlin put on Richard. Have you ever seen that before? Is that something Marlin does?"

He shook his head. "Ours is thunder magic. We're air-raisers, air changers and wielders. Didn't you know?"

My turn to shake my head. "Never heard of it," I said, because I thought it would piss him off.

"You don't know much, then, do you?" he said.

I reached out and patted him gently on the cheek. "Just answer the questions."

"We don't put magic into things. It's not what we do," he insisted.

"Where did Marlin get that thing, then?" I asked.

He shook his head, and however many more times I asked, he insisted he'd never seen it before.

"How's Marlin now?" I asked finally.

His face fell. "He's no different. We've been sitting with him in turns ever since." He sat up again, put out his hands, and said earnestly, "Do you know anything we should be doing? It's said the wolves have special wisdom and are known to be great healers. If you know anything that can bring Marlin back—the way he was—we'll do anything, I swear."

Great healers? Special wisdom? First I'd heard of it. "I'll tell you, if anything comes to mind. Meanwhile, I've glad we've had this little chat. I'll check in with you again, in case anything else occurs to you." I stepped back and changed and jumped off the roof.

Idiot! I'd calmed down quite a bit. I'd been counting on that huge size coming with the change. I fell off the building into empty space, had to reach out and claw for the neighboring rooftop. I changed as soon as I realized I needed hands *right now* and was able to find a foothold and swing myself up. This building was occupied, and fortunately, the door to the roof was on latch. I let myself in just as Honey came to the edge of the roof up above and cast around looking for me and calling, asking how he was supposed to get down. I hadn't a clue.

I walked down two flights of stairs nursing my hands, which I'd scraped on the concrete edge. Damn. I'd almost killed myself. The cold fury was still in me, I could feel it, strong and comforting. It just hadn't manifested that time when I'd changed. I needed more practice. But what I needed even more was information. In the meantime, I'd start with a map.

∞

CHAPTER FOURTEEN

All right, what I did next was not too bright. But lucky improbable chances are possible. I believe in coincidence. I believe in blind luck. I guess you can't make blind luck happen to you by getting a big map of the Hollywood area, drawing a circle with the dance studio in the middle, about thirty or so miles' distance in every direction, picking a sector, parking, and walking around trying to scent Richard, or Marlin, or both. That's how I spent half the next day. I didn't even bother calling in sick to work. I drove back out to Hollywood so early the next morning I didn't even hit traffic to speak of. I spent the whole morning with that map in one hand, trolling up and down streets with my window open, getting out and walking when I thought it would help. After five or six hours of this, I came up with nothing but a huge thirst and the overwhelming need for a lot of meat *now*. But I kept hoping. I kept thinking that around the next corner, or just across the street, or just over there, I'd sense him, that my feelings for him would guide me to him. But they didn't.

In a greasy spoon on Pico, standing in line for my food, I realized this was a stupid way to hunt. You don't try and find one rabbit in rabbit city. That's exactly why I chose Los Angeles in the first place. Was it love that made me stupid? Was I in love? With Richard?

But how could I not love Richard, when his every look, his every action, was designed to please me. I knew that, just as I knew it was how he was made. But that hadn't made me love him. He'd tried that on me, in the beginning, and it just pissed me off. It was not Richard's scent memory that stuck in the back of my throat. No, what made me love Richard was finding his wolf. I loved the man, however much of him was a man, because I loved his wolf. But he came forth a wolf, because I called it up. So was it Richard that I loved, or the Richard that I had called into being? And was that how he was made, right from the beginning? To become whatever the one he was with desired? Or was it how Richard, with whatever powers were left to him, stuck here for so long, ensured his survival by becoming whatever his master wished? So how could that be love? Or is some part of love simply naming something you liked *mine*, and then not letting go. But if you lost your possession, you didn't go hunting it with a map and a belief in coincidence.

As I stood outside, devouring my first hamburger, I thought of someone who might have a better way of finding Richard than I did. I ate my other hamburger and the onion rings in the car as I sprinted down the 10 away from downtown. There were two accidents. It only took two and a half hours to get back to Whittier. I crept along with my window open, just in case Richard had passed by this way. Really, really stupid, but just in case.

I stopped briefly at my apartment, got back in my car, gassed up just before the freeway, and then headed out ahead of traffic to Pomona.

By the time I reached the counter of the taqueria across from the car wash and the little park, I was hungry again, so I ordered myself a burrito, along with the bag of food for the Rag Man. I went back and sat on that same bench, which was distracting, because Richard's scent was there. It hadn't even been a week since he'd laid his greasy hands on the board in front of me. The Rag Man's food got cold. He didn't show up. But I wasn't starting from the empty air with the Rag Man. He had trails running all around this place. I went around to the back of the car wash and changed. I made myself small, went back to the taqueria, chose what seemed to be the most recent of the Rag Man's trails, and backtracked it.

The Rag Man wandered all around this area. There were traces of him going in every direction. But all the strands of a spider's web coalesce to the web's center, and all the trails of the Rag Man collected on one street, in front of a burned-out house. The walls were black, the windows were empty, the roof was gone, and the two floors were in a heap in the shell. I trotted along the chain-link fence that kept people out of the ruins, turned the corner, followed the fence into an alley, and found the place behind some bushes where the fence had been artfully sliced. The gap was scuffed with numerous footprints. I knew whose they were. I slipped inside.

He'd built a lean-to against the house where the porch had fallen in. He was huddled against the wall, holding himself, shaking with chills, though the day wasn't cold. I changed and sat down in the doorway until he noticed me.

When he stirred, and opened his caked eyes, I said, "I'm looking for Stan."

"Huh?" He blinked out at me. "Who's there?"

I came a little closer, so I wasn't backlit, and he could see me. "I'm Stan's friend."

"Oh, yeah, yeah." He tried to put on that smile of his, but he was ill. "Stan the man. Right. Where is he?"

"I don't know. I can't find him. I wondered if you could."

"Yeah," he said. "Yeah, all right." He rested his head against the wall and closed his eyes. "In a minute…"

I waited a little, then I told him, "I'll be back."

I went back to the taqueria and ordered more food. I got some bottles of water and some other supplies as well. I drove my car back to the burned-out house and parked in the alley. I took out the blanket I kept in the back, shoved it and the food bag through the fence, and pushed my way in after it.

The Rag Man had straightened up. He was sitting with one knee up, stiffly clutching couple of small stones, a rusty nail, and a twig of rosemary. "I'm not seeing anything," he said as I came in. "I don't see anything."

"Here," I said. "Have some of this." I handed him the still-warm bag of food, and he opened it delicately, fished out the tacos and made short work of them. He had trouble holding the burrito.

"You've hurt your hands," I said.

"Yeah," he said through his mouthful. "That's the way it is."

He hadn't quite finished eating before he leaned back against the wall again and closed his eyes. He didn't move when I slipped the blanket over his shoulders. I gently unwrapped the rags from around each hand. There were new burns on his palms, still suppurating, and crusty black scabs around the edges of his wounds. I poured a little water over them. He made a sound, but did not open his eyes.

"They needed me," he explained. "The Heiligen guys. Nice folks. I tried to help." He lifted his hands, to show what had happened to them, and winced.

He didn't react when I changed. Maybe he thought he was hallucinating. Or maybe he was too sick to be surprised. I lay down by his knees, laid my paw on his wrist to keep his hand still, and licked the wound on one palm and then the other, until the suppurating stopped, and all the stink was gone. Then I changed again, so I could wrap his palms in the gauze I'd bought at the little grocery, and put an ace bandage over each hand.

"Mm," he said, when I'd finished. "Thanks. Thanks, man. I didn't see anything. I tried. Sorry."

"I think that's because Stan's a demon," I told him.

"Huh!" The Rag Man's eyes opened then. "A demon? You don't say. That explains a lot."

"You can't scry a demon, right?"

"Well," he said. "That depends. You can't see him. You might see around him. And that could tell you something." He pulled himself up and began collecting things from the ground, a nail, a couple of pebbles, a coin.

"Won't it hurt?" I asked.

"Oh, yeah," he said. "Don't worry about it."

So I took out the comb that Richard had been using, that I'd picked up from my place, and gave him a few of Richard's bright hairs.

The Rag Man tried several times, but all he saw was darkness. His hands did not explode into flames this time, which was just as well. I didn't have any more bandages. When he dropped his telltales to the ground for the last time, he sat quite still, but his eyes didn't change. After a few minutes he looked at me sharply. "Something's coming. Be ready."

He had one more thing for me. As I backed out of his shelter, he added, "Watch out. Stan's going to hurt you."

I paused in his doorway. "I know," I said.

The sun had set by the time I got to my car. I drove back to Whittier. I had one more place to try that night.

Hellman Park closes at dark. I wonder what the cops thought of all the cars parked along the street outside the gates. Or maybe there were wards there, too, that I didn't pay any attention to. I could already hear the drums.

I made my way up the hill at a run, not because I was in a hurry, but because it felt good to run. I wasn't planning to interrupt whatever ceremony they had going that night. I just wanted to talk to the sorceress. I was about out of sources of information, and she was the only power-raiser I could think of who might know where or how I could look for Richard.

I slowed when I reached the hilltop overlooking the clearing where they had set up their circle and altar the last time. The drums were pounding louder and stronger than ever before. Breathless, open-voiced chanting carried on the wind accompanying the drums. When I looked down on their circle there seemed to be dozens of them, dancing around a bonfire, robes swirling, hands raised. After a while I saw there were only twenty or so women altogether, four or five drumming, and the rest dancing. It's hard to see a working clearly.

They'd built the altar to the east again, and the sorceress stood there in profile to me, quite still, holding her sword. All of them, drummers, dancers, and celebrant together were bound up in the trance of the energy they were raising. The sorceress swayed in the wind the dancers made, but there was no wind that I could feel up where I was. It wasn't protection and deflection they were working this time, but sustaining and maintaining the power they'd already raised and set in place. They were still working up to their full power. I lay down in the grass among the mustard flowers, put my head on one paw, and waited for them to finish.

I must have fallen asleep. I was woken by the sound of silence as the drums cut out altogether, the dancers froze on a shout, and the sorceress brought down her sword. There were words said, and the drums came in on a heartbeat as the women slowly walked the lines of power they'd raised around the circle, and wound the working up.

One of the drummers wasn't wearing a robe, a black woman watching the other drummers with calm, alert certainty, her djembe sounding bright and clear among the rest. I knew that woman, but out of context it took me a few moments to realize who she was, and be astonished. It was Yvette. From work. Drumming with the magic-raisers. What on Earth—? And what was I going to do if she recognized me?

What the hell. They were all still in trance. Maybe she wouldn't remember this or anything else the next day. Hey, I like fairy tales, and anyway, it could happen!

They women sang in closing. They thanked the powers and let them go. They quenched the fire, they hugged, they doffed their robes, and some of them started on the long walk down the hill. Cell phones opened, conversations to distant parts mingled with those with their neighbors. "I'm coming down, I'm on my way, I'll see you Tuesday…" When the sorceress had hugged her last cohort, holding her sword, now sheathed, in her hand, she turned up the hill and faced me. "Sister?" she said. "Did you want to speak to me?"

Damn. Yvette was still standing there, smiling at the other drummers who were talking with her, hugging her, exchanging phone numbers or something. What the hell. I trotted down the hill to meet the sorceress.

The women weren't so amazed to see me this time. Yvette glanced up in surprise to see a wolf come down the hill, but she was being cool because everyone else was. When I reached the sorceress, she nodded to me regally. "What did you want to ask me, Sister?" she asked.

I sighed. Too bad she wasn't a mind reader. Oh well. I changed. I nodded to the sorceress and moved so that my face would remain in darkness, and when the sorceress moved with me, I put my back firmly to Yvette before I started talking. But the sorceress said first, "Where is it? Did you kill it?"

"Kill—?" She meant Richard. "No. I didn't kill *him*. Listen, I need help. Someone's taken him from me, and I want him back."

"Taken him?" She sounded skeptical.

I shook my head. "There isn't time to tell you the whole story."

She smiled, looked around, picked a nice patch of earth, and sat down on it with her sword in her lap, folding herself up cross-legged with remarkable flexibility for someone her age. She gestured, and I sat down beside her. "I have time," she said. "Go ahead."

So I told her. Most of it, anyway. At the end she sat back on her hands, raising her face to the sky. There were the usual few scattered stars, but what lit her face was the reflected glow from the city below. We could hear the unending thunder of traffic from the two freeways in the distance. She looked tired. I wondered what she did for her day job.

"So," she said, "the demon seduced you, made you fall in love with it, and now it's been captured and you want to go after it. Where have I heard this story before?"

"It isn't like that," I said.

"No?" She sat up again and took hold of the sheathed sword in her lap. "I'm just sorry I didn't kill it when I had the chance."

"I stopped you for a reason. And I'd do it again."

She cocked her head at me. Her eyes were very blue. She seemed wise, but you're only as wise as your experience can teach you to be, and she didn't know Richard the way I did. "Are you aware that those things survive in this world by making themselves attractive, and making themselves useful here? But what they are, what they want here, no one knows. At least, no one that I trust for a truthful account has made a study of it. I gave it to you because I thought you'd be able to kill it, whereas...."

"You couldn't do it."

She shook her head. "I'd seen it, seen what it was, but I couldn't slay it when it looked so much like a man."

I didn't answer, but really, I'd felt the same.

"What do you know about the Eater of Souls?" I asked her.

She nodded thoughtfully. "Ah, yes. That's just the kind of cataclysm that would arrive in a place where the World Snake is expected. Just as your demon has."

"The Eater of Souls is here," I said, "or at least something like it." I told her about Darius, and about Marlin.

She looked skeptical. "Maybe Marlin and his Thunder Mountain Boys just blew a head gasket. You sure he didn't brain himself with his own working? I never thought those people knew just what they were doing. Too busy doing it—and enjoying it."

"They said Marlin went to drop Richard off somewhere. They said he was fine when he left. He didn't come back on his own.

One of them found him walking the street. When I met him—he was gone." I tapped my head.

"It could be a number of things."

"What about Darius? Did you know him?"

"Of course I do. If anything's happened to Darius…" Her hands came up in a gesture of aversion. "That would be a great blow to our cause. We're a proud lot, we power-raisers, and prickly. That comes with the power. Darius is one of the few that can talk to all of us, keep us all on the same page. As much as we ever are on the same page. The Thunder Mountain Boys should have been doing their working tonight, not Tuesday, for one thing—"

"They can't," I told her.

"Why not?" she asked. "Tonight the moon is full. They shouldn't even have to look at a chart to know—"

"They couldn't do it tonight because their studio's not available. It's women's jazz dance night tonight. It's Thursday."

The sorceress threw back her head and laughed.

When she'd had her fun I asked her, "If there is an Eater of Souls, where would I find it? Do you know anyone who's dealt with it before, and can tell me how to…"

"How to what?" she asked me sharply.

Was I a hero or not? Was I going to take the job? It's not like I had anything else to do. All right then. "How to defeat it," I told her.

I didn't like the way she looked at me when I'd said it. The way you look at a kid who's just said she can fly. The trouble was, I knew I didn't know what I was getting into. I knew I didn't know what I was taking on.

Be patient and wait, be patient and wait. Look, I can be patient when I want, but I had things to do! The sorceress told me she'd do a working for me, and find out more about the Eater of Souls, if it was here, where it was, and how to defeat it. She'd send for me when she had the information I wanted. And what was I supposed to do in the meantime? Sit on my hands? Suck my thumb?

Play with the mammals? Maybe I'd hunt me up another Thunder Mountain Boy just to see if this one said different things from the other one. I wondered if Honey had found a way off the roof yet. I'd have to ask him someday. If he made it.

I watched the sorceress walk down the hill into the dark after she'd told me to be patient, she'd get me that information, and I was pissed off. I thought for a second of finding out how big I'd be if I changed right then. I was angry, and if I was really big when I changed I could be on her in a single bound, give her back a little pat, and watch her roll the rest of the way down the hill....

"Hey, Amber!"

The last thing I was thinking about was meeting a coworker at that moment. I turned around, trying to find my coworker smile somewhere in my choice of expressions. I realized then I didn't have a coworker smile.

Yvette had on jeans and a long African shirt, and her hair was tied in some kind of kerchief. Not like at work. She was holding a drum decorated all around with beads and feathers and little bells. She held it like it was an extension of herself. She was radiant. Not like I'd ever seen her at work.

"Hey, Yvette."

She came over to me. "Is this cool or what? I heard the drumming, I came up the hill, these women treat me like I'm their long-lost kinfolk. They said—" She was rapt. I knew I was going to hear every word of her experience before I got away. "They said there's power in my drumming, and that I tune well with their power, and they—did you hear it? When we were drumming, there were voices in the drums. Like—spirits—answering us. It was fantastic."

"Yvette," I said, "where do you live?"

She looked down the hill and pointed. "There."

I started walking in that direction, and she followed after me, still going on about the drumming. I walked her almost to her door. When we turned down her street, about a mile from the park, she fell silent. When we neared her apartment, a rundown three-story old house that had been subdivided fifty years back, she stopped and turned to me, cocking her head under the streetlight. "Hey, Amber."

"Yeah?"

"Did I see what I thought I seen? When you came down that hill?"

I could have frozen her dead. It's what I'd have done with anyone else. Hey, I do it on principle. It's the way I am. But this was Yvette, and she'd covered for me at work that day, without my asking her to. I said cautiously, "What did you think you saw?"

"A dog. A big, black and gray—"

"It was not a dog!" I told her, outraged. "It was a wolf! Don't you know a wolf when you see one? A timber wolf, a Gray Sister, a Daughter of the—"

"All right, all right, shhh…" She had her hands up, shushing me before we woke the neighborhood. "A wolf, then."

"Yeah," I said. "So?"

"So," she stepped forward, "can you show me how to do that?"

I went to work the next day because I hadn't come up with another plan to find Richard, and I didn't want to spend a lot more useless hours driving around the city, especially not on the off-chance I'd happen to run in to him. I had no plans to be that stupid again.

I got a break from oiling the wall paneling because Pete, our boss, wanted the stage cleared of junk prior to the new boards being put down. I threw myself into hauling all the crap to the back and tossing it into the dumpster, working furiously to make up for what I ought to be doing right then and wasn't because I didn't know where and I didn't know how, which was finding Richard and getting him out of whatever it was he had gotten himself into. I kept trying to suppress what he'd said about how the Eater of Souls had treated him last time. It's hard not to think about what you don't want to think about. Funny how it's always,

always there.

At lunchtime Yvette came and got me with the assumption that the two of us would go out together, and I went, thinking with amazement that I had a friend. An ordinary friend. And also, how easy it was. You just go along, and you don't kill them or anything. We went to the enchilada place again, which was great because those things are really good. She asked me some questions about being wolf-natured. She said "werewolf," but I told her we don't call it that. She thought I could bite her and make her one too, but I explained you had to be born to it. Then she gave up on that and we—she—talked about drumming.

She's recently gotten out of juvenile hall, where she's been held for almost four years for beating up her mother. Except she wasn't the one who had beaten up her mother, who was left in a coma for months and was brain damaged afterwards. It had been her stepfather, and she'd been delighted to go to juvey because it got her away from him. When he accused her (and she'd been big when she was sixteen, just as she was now), she'd confessed and never said a word more. She liked juvenile hall, she said, because it was orderly, all the meals were on time, and school was easy. She'd gotten her GED the last year. Also, until the funding was cancelled, there'd been an African music group, and that's where she started drumming.

That was something about having a friend: you heard new stories. I felt an impulse, when she told about her stepfather, to find out where he was and go kill him—I could identify with her about stepdads, really—but I figured that could wait. Since he lived somewhere in the greater L.A. area, he might soon be swallowed by the World Snake anyway, and that was good enough. If not, there'd be time to go after him later. Him first, and then, who knew? Maybe I'd go after mine. The rage burned in me suddenly at the thought. I'd have gone after him a long time ago, but my mom told me not to. Which is what I never understood. My mom was important. Even my dad deferred to her, along with the whole rest of the family. How could Ray come out of nowhere and just take everything over? Why didn't she stop him? Why didn't she let the rest of us take him out? Why didn't she go after him herself? Why did she let him do the things he did? And his horrible boys, too.

I'd been roiling under these questions for years. Getting away had distanced me from the family problems, but thinking about stepdads brought it back again. One day, I was going back there to work everything out. My way. I banged on the table without thinking, interrupting Yvette in the middle of a sentence and startling the half-dozen other customers in the tiny store-front restaurant. I got up. "It's time to go."

I finished clearing the stage that afternoon, tied up the curtains out of the way, and got out a mop and bucket to wash down the whole huge stage. Rotten boards would be replaced after that, and the whole thing would be sanded and painted anew.

What would I do that night? I thought I'd go back down to Costa Mesa and see if Tamara was around, if she'd learned anything, or if she could tell me where or how to find Richard. Or maybe the sorceress from up the hill would have completed her working already and found out who I should talk to next. I thought about introducing Yvette to Tamara, as she'd probably like the shop— and then shook myself. She might be a friend, but she wasn't going to get involved in my whole life. Maybe next time. If nothing else panned out, I could go back to the dance studio and see if I could track down another one of the Thunder Mountain Boys. I smiled at the thought. I really enjoy hunting.

I grabbed a hamburger on the way home so I didn't have to cook. I was going to change out of my work clothes and go on my way. I had to drive around a huge silver limousine that was pulled up in front of my building. I thought nothing of it. Someone rich might be visiting Whittier College down the street, or they might have offspring there. I parked my car in the carport, came around the corner to my steps, and stopped. There was a young woman standing on my walkway. She wore a long, voluminous robe obviously covering her clothes underneath, and a scarf over her head, wrapped around her neck to keep it in place. She was holding what looked like a green triangular jewel suspended on a thin, almost invisible chain, and she stood very still, watching it move.

I said, "Hey." I was expecting a couple of things: Tamara was supposed to get in touch with me, or the sorceress might send a message. I added, "You looking for me?"

She looked up at me with dark, luminous eyes. As I came closer, the jewel began to swing back and forth towards me. She glanced down at it, and then tucked it up into her sleeve and looked again at me. "Yes," she said decisively. "I am." She had an accent, but I couldn't place it.

I said, "Did Tamara send you?"

She looked…expensive. The fabric of her clothes was new. She wore gold earrings, gold bangles on her wrists, and several rings with flashing stones. I couldn't see the sorceress and her crew hanging out with someone this exotic.

She didn't answer the question. She said, "I was sent to bring you with me. My father wishes to speak with you."

"And he is…?"

Her head went up and she spoke with scornful pride, as if I should have known who her father was by looking at her. "My father is Sharrif Ibrahim Mechad Ibn al Hassan. Surely you have been expecting to hear from him?"

Well, someone must have gotten in touch with him for me. Maybe it was even Darius, before he was attacked. All right, I thought, I'll bite. After all, what could happen?

"Just a sec," I said. "I have to change. I'll be right with you. You can come in, if you want."

She did. When I came out from my room after the quickest of quick showers, dressed in clean jeans and a sweatshirt, she was standing in my living room. She'd gotten the green jewel out again and was watching it swing wildly to and fro around the room. When I came in it changed directions and swung just as wildly toward me. Funny, she didn't seem to be moving her fingers from which the chain hung at all. Well, there were all kinds of magic. I should be used to it by now.

"Ready," I told her.

When we went outside, the big silver limo had pulled up in front of the walkway. The driver sat straight-backed with both hands on the wheel, staring straight ahead. Beside the car, a heavy-set guy in his thirties stood holding open the backseat door. He was dressed in a long black button-down coat that hung almost to his knees. Both men had short beards and wore dark turbans. I moved away from the young woman toward my carport.

"I'll take my own car, thanks," I told her.

She held out her hand toward the car imperiously. "My father has commanded me to bring you to him." The man holding the door bowed slightly.

"I'll follow you," I said, stepping further away from her. "My car's just up there."

She glared at me, lifting a hand and making a little sign in the air. There was a crack in the air, like a localized explosion of thunder—or did I just imagine it? I shook my head to clear it. Then I stepped away again and trotted up the hill to the carport. I didn't know where I was going. We wolves like our independence. It's part of our nature. L.A.'s a really big town, and it's a really long walk almost everywhere. I didn't want to be in a position where I couldn't get home without asking.

€S&#x03;

CHAPTER FIFTEEN

When I drove down the alley to the street, the limo had turned around and was waiting. The woman leaned out the window to wave at me to follow them. I waved back. The limo set off at a stately pace, adhering to the speed limit at every instance, and pulled eventually onto the 605 going north. I wasn't surprised when, after extensive signaling, the limo took the off-ramp to the 10 heading for the city. We hit traffic immediately. I trailed them slowly stop-start for half an hour or so, until the pace picked up again and I was able to get out of second gear—always a pleasure. We caught the 405 North eventually and got off on Sunset, heading toward the ocean. They signaled a while later and pulled into a side street, and I wasn't a bit surprised when shortly afterwards the limo pulled into one of those gated mansion driveways that abound in that area. The lot was surrounded by a high stone wall. I parked across the street while the gates slid smoothly open to let the limo in.

The woman waved to me from the car to follow her. I crossed the street to do so. She leaned out the window. "No," she said, "park your car in here. That way it will be safe."

I looked up and down the street. There were cars parked here and there whose fenders were worth more than my whole car. I shook my head and smiled a false smile at her. I'd come to get information from her dad. I was liking her less and less.

"It'll be fine out there." I waved dismissively at my car, and walked along the limo and through the open gate.

Inside the gate, invisible from the road because of the high wall all around it, was a large lawn cut by a circular cobbled drive that forked near the house. One leg led to the front of the house, and the other curved around to the back. I assumed this was a front door visit, so I headed that way.

The door opener got out of the car. With a little bow he led the way toward the front steps. The car went off to the right, toward what I assumed was the multi-garage facility that would go with a place like this. I made a few long strides and caught up with my guide.

"Who are you?" I asked.

He made the same little bow once again and motioned toward the house without breaking stride. Not very bright, I thought, or— then it came to me—maybe he doesn't speak English. Interesting.

"Where are you from?" I asked slowly.

All I got was the same little bow again, but we were at the house by that time, and maybe it just wasn't time to talk. The house was huge. It was like a wedding cake, set on tiers, with a balcony circling each floor above the ground floor, big enough to be called a patio rather than a mere balcony. And there were gardens on each one, so the thing looked like a wedding cake with trees and bushes sprouting from it. It was painted a pale pink. Yuck.

The front doors opened as we mounted the steps, and when we got inside, there was no one there opening them. I think this was supposed to awe me or impress me, but I'd seen stuff that good at the grocery store, so what the hell. The doors closed behind us.

My ears went up as though I were in my other nature. I move my head from side to side, trying to be unobtrusive about it;

something was really wrong.

The front hall was large, though dark after the bright sunshine outside. It was higher than it looked from the outside. The floor was tiled with intricate little black and white tiles, and there was a large fountain in the center depicting a rock mountain, with little streams trickling off it in all directions. A pool surrounded it, like a little moat. Of course, there were fish in the moat. The walls were darkly paneled, and I shot an appreciative glance at the shine they'd achieved. A lot of linseed oil polishing had gone into them. The walls were covered with old Persian carpets and faded colored tapestries.

The place wasn't new, obviously, and the stuff on the wall was pretty darn old too, so I should have been experiencing a wild array of exotic scents of different strengths and ages. I should have been able to sense the history of the house and the people who lived there. I should certainly have been able to smell who had crossed that floor today, yesterday, even this week. I lifted my head, trying for another layer of air; I even thought of changing, because I could hardly sense anything. Tiny signals were getting through that should have been enormous. I could just sense the man beside me. The water, yes. And a tiny bite of the linseed oil, all right. But not at their usual volume, not with the usual detail. And everything else was faded, dampened down, almost as though I was trying to smell things underwater, and that, let me tell you, is practically impossible. I rubbed my face just to see if I had mistakenly and without noticing gotten a wet towel over my nose, but no.

Before I could figure out what was going on, one of half a dozen dark doorways leading off the hallway illumined briefly, and another manservant appeared. He stepped out beside the door and bowed me toward it. The man beside me bowed simultaneously, gesturing toward the door as well.

All right, I could take a hint. I crossed the hall, shaking my head a little as though the problem with my senses was in me, like a headcold or something, and I could somehow clear it.

The man at the door was dressed in the same smooth buttoned-down coat and turban as the guy from the car. For a second I thought it was the same guy. I even turned and looked back, but the other guy was still there. They were just dressed alike, I told myself, because my real way of telling who was who was by smell, and I could only faintly smell either of them. This was really bugging me. I wondered how soon I could leave.

I walked past the second guy and into a large room that was obviously the study and library of someone who was into a whole lot of different things. Three huge Persian rugs covered the hardwood floor. Bookshelves stood against the walls, higher than anyone could reach, and there was a ladder on a track so that someone could reach them, just like at Darius's bookstore. A huge dark wood desk sat at one end of the room. Across from me, the only break in the shelves of books was a huge fireplace. Everything in the room was oversized, as though to infer that a giant lived there. But there wasn't a giant in the room. The young woman was there, standing beside a large leather chair next to the fireplace, where a roaring fire was burning. In the chair sat a middle-aged man who turned to me with big friendly eyes as I came in, and motioned me to come over to him.

I still couldn't smell anything. He was dressed in a white robe over a black gown, over white pants, and white leather slippers. Or so it seemed. The fact was, he was hard to look at, like a working is hard to look at. The hair on my arms went up, though it was warm in the room because of the fire. He stood up to greet me. He wasn't that tall, but he seemed to fill the room nonetheless. That wasn't right either, because everything else was so large.

"Welcome," he said, with a broad, gentle smile, and a graceful gesture of his hand. His face was long and thin, with a meticulously cut beard framing his mouth and cheeks. He had deep-set eyes that looked saddened by all that they had seen, and yet they were luminous, like his daughter's. His beard was dark, but a white turban hid the hair on his head. "My daughter has guided you here safely; I am so glad. She would be delighted to perform introductions, but she is mortified that she did not catch your name?" He put a little question on the end of that, and with it came a little pull in the air. At the same time, he motioned me to sit down in the leather chair opposite his.

I looked at his daughter instead. I had my mouth open a little, trying to bring scent into my nose that way. Hell, my senses were so bad, I couldn't tell exactly if it was his daughter—I mean, the same young woman I'd met outside my apartment. She was dressed the same, all right, but she'd pulled her scarf up so that it covered the lower part of her face. The top part of the scarf had dipped so that it covered her forehead to her brows. She didn't look morti-fied. She looked pissed off. She looked like she'd just had a major chewing out from Dad. Somehow this made me happier.

"Actually," I said, "I didn't catch her name either."

His brows rose, and he turned and spoke to her mildly, the syllables flowing from his lips like water in a language I'd never heard. She bent her head at his words as though she was bracing herself against a storm. Though I couldn't understand the words, the effect was impressive. When he finished speaking, she bowed, then backed away a few steps, and walked to the wall. When she got there, one of the bookshelves opened. She slipped swiftly through this doorway and then it moved back into place.

Her dad watched her go, too. He waved at her back with one graceful hand. "Ah, my daughter. I sent her on this small errand, she hoped to execute it perfectly, and now she has embarrassed us both." He put his hand on his heart. "I am Ibrahim al Hassan. I am honored to receive you beneath the hospitality of my roof. My daughter tells me you have been expecting to hear from me."

It must be Darius, I thought, who'd sent me to this guy. I didn't have to like him.

"Please," he said. "Be seated. We will have tea together, and you will tell me how I may serve you."

Not being able to smell him properly really had me on edge. How was I supposed to know what he was feeling or thinking? How was I supposed to know if he was lying or not, or even if someone else came into the room? He motioned me once more to be seated. I sat down when he did, but with my feet still under me so I could get up in a hurry if I had to

He raised his hand, the door I had come in through opened, and another man, dressed in the same turban and long buttoned coat, came in wheeling a silver cart. On it was a curlicued silver teapot, two tiny tea cups, and three little covered plates. The man—and this was a different man, I could tell because he was definitely younger and shorter than the other two—poured the tea, distributed plates, and then handed around the covered plates, which contained little sandwiches and sweetmeats. My host loaded his plate. I took one of each and set them, together with my teacup, on the table beside my chair.

I couldn't smell the new guy either. People who go blind must feel like this. I started planning my way out of this house. I'd lost my sense of smell when I came inside the door of this house. I wanted to get out and be sure that I'd get it back as soon as I was outside again.

"Thank you," Ibrahim al Hassan said to the servant and waved him away. "We will serve ourselves now."

"How many servants do you have?" I asked. I wondered if there was one guy whose only job it was to brush Ibrahim's teeth each night.

"Oh, no servants," he said genially. He held up a tiny pair of silver tongs and proceeded to add lump after lump of sugar to his cup, until it overflowed. He slurped it with relish and added two more lumps. "Sugar?" He offered me the bowl with one hand while he slurped away again at his tea. I shook my head. He drank more tea and put one of the pastries in his mouth, tasting it with obvious enjoyment. "What was I saying? Of course. Not servants. These are my children. My sons and my daughters. They serve me far more faithfully than any servant ever would. And how many, you would ask me," he went on, waving away my next query as he poured himself a second cup of tea and filled it with sugar as before. "And I am ashamed to answer I do not know, exactly. I have had many wives. In my culture, it is expected that a man such as myself, an important man, would have many wives, and concubines also, by which to have many children. It is good—how do you put it here in America? It is good for the race. I can only tell you that I have completely fulfilled my obligations in that regard." He waved one hand gently in the air as he spoke, while drinking tea or eating with the other. He exuded kindly geniality. He seemed like a really nice guy.

He went on, "Children make much better attendants than servants, I have found. For one thing, they are completely loyal, even unto death. And they have good reason to offer me their service. Each one of them, you see, is hoping to become my heir. In our tradition, you must understand, only one will inherit. And he or she will inherit everything." He waved a hand around the room, still clutching a little pastry. "It gives them—what is your lovely name for it?" He looked up, reaching for the word, then smiled benignly as he found it. "Motivation. Yes. It gives them motivation. My smallest wishes, instantly obeyed. They are good children, I tell you."

I didn't sip the tea, and I didn't eat the food. I don't eat things I can't smell. Ever. That's something we learn when we're pups. And if nothing else, I *should* have been able to smell the food.

"So a girl could inherit too?"

He nodded while he finished chewing. "Oh, yes, I have told them so. I care not the gender of my heir. I care only that he—or she—has the necessary qualifications. The necessary craft. What is your name?" He asked me then, and reached out as he said it, and described a little shape in the air.

The air tightened. There was definitely something going on here. Something I couldn't—smell. I thought about my answer for a moment, and then looked past his hand, still stretched out towards me, at his face. Suddenly, it seemed as though his face was old, lined, his beard gray, his mouth misshapen by missing teeth, and his body shrunken in his chair. I blinked. No, same middle-aged guy, same benign smile, same kindly eyes.

I said, "You're a magician, aren't you?"

He looked annoyed for an instant, and then his face smoothed again. As though as an afterthought, he added a laugh and a wave. "Of course. But you knew that. How else could I help you?"

There was a fly in the room. It buzzed around his head for a moment, and then went to land on one of the plates of cakes. I saw his eyes follow it for a moment. Then the fly came and buzzed around my head. I shook it away from my eyes.

"Have you studied demons?" I asked, partly distracted by the fly that seemed to want to land on my ear. I don't like flies.

He opened his hands. "Yes, of course you would ask me that. It is my life's work," he said. "The study of summoning and direct-ing the demon-kind. My library—" He gestured to the books all around us. "—you will find is the greatest collection that exists today on Earth of demon lore. Yes, if you seek to know about the demon kind, I am the one to ask."

I sat considering him for a moment. If he knew all about de-mons, I should ask him a hundred questions, just to see what he said. But if I couldn't tell his truth from his lies, his answers weren't going to tell me anything.

I got up to go and look at the books. I took a swipe at the fly as I went. I struck it with my hand and it sped away, buzzing. Funny that in a house so big, so well-kept, with so many ser-vants—all right, children—he couldn't keep out one persistent and obnoxious fly.

The books were obviously going to be no use to me. I couldn't even read the names on the spines. I didn't know what languages they were in. They might have been in every language, because I saw lots of kinds of alphabets. Bunches of the books were actually scrolls kept in boxes and labeled with what may have been Arabic or something like that. He got up and accompanied me as I looked at the backs of books. Occasionally he pulled one out and opened it, offering a continuous commentary.

"The Magus Apollonius," he said, taking a thick ancient volume out of my hand, "claimed to have had thirteen demons in his direct control. He claims also to have used them to destroy the city of Abuchiya in 760 A.D., when the Caliph of that city offended him."

"Where's Abuchiya?" I asked.

He waved his hands gently. "No one knows. No one has ever heard of it. Of course, Apollonius did claim to have destroyed the city for all time, but it's probably just a story."

I reached out and turned the pages of the book he still held open in his hands. It was huge, so large you couldn't hold it with just one hand. Paper is a really good source of trace scents, since it absorbs the oils of peoples' hands really well. The book was centuries old, the pages dog-eared and stained where people had studied them for extended periods of time. I wanted to put it right against my face and breathe in deeply, but thought I'd better not in front of him. As it was, I couldn't smell a thing. The words were written in a language and a script I didn't know. There were diagrams, one or two of which reminded me of things I'd seen in Darius's room. Then I turned a page and found a picture.

A magician in a robe was summoning—staff in one hand, book in the other—a creature in the shape of a lizard or crocodile but with a human head that had appeared within a pentagram inside a circle, crawling out of a hole of darkness.

"Have you ever called up a demon?" I asked Ibrahim al Hassan.

He looked down at the picture, and then closed the book. "Those of us schooled in the science of the demon-kind often call up the unholy ones to do our will. It is a great endeavor and full of danger. It takes an unusual talent, boundless concentration and skill. It is an ability so rare that, unfortunately for me, not one of my children has it. In fact," he said, looking at me with his wide eager eyes down his long nose, "were I to discover someone who had that power, so rare and so great, to call a demon to his will—or hers—I would be tempted to make her my heir. My one heir. Heir to my library, my knowledge, my craft, and of course…," he waved his hand around the room, "the other riches and treasures I have accumulated in the service of knowledge throughout my life." He waited expectantly, watching me, one hand still in the air.

"What would happen to your children?" I asked. I wandered along the shelf, running my fingers across the spines of books so old that pieces of them disintegrated as I touched them. In the corner of my eye I saw him watching me. He lifted one hand magnanimously.

"My children know well that when one is bound to the service of a great craft, as I am, personal considerations may not get in the way of the furthering of knowledge. No, my heir must be the right person, whether he—or she—is of my own blood, or not."

"I'll bet your kids would be awfully mad," I surmised, "after working for you for all those years and all. I bet they'll go to court." I was thinking aloud, just riffing to keep the conversation from settling anywhere serious. "I'll bet they tie up everything for years and years, since they are your kids, and after all they did for you."

"Oh no," he said simply. "We have another custom, where I come from." He closed the large book and put it back gently in exactly the space I'd taken it from. "No matter how many the children, there is only one heir. One heir." He held up a single long finger, to help me count. And he smiled that benign smile again that was beginning to chill me on the inside, as well as put the hairs up on my skin. "It is the first duty of the appointed heir to assure that she—or he—is the only heir after all. Of course, the chosen one, the one skilled in the craft, and able to call demons to her will, shall have no difficulties in this regard. No difficulties whatsoever."

I got it. I wondered if any of his devoted children were listening right now. What a great dad.

"That's something I always wondered," I said suddenly. "I mean, I've heard of people calling up demons and controlling them and making them do your will and all, but what do you do after that?"

"After that?" he asked.

The fly came back. It had buzzed around the room somewhere, probably laying millions of eggs on the sandwiches and pastry that still lay on the little plate by my chair. It buzzed around Ibrahim al Hassan's clean white turban. He took no notice. I waved a hand as it buzzed by my head.

"Yeah. After that. When you're done with it. How do you make it go away? I mean, you don't want a demon around all the time. You don't want it coming around and bothering you when you didn't have anything more for it to do. How do you send it back where it came from?"

Ibrahim al Hassan stared down his nose at me, and one of his long-fingered hands crept up to stroke his beard while he considered me gravely. With his other hand he suddenly batted at the fly. "But you don't simply send it back," he told me. "No one of any conscience would do that. Demons come from the darkest realms of Hell. We who have the power and the craft call them to do our bidding, but when we are finished with them, as you say, we destroy them. Thus we commit a righteous act." He lifted a hand and, with the other, he pointed at the fly, which was crawling along the bookshelf. It stopped crawling.

Behind him two of his children came into the room. Each of them carried a fly whisk. One was a man and the other was the same young woman who'd come and picked me up, or it was her sister who wore the same clothes. They advanced to where their father was pointing, and the girl brought down the whisk with sudden ferocity on the book where the fly seemed to be pinned. She examined the whisk for traces of what she'd killed, and then the two of them went out of the room without a word, and without a glance from their father.

They weren't like any kids I'd ever seen.

"Of course," Ibrahim al Hassan continued, as though nothing had happened, "it is not unheard of for a young adept who has succeeded, beyond all hope and desires, in calling a demon into her service, to give the creature over to a master of the craft to be bestowed wisely. That is often the best course of action, in such a case."

He put out a hand as though he were going to put an arm around my shoulders, and I moved on smoothly before he could reach me.

"Well, that sounds like a great idea," I said.

"Yes," he answered, following me. "An excellent idea, and so easily done, since all the adept requires to make the problem go away is the demon's name, correctly pronounced." He shot me another look, and his hands curled in a gesture towards me. I thought about chewing on those hands. If you do it thoroughly you can separate out all the little bones. It takes a while.

Al Hassan went on talking. "Ancients of the craft, such as I, consider ourselves to be at the service of young adepts, to guide their footsteps and answer their queries, and help them in their trials. It is one of our most sacred responsibilities." He put both his hands on his heart, and smiled his beneficent smile at me. I smiled back. He sounded so sweet. So healthy and kind. I wanted to eat him for dinner. I couldn't imagine what he might have up his sleeve, though, so I didn't try. I bet he was poisonous, anyway.

"Are there any books in here about the Eater of Souls?" I asked, gazing around at the huge collection.

"The—?" For a moment it seemed like he didn't know what I was talking about. He lost his focus and looked around the room. "The Eater of Souls, ah, yes. I should not wonder at your question. This region is expecting…" He smiled a different smile then, one that showed his teeth. I answered with a toothy smile in my turn; I couldn't help it. It was all I could do to keep from putting my head down and growling as well. He reached for the right word, and found it, "...visitation, am I correct? Yes, from the World Snake. The Eater of Souls would of course take the opportunity—but you and I cannot be disturbed by these little occurrences. The pursuit of knowledge and the understanding of the many layers of truth is a greater calling, one might even truthfully say a holy calling, and we of its faith must not allow ourselves to be distracted. Now come, let me show you my work place." He held out his arms, beneficent, generous, to conduct me to a doorway across the room.

I turned into the middle of the room so as not to be herded. "But if I just wanted to know, like you said, to have more knowledge..." This was like that game I'd seen girls play in middle school, trying to look stupid so the guys would feel smart. It's amazing how often the guys fall for it. It's amazing how stupid they'll believe a girl can be. Ibrahim al Hassan fell for it too, or else maybe he just enjoyed being the smartest one around, and telling you about it.

"Ah, of course, of course. A child after my own heart, I knew it." He returned to his chair, gesturing for me to follow him so that his robe flowed around him in a gentle swell. "Sit down, yes indeed, sit down and we will discuss the matter." When he had seated himself he absently reached for his teacup. He frowned at the half inch of brown liquid left in the cup. It must have been cold.

"What must you know about the Eater of Souls? Well, you must beware of her, of course. She makes no distinctions in the quality of the souls she devours." He finished off the last little sandwich, and then stabbed with one damp finger for the crumbs on the plate and waved the finger at me as he made his point. I should have been pretty hungry by then, as I hadn't eaten since lunchtime, but somehow I'd lost my appetite. "You, or even I, are the same to her as—as one of those people in the street out there. No distinction."

I frowned at his words. So far, the Eater of Souls had favored power-raisers pretty forcefully. "We don't taste any different? Any better?"

"No."

"And how do you stop her? If you meet her in the street, I mean. What do you do?"

He'd given up on the remains of the tea. He leaned back in his chair, smoothing his robe about him. "I, of course, would not meet her in the street. But what should a young adept do, who wished to keep her soul after all? A young adept, such as yourself?" He smiled that benign smile again. It really made me feel as though I were going to be the one for dinner. Not a feeling I like. "First of all, you must not meet her gaze," he said, leaning forward and fixing me with his own. "Her gaze is like that of the snake, that penetrates the mind. She can see your soul, you know. That's how she knows what it is she is after."

His gaze held mine and I couldn't tear it away. I felt a growing numbness in my gut, and I realized that it was fear. Inside my chest the cold ball of anger that I'd nurtured for days swelled up suddenly in answer. I blinked back at him, glanced away as though unconcerned, then met his gaze again politely. I felt like I was growing larger. He didn't seem to notice. He looked perturbed for a moment, and leaned back again in his chair.

The door opened and his daughter came in. I wonder if I imagined the angry stare she gave me before she bent to her father's ear and whispered. His face lost its benign expression and settled into one of tight, hard anger. He rose up from his chair, and all of a sudden he looked bigger too, and stronger, and older, and nowhere near so cute anymore. His daughter backed away from him, pulling her scarf over her head, bending to make herself smaller. It was easy to see what this family was like. I was out of my chair too, but he held up a calming hand.

"Forgive me, my dear guest. Something has occurred that requires my attention. My immediate attention." His daughter was about to follow him out but he waved his hand at her. "My daughter will entertain you. More tea, perhaps?"

He was already most of the way to the door, moving darn fast in that robe. Two of his sons met him in the doorway and an intense, low-voiced conference began before they'd even shut the door behind him.

No doubt about it, the daughter was eyeing me with hostility. I wondered if the kids listened in on their dad. With the future he had in store for all but one of them, I wouldn't blame them one bit. He must be pretty powerful, I realized, if he could keep this bunch from taking him out in his sleep.

I smiled at the daughter, and took a stab at random. "Lisa, is it?" Almost every woman I know is called Lisa. Or Laura. Or Sue.

"No," she said.

"Sorry. Laura, then?"

"My name is Maryam," she told me. Then she looked sideways at me and smiled. "What's yours? My father didn't tell me."

"Do you live here all the time?" I started to walk around the room again, and she followed me.

"Of course not. We have houses—many houses. In Cairo. In Paris. In South Carolina."

"South Carolina?" I asked, surprised. "What's there?"

She looked down, looked away, shrugged one shoulder eloquently. "We go wherever my father's experiments take him. It has to do with the latitude—and other celestial considerations," she added airily, and she waved her hand just like her father did.

"Aren't you going to show me the balcony?" I asked, continuing toward the door.

"No," she answered, but she followed me.

"That's funny. Didn't he tell you? I was telling your dad that the balcony with all the trees and shrubs looked so beautiful from the outside, and he said you'd show it to me. For just five minutes, that's what he said."

She looked sulky; she looked like it was the last thing in the world she wanted to do, but she led me out of the room where four of her brothers or half brothers were congregating in the hall. She waved them away with a few words in a language I didn't know, and they retreated to their four respective doorways. I figured their presence meant that I probably couldn't just walk out of here. But I was going to see what I could do about that.

We went up the stairs and I admired everything out loud, the tapestries on the wall, the handsome dark paneling that continued up the stairs, the marble stair rails, for the gods' sake. She swelled and thawed a bit in the sight of all the things she had that I didn't have. She'd seen my apartment. When I said I'd never seen anything like the huge painting at the head of the stairs, where a bunch of people in robes looked on in open-mouthed horror as the guy on the throne's servants offered them a severed head, she knew it was probably true.

There were a number of doors off the upstairs hallway. She led me through the center doorway into a sunroom with wicker chairs and potted palms placed on a tile floor at strategic locations, and a wall of windows with a set of French doors in the center. She opened these and let me out onto the first floor balcony. I could feel the cool breeze that came up the side of the house, but there were no scents in it. Large square planters held ferns and shrubs and even a couple of palm trees leaning out from the balcony for more light. Along one side was a box of roses, and boxes of late tulips and irises stood at intervals along the balcony railing. Two of her brothers were stationed along the railing. They moved closer to me when I went to admire the view out over the front lawn. I smiled at them like a pup, ducking my head and making myself small. My action didn't seem to have any effect on them. I thought, now or never.

I unleashed all the fear I'd been feeling, I opened up to the cold anger that I harbored in the bubble by my heart, I threw myself into the air as angry and huge as I could make myself, and I changed.

My front feet hit the rail as the two men leaped for me, but I was past them, and then my back feet pushed off the rail and I launched into the air, and I was huge, I was enormous, I was not going to fall forty feet to the pavement below and break my legs and be trapped here, I would fall not even half my body's length, and I realized this with joy as, like a blow, my senses returned to me and I could smell everything, the house, its filthy repression still clinging to me like a layer of soot, I could smell the garden, the breeze, the tales told by little tangs in the air and I leaped into it with all my heart out of joy at seeing I was only two strides from the wall, I was going to make it, I was going to be free, when, on my second stride, I almost turned in the air with a yelp, because I smelled Richard.

∞

CHAPTER SIXTEEN

I stood for a second, still inside the wall. I was casting about, trying to gauge where Richard's scent was coming from. Up on the balcony where I had leaped, Laura or Suzie was screaming and waving her arms, and bunches of her brothers and some sisters had joined her. It was quite a family. Down in the garden more brothers were converging on me from both sides of the house, and some of them looked to be pretty darn old, hobbling toward me in the same long dark jackets, pants, turban, sandals, holding gardening rakes or shovels. I put my head down and growled at them, and what was funny was none of them hesitated for an instant, like they didn't know enough to be afraid of me. When the brother appeared on the balcony with a rifle, that made my mind up, and I hopped onto the wall. I walked along it to where I was sheltered by a tree and I changed. If there are guns involved, you don't want to look like a wild animal; people won't help you then. They'll help to shoot you down.

I scanned for Richard. I didn't believe he'd be out in the yard, but that's where I'd scented him. On the other hand, he could have rolled naked and sweating all over the floors of that house and I didn't know that I could have smelled him at all. More people were converging in the yard—how many kids did this guy have? Twenty? A hundred? He must have been a busy, busy guy for a long time. I could still smell Richard's scent, the tiniest touch of it—and then I realized where it was coming from. It was on me. In tiny amounts: on my ear, in my hair, and on my hand. When had I touched—of course. It was the fly.

I hopped off the wall and onto the sidewalk, and quickly crossed the street. The gates were closed. Funny, I couldn't hear any of the hullabaloo out here, not even Suzie screaming from the balcony like she had been just a moment ago. I was trying to think what to do. Obviously, there were powerful magics in that house. Obviously, Richard must be somewhere that that fly could wallow all over him before it had a go at me. Obviously they didn't want me to leave. I had the choice. I could leap back over that wall and try to take out the whole family, which chances I didn't think very much of because the guys on the ground hadn't been afraid. There were enough of them that I wouldn't have time to bite them all before I'd be at the bottom of a dog pile. And of course there was that gun, which wasn't good.

But Richard was in there. And didn't that make this house— I stepped backwards as I realized it—the house of the Eater of Souls? Did the old wizard have the Eater of Souls inside? Or was he the Eater of Souls himself, that kindly old guy with the big library and the bigger family? Did he have as many kids as he had books? Did he have more at his other houses? And where were his wives? It boggled the mind. My best chance was to get the hell out of there before I was turned into a driveling idiot myself, and the next step was to tell the Thunder Mountain Boys, and Tamara, and the sorceress, that I'd found the Eater of Souls and—where the hell was my car?

I'd parked it right across the street from the gates. I knew exactly where I'd parked, and my car was gone! The bastards! So, when Suzie said it would be safer inside, she'd meant it. It wasn't good enough for this neighborhood, so it had been hauled away? The local private police could see it didn't belong and had taken care of it? Or al Hassan's boys had picked it up bodily and carried it away inside. Well, then, at least my parking outside had given them that inconvenience. Good.

The street was still quiet. No one ever goes outside on streets like that. Nobody takes neighborhood walks. They live in their walled mansions like cocoons. The gates of al Hassan's place were closed, and I didn't even see any of the children looking out through the bars. Dark had fallen. Over there, on the eastern horizon, the moon was rising, extra large in the haze, and full. Still, they knew I was close by, and if I was going it was best I went soon. Now, in fact. But it was a long, long, long way back to Whittier from here. Damned if I was going to walk it as a human. Humans are slow walkers. I moved along the street into the shadow of a hedge and changed, going as small and humble as I knew how. I turned and started back along the street—and there was my car! Right where I'd left it! Damn, how'd they do that?

I changed back without even looking around—and damn if the car wasn't gone again. But I knew right where it was then, and I walked forward until I touched it. Just as I ran into the bumper it exploded back into my sight as though it had manifested before me at that moment. I didn't worry about why. I worried about how soon those gates across the way were going to open. I unlocked the door, sweet-talking the car as I slid in because the gods forbid anything should go wrong now. But the engine came to life as soon as I turned the key—I love that car. I turned the headlights on bright to offset the possibility that I was driving a car that only I could see, and I drove on out of there.

What should I do? Richard was back there. I turned right at the next major street. No one seemed to be after me. I should go back, scout the house, find a way in there—and lose my senses again and not be able to find him. I turned right again at the next light. I knew where he was. He was somewhere in that house. All

I had to do was go back there—and get mobbed by that multitude of children. He had some awfully old children, too. How old was this guy? Was he the Eater of Souls, or had he been about to conduct me to whatever that was when his son called him away? I turned right again. And where was Richard? Had the fly been on him, or had Richard turned into a fly? After all, I'd seen him turn into a wolf once. Did this guy know how to get Richard to change? But if Richard was a fly, he was dead now. I'd seen them do it. Or—I turned right at the next light—was he back in his original body, all scars erased?

I'd circled the neighborhood one and a half times by now and had come no closer to a plan. I couldn't go back in there, much as my wolf blood wanted to start biting something. I needed help. I needed to know more. I needed—a pack. Damn. I was a different kind of wolf, that's what I'd always believed about myself. I didn't need family, like the others did. I was a lone wolf, and I went my own way. All right, well, this time I needed help. And I knew the first place to look for it.

Heading down the 5 to Costa Mesa on a Friday night, I hit traffic. I was two and a half hours in second and sometimes, blessedly, in third gear before I got onto the 22 and mercifully was able to make fourth at last.

Tamara's shop would be closed at this time of night. How was I supposed to find her, even if she was in town? Then I remembered what Richard said about the wards around that place. All I had to do was go and break them, and someone would come to see what was up. As it turned out, I needn't have worried. The moon was full, and Tamara's Ethnic and Tribal Music Store was hosting a party. I noticed the parking problem before I heard the music, but as I cruised by the shop I saw the drum circle and the dancers in the little courtyard, tiki torches lit all over the place, colored lights strung in the trees, and the people milling around, eating, drinking and talking. I finally found a parking place about three blocks away, and even from there I heard the drumming loud and clear. Also, I smelled meat. I trotted back to the store.

The moon had risen high above the crowded buildings, the power and phone lines, and the streetlamps, but the moonlight was drowned out by all the ambient city lights and the torches that surrounded the music store. Smells of barbecue wafted from the back of the store. Someone was grilling chicken and beef. My mouth opened as though I were in my other nature. I was hungry.

There must have been twenty drummers in the little courtyard, drowning out a couple of fiddle players and a bass player, but blending well with the dozen or so people wielding shakers and rattles, banging on bottles and sticks, and the two guys standing side by side, wearing hats like little red pots and blowing down didgeridoos. The dancers, both inside and outside the circle, made the drummers and other musicians almost invisible.

I smelled meat, I smelled spilled beer, I smelled sweat and excitement, and something akin to joy. Amid all that gathering, I caught the scent of someone I knew just before I glimpsed her among the drummers. Yvette, my friend from work, had found her own way to the music store. Not too surprising, if someone had told her she could go there and drum. She'd changed her hair. She was wearing it combed back now, and had braided it with tiny beads and little glinting gemstones, red, white, black, gold, and blue. She was watching the other drummers with quiet intensity, and pounding away on her drum, stamping a little in time.

The dancers and drummers weren't doing a specific working—no one had organized them—but the buzz of magic that was always present in the music store, a remnant of workings in the past, was fully alive in this joyful, pulsing noise. It may not have been a working, but magic was there.

I didn't see Tamara outside. I made a circuit near the barbecue, but they weren't giving out food there. A couple of guys were grilling up a huge stack of skewers full of meat, laughing and talking. One of them was the biggest bear. I had an urge to warn the two straight humans that a lot of their food might be missing before long, but who was I to interfere in the doings of the bear kind?

Near the front door I found the food tables, where I reached past slower, less hungry people and grabbed a handful of skewers, plain and marinated, chicken and beef, as my stomach was telling me quite clearly by that time how long it had been since I'd eaten. I scarfed down four of them standing there. Then I headed for the door. Another one of the bears confronted me as I stepped through the door—the smallest one, whose name I hadn't heard. I expected to be told to eat that stuff outside, or at least to be asked what I was doing, but instead he nodded me toward the door to the back room.

"They're waiting for you," he told me, and moved away.

I walked slowly toward the back door, chewing as I went, wondering why they would be waiting for me. Jacob stood by the closed backroom door.

"What's going on in there?" I asked him, tearing the meat from the last of my skewers.

"Meeting," he told me. "They're expecting you."

"Nobody told me," I said defensively.

"They knew you'd be here," he answered.

"Yeah?" I asked. I didn't think it had been that easy to get out of that house. I wish I had known I was going to make it. And I sure could have used some help with the traffic!

"They have their ways."

He opened the door to the office and pointed to the trash can where I could drop my skewers and my napkin before heading into the back room where the meeting was being held. The noise level in the back room was loud and shrill. "What's everyone so upset about?" I asked Jacob.

He looked at me in surprise. "Didn't you feel the earthquake? This afternoon? About a five point five."

I must have been on the freeway. The voices beyond the door rose again. Some man on the other side of the door was shouting, and then other voices rose over and drowned him out.

Jacob sighed as only a bear can. "They all think they know just what it means, and what we all need to do about it." He opened the door for me.

I had no idea why they wanted me there. But I sure knew what I wanted from them. I walked through the door and lifted my head and took a breath to take in the gathering. Every chair was filled and people were sitting on or leaning against the counter that surrounded the backroom. Tamara, in a new red and purple turban, sat at the head of the table with a bent old woman wrapped in a patterned green shawl beside her to her right. On her left was a skinny guy with a self-satisfied smile, who kept reaching to touch her hand or brush her shoulder, though she was leaning a little away from him. He had long graying hair tied back in a ponytail, and a deep tan. A white scarf was draped over his shoulders. Behind him, two women, one older and one young, stood in attendance on him, also wearing white scarves. There was a group of priestesses across from them, obviously priestesses because they wore shiny clothes and diaphanous draperies and many rings. They were telling everyone what was what, at the same time. Through a break in the noise I heard one saying, "The answer is not to be belligerent. Violence will only enrage it. We must speak to it—"

"Commune with it!"

"We must stop it with any means, and at all costs!" A black-robed man with an impressive beard shouted her down, and the clamor of voices rose again.

I smelled three of the Thunder Mountain boys before I spotted them near the foot of the table, well-groomed and elegant in expensive casual clothes. I almost smiled because one of them was Honey. I guess he'd found his way off the roof after all. He didn't meet my eyes. I expect the women from the Wiccan group may have greeted me, but they were involved in an intense argument with a group of Goth kids squeezed against the counters, holding, of all things, wands.

On a stool at one end of the table a girl sat bent over a chess board, playing against herself. A trio of bearded guys stood against the wall, the shortest one bellowing down the table while the other two tried to contain him. In front of them a heavy-set guy with short, stringy hair and glasses, sat back in his chair with folded arms. He had a sword on the table in front of him. An older guy, with long white hair and merry blue eyes was whispering in his ear, and the sword guy was trying not to laugh. Magic users. People of power. Working together. I could have had a good laugh myself.

There was a lot of shouting. All of this noise together with the drumming outside created a din that made the hair on my nape rise. No one looked at me. Well, this wouldn't do. I jumped onto the table and made sure I landed hard. That silenced them. They turned to look at me as I walked down the table, and Tamara rose at my approach.

I didn't wait for courtesies. "I've found the Eater of Souls, and he has my demon. Does anyone here know how to kill him?"

I don't suppose I should have expected an answer, or at any rate, one that I could hear or make any sense out of. It seemed like every one of them answered at once, and now most of them were on their feet, and everyone was shouting at the same time. I jumped down next to Tamara. The touchy man in the white scarf had risen, too. He reached out his hand to me, his eyes wide. I showed him my teeth and he backed off into the comforting arms of his supporters. I turned my head, feeling someone's eyes on me. The old woman in the green shawl still sat beside Tamara. She looked me up and down with deep, hard eyes. I almost shivered.

The angry robed man down the table raised his voice over the noise to tell me, "This meeting is not about the Eater of Souls!"

"It's about the earthquake!" one of the priestesses shouted. "I foretold there would be a second quake, and it means—"

"It's about the Worm We Do Not Name!" The robed man's

voice rose and drowned her out. "That is our enemy. We were just getting on track when you got here."

Tamara only said, "Welcome, Sister," and smiled a long-suffering smile. I nodded to her, almost smiling back. I didn't mind being called Sister by her.

Then the little dark woman on Tamara's other side lifted one hand and, after a moment, the noise ceased. When there was silence, she pointed to me. "Who is this?" she asked.

Tamara pitched her voice loudly, as one does for the partly deaf. "Mama, this is the daughter of the wolf kind that I told you about."

"The wolf girl?" she repeated in the silence.

"That's right, Mama."

"What does she want?" the old woman asked in a querulous voice. It did not go with her steadfast eyes.

Tamara looked at me briefly, and then answered for me. "She wants help in defeating the Eater of Souls. She says she's found *him*, and that he has her demon." She gave me a sharp look, to remind me of her message that the Eater of Souls was not actually a man. I knew what she meant. I hadn't seen al Hassan actually do the trick where someone's mind was taken away, but then, since I was the only one in the room with him aside from his children, I thought it was a good thing I'd missed it.

Uproar followed Tamara's answer. There were fierce arguments going on about what to do next, when to do it, and what good it would do. The Thunder Mountain Boys seemed to be making a case to throw me out. The sword man was looking around and laughing. The chess player defended her pieces from the women next to her leaning over the table. The touchy guy reached out to me again. I looked at him at let my eyes turn gold, and he backed up fast.

Then the old woman grabbed hold of the edge of the table and drew herself slowly to her feet. Tamara extended a hand to support her if she fell, but she was careful to do it out of her mother's sight. The old woman held herself upright with both hands on the table, and then she turned to me. "What do you want?"

By the time she finished speaking, the noise had died again. Everyone in the room waited for me to answer the old woman. I spoke strongly and clearly.

"Inside his house, I can't smell anything. I need to know how to beat that. He's got hundreds of servants, his children, and they're not afraid of me. I can't kill them all. I don't know where Richard—my demon—is. If I can smell him, I can find him. I want to find Richard. And I'd rather not have my mind wiped by the Eater of Souls while I'm at it."

"How do we know—" a piercing voice began from down the table where a soulful young woman with long blond hair in a long gray gown was speaking. "How do we know that the Eater of Souls isn't you?"

I looked at her, and she stepped back. That's not the sort of question I answer. I looked back at the old woman.

"We've all seen Darius. We all know what happened to him," the young woman continued, her voice pitched so that the old woman could hear. "*She* was the last to see him." She pointed a limp finger at me. "She said so. How do we know—"

Uproar again. Voices came out of the din, and none of them said anything that was of any use to me.

"We cannot divert our resources—"

"This is not what I came here to talk about—"

The old woman reached out and took my hands, transferring her weight to them from the table. She was pretty small—I topped her by more than a head—but her hands were very large. She opened my hands with her own and peered down at them, raising them close to her eyes and then holding them far away, adjusting her focus. She breathed a whistling breath as she stared down at them. She had a spicy smell to her, a clean scent, with just a touch of musk, and the tang of the soap she used on her hair. Her dark skin was deeply lined. Her eyes, slightly filmed with age, were calm and certain. I waited, my hands in her grasp and, as I stood there touching her, some of the fury and fear that I'd been carrying since I'd decided to leave that awful house dissipated. I felt my feet on the ground, her warm touch on my hands, heard her breathing, and slowly my certainty returned to me. What a strange old woman! I liked her. After a few moments of peering she put both my hands together and patted them, and looked up into my face. She cupped my cheek with her hand, and I let her, and didn't snarl or bite. She grinned then and reached for Tamara.

"I'm going to lie down," she said. "I've had enough of this." She toddled toward the back door of the shop. The third bear stood there. He held out his hand for her, and she took his arm. Before she got to the door, she turned and said over her shoulder to Tamara, "Give the wolf girl whatever she needs. Don't forget. It's important."

The argument in the room had already returned to its roaring pitch. Some people hung tiredly in their chairs, while others were on their feet yelling at people to hear them. The sword man and his friend were pushing their way to the shop door. I figured I'd done what I came to do. I went out the back door after the old woman. I watched the bear conduct her slowly across the courtyard while people fell out of his way as soon as he neared them. He opened the door of the next house for her. I guessed that's where Tamara lived, and maybe her mother, too.

I stood on the back steps, plotting a trail through the crowd, which was thick at this end of the courtyard. And I wasn't sure what to do next, except I knew it would involve more food, and plenty of it. I turned as someone came out the door behind me. It was Jacob.

He nodded to me by way of greeting. "Tamara said to tell you to come here tomorrow. She'll get you what you want." He cocked his head and advised me, "Don't come early. She'll be up all night with that lot in there."

"What's the meeting about?" I asked.

He looked disgusted. "They want to coordinate their plans for the next new moon. They're better off working by themselves and hoping all the pieces fit together." He looked up at the moon, now topping the sky. "They've wasted tonight. They could have been out there doing something."

I nodded to the fire circle. "Isn't that something?"

He shook his head. "Not enough. Not what it could have been." He turned to go back inside. "See you tomorrow."

I went back to the food table and grazed on meat skewers that just kept coming from the barbecue, and piles of pretzels and chips and guacamole, and even some vegetables, mostly for the tasty white dip that went with them. There were bowls of some African thing that you wrapped up in flat bread and ate like a burrito. I used the bread to wrap up a handful of chicken, instead of tearing it off the skewers, just for variety. At a table on the other side of the door, a pair of young women were selling soft drinks and bottled water. The beer was coming from someone's cooler deep in the crowd. I got myself some water. I don't drink things that spit at me.

"Amber? Amber! What's up with you? What are you doing here?" Yvette came toward me, an elongated can of beer in her hand. If I'd depended on just my eyes, I wouldn't have recognized her; she looked happy.

"Hey, Yvette," I greeted her in return. "You come for the drumming?"

"Yeah, some of the women from—you know, last night—they told me. The ones I'm drumming with. They're over there." She pointed. I took her word for it. "What are you doing here?"

I spoke the truth without thinking about it. "I came to get some help."

"Yeah?" she said. "What's going on?"

I studied her. For all the insult of the bear the other day, wolves aren't really known for discussing their business. And I had kept my own counsel from the time I realized I was on my own, and that was back when my dad disappeared, and my mom stopped answering my questions. So my instinct was to brush Yvette off when she asked me my business, maybe with a smile that showed my teeth and taught her the lesson not to ask me again. But we'd begun to be friends. And she hadn't freaked out when she saw me in my true nature on the hill. She wasn't freaked out now, though she knew what I was.

I said, "You know what's going on? I mean, with the Wicca group last night, and all these guys?" I made a motion including all the various dancers and drummers, shakers and players around us.

She nodded. "I hear the city's going down, and people who can raise power, through drums or by dancing, or whatever, are doing what they can to stop it."

That was a drummer's answer, all right. She probably thought the Wicca ceremony the previous night had been all about the drummers, with the celebrant and the dancers just hanging around to help out.

"That's right," I said. "So nobody has time for the other enemy that I've uncovered, but he's got something of mine that I want back, and I want it before—as you say—the city goes under."

"I'll help," Yvette said, taking a swig of her beer.

I was going to ask her what she thought she could do to help me, but then she looked away from me, and headed off back to the drum circle. Then I realized something about the drumming had changed.

Tamara had joined the circle of dancers. She'd shucked off her outer clothes and was wearing a robe of dark blue that looked like it was covered with stars. Suddenly the drummers were making a pattern that was like a maze for Tamara to dance through. There was a shift among the bodies of the musicians. Drummers who had been taking a break went back to their drums. I saw Yvette sit down on a camp stool and right the drum she had leaned against it. She listened for a few moments, joining in on the heartbeat, and then she found her place in the pattern, and laid in a rhythm loud and clear on her own. The drumming was hard, sharp, intoxicating. I couldn't help moving to it where I stood, and neither could anyone else. If it hadn't been a working before, in that circle, it sure was now.

Tamara turned and twisted, reached up and reached down, and it seemed she was climbing the sounds of the drums the way she might have climbed a ladder. Suddenly the fire flared as high as she was, though no one had put on any more fuel. Other dancers joined her, so the pattern repeated in the air, even as it changed constantly, over and over like dozens of mirrors repeating an image to infinity. The drumming began to echo in my head. I heard voices, as though a group of people had started chanting, but I never saw who was making the sound.

In the crowd of fire dancers I saw the three Thunder Mountain Boys, perfectly in step, perfectly in synch, even when their movements opposed one another, harmonizing somehow with the other dancers even as they kept to their own space, close by the fire. Honey briefly met my eyes from across the circle, then spun away.

I saw others that had been in the meeting taking their places around the circle. They held up their hands, speaking words that couldn't be heard over the drumming, whether of blessing, invocation or admonishment, no one could tell. People who weren't dancing picked up sticks and tapped on bottles or cans, snapped fingers, or clapped hands. The force of the circle shifted, became stronger. I made a circuit of the circle from behind. When I walked along the sidewalk I saw a cop car cruise by. Both of the cops stared straight ahead as though they couldn't see or hear the party in full roar beside them.

I stood behind the drummers for a few moments, watching Yvette and the others. I swayed as I stood there, in time to the drums. I recognized two women from the Wicca group on the hill. I was going to move on, do another circuit, but the pounding of the drums was reverberating within my heart and in my blood. My feet started to move before I did. I made my way between the drummers and was dancing even before my feet entered the circle. I danced without thought and without plan, but before I'd gone twice around the fire I found I was certainly dancing with intention. The cold anger that sat upon my heart like a hitchhiker opened and enlarged. I danced the fight I would fight with the Eater of Souls. I danced how I would stalk him through his great house, using every wile I knew from my own experience and from that of my people of old. I danced how I would knock down and take out every one of his children who got in my way. Even if there were legions of them, still they would be defeated. I danced how I would chase down the Eater of Souls, how I would take his head in my mouth up to the shoulders, and he could do what he would in the darkness inside my gullet, before my teeth came together and snapped him in half. I danced how his blood would taste when I drank it. I danced sweet white human meat, with lots of fat, like bacon. Yum.

Then I danced how happy I would be to find Richard, imprisoned, not dead, in one piece, and my own again. I didn't dance anymore than that, though the thoughts were there. After all, I was dancing in public. I leaped from one side of the fire to the other in a single bound. I found myself looking down on the head of Tamara, though she too towered beside the fire. I saw that I was dancing now on paws and now on feet, as though I had eight limbs instead of four, and I realized I had taken in the lesson Jacob had shown me: for the first time, I was wearing both of my aspects at the same time. So then I danced the joy of both my natures, the power and passion of two-in-one.

I danced as though the whole circle was mine, and the drumming built the halls I hunted in. The three priestesses spun past, whirling like children. The Thunder Mountain Boys stamped and turned to their own choreography. The chess player jumped up and down. The Goths spun through the circle like wraiths. The priests stalked the edges. Shakers and drummers stamped in and around. People leaped close to the fire and then away, but even though the crowd dancing around the fire grew and spilled out to the sidewalk, no one collided, and no one got in my way.

Tamara seemed to take up the whole world herself, with her sky-robe swirling around her, her hands and hair wild, her face entranced. Then all at once the other dancers seemed to twirl away. The circle near the fire was clear, and there I saw a small dark shape, wild and intense, powerful and profound, and then the drums found her heartbeat, and she began to dance as though the moon, the stars, the air, the city, the distant traffic, the drumming, and every one of us were the pattern that she danced against. It was Tamara's frail mother, who, when she took my hands, had not been able to stand unaided. Now, in the relentless rhythm of the drums, she danced down the moon.

Later on I thought that I dreamed it. The next thing that I remember at all clearly was waking up in the back seat of my car, still parked on the street near the music store, really thirsty. I fumbled with the door handle for several moments before the thought occurred to me that it would be a lot easier to open the damn door if I had fingers on my paws. I was so tired it took me a few seconds to change.

The sun was rising through an early morning haze. The streets were still. My ears were still ringing from the sound of the drums. And I ached with exhaustion. It was chilly, and my sweatshirt was damp with sweat. My hair needed brushing, my teeth needed cleaning, and my mouth was dry.

The music shop was dark, but half a dozen people wandered around outside like zombies, cleaning up the mess from the all-night party. In the courtyard three of the four bears sat nursing large mugs of coffee in their big hands. They nodded to me. Jacob read my unspoken need, took me in the back door, and poured me a styrofoam cup of coffee from an industrial-sized pot. It tasted awful. Just what I needed.

"Tamara's not back yet," he told me when my immediate needs were seen to.

"I know," I said. "You told me not to come till later because Tamara wouldn't be up yet. I'll wait. It's not worth driving home and back now." I sipped the hot, bitter liquid.

Jacob was looking at me in surprise. "Didn't you know? The old lady had a seizure early this morning. The ambulance came and took her away not an hour ago. Tamara went with her to the hospital."

I stared at him. "Her mother?"

He nodded. He looked fierce, and the scar on his brow knotted under his frown. "No one expected her to dance. She hasn't danced since—not since I can remember, anyway. Tamara about had a fit when she came into the circle."

"I remember her dancing," I said. I shook my head, trying to clear it. I remembered the dancing as though it had gone on forever. And I couldn't remember a thing after that, until I woke up in my car.

Jacob was smiling now. "Yeah, you were dancing pretty wild yourself. I didn't know the wolf kind could dance like that."

Actually, I hadn't either. But we are known for keeping our secrets, so I just smiled and said, "You'd be surprised what the wolf kind can do."

But he shook his head. "I don't think so."

I was pretty sure that what the bears had been doing during the dancing was cleaning up the food, but I didn't mention it. One should be kind to bears.

We went back out into the courtyard where the other bears feigned being deeply involved in sitting and coffee-drinking, so deeply involved that they couldn't possibly help the others clean up the mess. I joined them. It pays to learn the ways of your cousins, especially when you feel like a truck ran over you.

The biggest bear was Aaron. Close up it looked like all of the features of his face were oversized, but this just added to the impression of his great size. "So what's this Soul Eater?" he asked me.

"I don't really know," I said. "I've seen two men that met him. They're both supposed to be pretty powerful magic workers—"

"Marlin and Darius," Jacob said, nodding. "They are both very respectable sorcerers."

"In different ways," said Sol, the smallest bear.

"In very different ways," Jacob agreed, and there was a general bear laugh, louder than necessary, and going on for longer.

"So what does he do, the Soul Eater?" Jonathan, the third-biggest bear, and the quietest, asked.

I shrugged. "All I know is that when I saw them after they'd met him, the only thing they could say was, hi, how are you, and can I help you. That kind of thing."

The bears exchanged glances that were fierce and hard.

"I know Darius," Jonathan said. He shook his head.

"We all do," said Aaron. "He wasn't like that."

They nursed their coffee thoughtfully for a moment.

"So, what are you going to do?" Jacob asked me.

They all looked at me. What could I say? I shrugged. "I'm going to go back in there, and I'm going to hunt him through the halls of his mansion, and when I have him backed against a wall, I'm going to tear his head off."

There was another bear laugh, and I joined it with a wolf grin, which is a lot like a snarl.

The sun had long broken through the haze when Tamara pulled up in front of the store. She got out in a hurry, slamming the door of her car hard. She was wearing the same clothes as she had the night before, and wrapped her night blue shawl close around her in what was almost a protective gesture as she walked toward the store. The bears stood up when they saw her. She glanced at them, and then caught my eye. She motioned me to follow her as she climbed the stairs rapidly, seeming almost to fly up them with her usual grace. When I entered after her, she turned on me. She looked exhausted. Her eyes were sunken with sleeplessness and grief. Her attitude, however, was sharp as ever.

"Here." She held out something in her hand. "This is what you came for. I hope it's worth it to you. It may cost my mother her life."

I took it. It looked like a small round circle of flesh, about as big as my thumb. It was dark brown, almost black, and not very old. There was a hold punched in the top and it hung from a length of black cord. I smelled it, and looked up, startled. There was a white bandage around Tamara's upper arm. Under my glance she cupped it in her other hand protectively.

"My mother said it was important." She shrugged. "I would think that saving the city would mean more at this time. But she has always been—" She seemed to smile then, but as her mouth widened I realized she was trying to keep from crying. "Stubborn," she said finally, closing her mouth hard on the word.

"What does it do?"

She waved a hand. "It's a focus point. When the magic of that house surrounds you, this will provide a focus for you to find and keep your senses."

"I don't feel anything," I said doubtfully, looking down at the little scrap of skin. If it were magic I ought to feel a tingle or something.

"If I tried something on you right now, you'd feel the difference. But to tell you the truth, I'm too damn tired." She dragged out a chair and sat down in it, almost awkwardly. "Get me some of that coffee, would you?"

I got her a cup, brought her the sugar she asked for, and found the milk in a small fridge under the counter.

"Thanks," she said.

"Thank you," I said in return. "For this."

She raised her hand tiredly, waving me away. "Go on, then. Go find your demon. And kill that thing, whatever it is, if that's what's deprived us of Marlin and Darius now of all possible times…" She trailed off, staring into her coffee. I was about to go when she raised her head again and looked at me. Her eyes were bright with tears, but this time when she looked at me, she saw me. "If you find that demon of yours…" She shook her head. "Be careful."

"You told me that before," I said.

"Yeah, well, I mean it." She got up then, took the talisman from my hand and slipped the cord over my head. "Here. Go with my blessing."

She laid one hand, cool and light, on my forehead. After a moment, she laid the other hand beside it.

For a moment her scent, so close to me, gave me the impression I was walking through a dark forest and was about to step into a brilliantly lit glade just ahead. I looked up, startled, to meet her eyes, but hers were closed, and then the impression was gone. I went out the front door, where the store had just opened up, and I was still trying to grasp the impression of that vision as I got into my car. I'd reached the freeway before I realized, suddenly, I wasn't tired anymore.

ᛃᛃ

CHAPTER SEVENTEEN

So now I was supposed to drive to L.A., hop the wall, and attack the Eater of Souls in his lair, relying on the little brown talisman around my neck to fend off evil and save me from a life of vacuous inanity? In broad daylight? Right.

If I was going to enter the grounds of that house again, it was going to be dark, and no one was going to know. I was going to smell my way to wherever Richard was and find him, and chew him out of whatever it was they were using to hold him down, and get him the hell out of there and go home. That's it. So what was I supposed to do? Go and hang around that mega-upscale neighborhood in my little Honda Civic? I was nowhere near well-groomed enough to fit into that neighborhood.

I went home. I fried myself up a pan of steaks. And then another pan, because dinner was a long time and a lot of dancing ago. I took a shower, because pouring hot water down the back of your neck is a cure for almost everything. And then I lay down until the sun set. I may even have slept.

I parked a long ways from the house. The moon was already riding high in the east, in its last night of full, just one corner looking a little shaved. I'd hunted by its light thousands of times. Tonight would be no different. No, I told myself. It would be better.

I assumed he must have wards out; any two-bit sorcerer would have wards out. He hadn't sensed my nature when I was in his house, I was pretty sure of that. That he knew it now, I had no doubt, but I still thought it would probably be harder for him to read my presence in my wolf nature than as a human, since he might not know exactly what to look for. So I changed beneath the hedge of a mansion two streets away, and trotted along to the house as the smallest, most harmless canine I could make of myself. I stopped to sniff a few times—studly poodle, been eating pork, also milkbones, and also (did his mumsy know?) dead possum—and even to pee. Not till I crossed the street and stood under the wall of the house did I seek for that cold hard knot of anger sitting over my heart, and allow it to grow. As it grew, I grew also. I hopped lightly onto the top of the wall.

Nothing stirred. The grounds were empty. Most of the lights in the house were out. Over to the right, a window stood half open. Good. And if that didn't work—I glanced up—there was always the first-floor balcony. I'd stepped off it getting out of that place. I could step up there again. It seemed awfully high from where I stood, in the shade of a tree on the top of the wall. I nursed the cold anger that had taught me to grow and felt confident. I could do it if I had to. I leaped lightly off the wall and into the grounds.

At least, that was the plan. As I jumped, something hit me from several directions at once, knocked me off balance and onto my side, and entangled me as I fell to the ground. I landed with a thump, kicking and snapping for all I was worth. A net. Not of rope but of wire, and as the moonlight glinted on the strands, I knew, the wire was silver. Idiots.

People appeared. I struggled, whining and shrieking what I hoped sounded like painful shrieks, and then I changed and lay still.

Ibrahim al Hassan swept his long white robes and his crowding children out of his way with the same gesture and squatted beside me. "Just as I thought," he said, looking me in the eyes. The moonlight caught his liquid eyes, large and kindly as ever as he studied me. He stood up abruptly. "Bring her."

They must have had everything already planned, because he didn't give any more orders. They handcuffed me where I lay before they untangled me from the silver net, with silver handcuffs, no less. They put silver manacles on my ankles as well, as I moaned and protested. I don't suppose I needed to bother. The kids didn't take any notice of anything I said or did. When my ankles were connected by a reasonably long chain, and my hands were cuffed tightly behind me, they removed the net and hauled me to my feet. A whole crowd of them escorted me inside the house, but most of them found other business once we entered the hall. I took a deep breath as I stepped through the door. My token was still around my neck and, sure enough, I could smell. I almost forgot to moan and cry and carry on for a minute.

The daughter, Suzie I think her name was, stood by the library door, waiting to conduct me inside. Two of the boys escorted me in. Al Hassan waited inside, standing by the fireplace.

He clapped his hands as they brought me towards him.

"Good!" he said, "Very good! I am pleased with you, my children. You may tell the others. Come," he said to me, "let me look at you." He hauled me forward by my shoulders, turned me around, checked that the handcuffs and ankle cuffs were good and tight by yanking on them hard, then turned me around to face him again. I cringed and twitched.

"You caught me," I told him, "fair and square. Now take these things off me! They hurt!" I added a whine. What did he know about kids? His were zombies. "Please?"

"Oh no," he said, a pleased smile on his face. "No, no, no, no. I know too well your powers, you see. I have done my research." He waved a hand at a pile of books on his desk on the other side of the room. "Tonight, the moon is still full. When it has set, then I will consider removing those silver restraints. But not before that, no. Do I want a werewolf loose in my house? Heaven forefend. But you, you—my twice-welcome guest. How happy I am that you have returned, almost as though you knew it was your fate to do so."

I just stared at him, eyes wide. What the hell was he talking about?

"Twice-welcome," he continued, "I say because, in the first case it has come to my knowledge—and do not ask me how but let it be sufficient to know that one such as myself has ways of discovering these things—that you, of all people in this late and decadent age, have succeeded in doing what my kind have spent their lives striving to do—and for that alone, I of course desired to bring you as an honored guest beneath my roof."

I didn't understand what my two natures had to do with people striving to do things. You have to be born what I am. It doesn't come any other way. That nonsense about getting a bite from a werewolf making another werewolf—if that were true, the world would be peopled with our kind. It's not like we hold back, after all. I didn't say anything. My idea was, the less he knew about me, the better for me, and the more he kept thinking for himself, the more he got it wrong, and that was good for me too.

He went on. He really seemed happy to see me, and he was the kind of guy to share his happiness by talking. "That is why I invited you here first of all. You have succeeded in summoning a demon. How wonderful! How praiseworthy! You must show me your methods. We have so much to learn from one another. You must be as delighted as I that we have found one another."

I opened my eyes wide at him. "I summoned a demon?"

"Oh, my child." He moved to put an arm around me, but I stepped back just far enough so that he missed. He continued, unperturbed. "You mustn't try to deceive me. Remember, I have my little ways of learning these things."

"Oh yeah?" I challenged him. "Like how?"

His hand swung in the air again. "Your demon told me, of course."

"My demon...?" I started, unbelieving.

He greeted this with a laugh. "I am not saying that he meant to do so. I am not saying that. But again you must remember that I have made this area my study for many, many years—more years than you can imagine," he added, leering into my face for a moment. "And there are many techniques for inviting cooperation from those who would withhold their knowledge unreasonably. What do you call him? Stan? Amyas?" Again, the leer in my face, as though he were crowing over knowledge that I would be surprised that he knew. "Amyas has told me many things about you. How to find you, for example. He told me that."

I remembered his daughter standing outside my house with that pendulum thing swinging, and how it went wild inside my apartment, where Richard had spent time. It occurred to me that this guy might be lying through his beard. Richard hadn't, after all, told the guy what I called him.

His hand was waving in the air again. "But then I learned another of your secrets, and I see that I must treat you with more respect this time. I wonder if you chose to be a werewolf, or if you were attacked, and the powers of the wolf have simply been added to your other, considerable abilities. We must discuss this at some time, but first..." He looked me up and down, and then walked around me, grabbing my handcuffs hard and yanking on them when he was behind me. I cried out. I hoped it sounded girlish.

"You will have learned already, through your many disciplines," he told me, "that pain is one of our best teachers. It is my hope that your current... discomfort... is teaching you that your only course is to obey me in all things as long as you remain under my roof." He reached down and grabbed the chain on my ankles. He jerked hard, to one side, and I couldn't help falling, and falling hard with my hands behind my back, onto my hip and shoulder. I got to my knees and then to my feet while he watched me. I didn't mind the bruise or two. When he came close to me I smelled what he was trying so hard to hide, with all his servants, and his great house, and his great power, and his great wealth so abundantly on display. I smelled fear. Long-held, ancient, tamped-down, but nonetheless omnipresent, his fear. I was almost smiling as he led me to the next room. I just had to find out what the hell he was afraid of.

"Your last visit was interrupted," he said, as he conducted me across the room, "just when I was about to show you my work room. And too, just when I was about to explain so many things to you. I wanted your cooperation, your collaboration, even. I mentioned—but of course it was only to deceive you, you understand that—that it was one such as you that I would, in time, make my sole heir. But my children would never stand for such a thing. Never."

He walked to one of the bookshelves. It opened smoothly like a door as he approached it, and he waved me into the next room, dimly lit as though by lamplight, but no. By something else.

The walls of the next room were lined from floor to ceiling with a jigsaw puzzle of shelving, the dividers creating innumerable niches of various sizes, jammed with small glass bottles. Each bottle emitted a tiny luminescence, each with a slightly different shade of color from a dark deep purple to a white so pure and clear, it was entrancing. I couldn't take my eyes off them. The glass vessels came in all colors and shapes, some as tiny as one of my fingers, some so large that I would have had to hold it in both arms. The shelves were stuffed with them, shining like little suns, here a green like the forest leaves in sunlight, here a yellow so pale it was almost white. A huge bottle whose glass was blackened nonetheless emanated a glow of cobalt blue, in a nimbus around the dark glass. A tiny, plump bottle glowed red like a bright ripe apple. A tall, thin one with a long neck shone black as a moonless night. On one shelf half a dozen different bottles glowed in variations of white, from the fist-sized clear one that glowed with a warm, inner fire, to an opaque crystal that looked like a luminous stone, and could only be identified as a bottle because it had the same wax and glass stopper as all the rest. There were hundreds of them. There may have been a thousand.

High on a shelf to the right, perched precariously in a crowded niche, stood the little blue bottle that Richard had kept in his pocket and I had once touched. There was no mistaking it.

Al Hassan had followed me into the room. "How many...?" I asked him.

He opened his arms. The light from the bottles lit his face like a figure in a church. He looked rapturous, even holy. "Ah, my collection. What do you think of it, eh?"

"You're the Eater of Souls," I said. "How many—?"

I broke off as he started laughing. He laughed and laughed. "The Eater...? Oh no, oh no. You must not think that. The Eater of Souls is nothing like this—wasteful, an appetite, that is all. I—" and he leaned close to me again, to impress on me what he was saying. "I am a collector. A connoisseur, you might say. And this is my pride, and the fruit of my not inconsiderable labors."

"They are souls," I said, staring at the bottles uncertainly.

"But of course they are. I would expect an adept such as yourself to recognize them at once for what they are."

"But if you don't eat them," I said, "what do you want them for? And where did you get them?" I asked the last question to see what he'd say, but I was beginning to suspect that I knew.

He stepped closer to the shelves and stared up at them with greed as though he did not already possess them all. "Oh," he said over his shoulder, "so the little adept does not yet know everything. I see that I may still teach you something after all." Then he pulled me through the open doorway to the left, into his lab.

I had to stop myself from ripping away from him. The sense memory of that room screamed at me, with terror and pain, hatred and despair. I jerked as we crossed the threshold, but he just grabbed me harder and pulled me in.

"You see," he announced with a flourish, "my workroom."

A stainless steel operating table gleamed under the ceiling lights. The counters were strewn with books and equipment. A set of pincers, laid out from smallest to largest, tiny to immense, stood by a modern gas burner. A heavy, iron-banded door at the far end of the room lay between two sets of shelves stuffed with more books, scrolls, and tools. I took that all in at a glance because it was hard to look at anything but the table, the source of the emanation of past suffering. The leather cuffs at each of the corners, ready to secure unwilling subjects, were stiffened with years of sweat and blood. Some working had been done to damp the fear in the room. The working had been done over and over, but the fear still won through.

The wall next to me had a set of three shelves, one crowded with bottles that held more souls, stoppered and glowing with that eerie luminescence. The shelf below was full of the same bottles, but these had no stoppers and they did not glow. They were empty.

Through the far door two of his children materialized, a son and a daughter, and came to stand with bowed heads and clasped hands next to that ominous table. I turned to him.

"Of course," he said with a laugh, "I may teach you some things that you may not want to learn. My children—" He gestured to the two standing unmoving by the operating table, "—have learned a few things of that nature. But I am their father. I teach them what I will. Why else do we have offspring?"

This guy was beginning to scare me.

"You mean some of the souls come from…" I nodded toward his children.

"Some from them, some from others." He herded me toward the table, and all the nice smiles and expressions were wiped from his face. "At the next full moon, one will be from you. Would you like to choose the vessel I will put it in? I sometimes allow that, in those whom I especially favor. And I will favor you, I will, because you are going to be so useful to me!"

"Yeah?" I asked him. "What am I going to do for you?"

He turned to his children. "You see? Already she asks how she can help me. She should be a model to you. Ingrates. Fools." He took a long step and cracked the nearest one, the girl, upside the head. She was knocked sideways by the blow. She caught herself on the table, straightened, and then stood as she had been before, though the shawl that covered her head was now a little askew, and there was a dull red mark on her cheek. She stood there without expression, as though nothing had happened, but there were tears in her eyes.

He turned to me, his eyes limpid once more with passion and kindliness. "Seekers of knowledge such as you and I know that sacrifices are always necessary if there is to be advancement. I, for one, have never hesitated when such sacrifices must be made, and I expect no less from my family, and…" He sized me up with his eyes. "—from others of my discipline. Yes, I require souls. I must have souls. For how else am I to live, and perfect my art?" He snapped his fingers at his children, and they seemed to know immediately what he wanted, for the guy came forward instantly and brought a chair from the wall, which he held as his father seated himself. They didn't offer me one. I gathered my status had changed, now that I was wearing handcuffs.

His hands rose once again as he explained himself, the shadows of his sleeves crossing and re-crossing the floor and the walls as he spoke. "You must know that I am descended from the family of magi, the so-called apostates of the true line, who discovered the means, crude but effective, of sharing the life-essence of another being. Of strengthening their own souls from those of others. I have gone far beyond others of my family in this study. At first this practice was used only to guard and enhance the life of the head of the family. But I have realized—" His voice rose suddenly as he turned to include his children in what he was saying. "—as my father did before me—" He turned in his chair and finished at a roar. "—that the strength of the head of the house *is* the strength of the family! That what benefits me benefits us all!" He turned back to me, smiling again. I smiled back. I let my teeth show. I don't think he noticed, or maybe he didn't know what that means.

His chair had been set so that I was standing in front of him. I walked away now, moving along the shelf of vessels, looking at one after another. I wondered what you could tell about the person who had owned the soul by scenting it. I wondered if people who had done evil had differently-colored souls from, say, those of children, who hadn't had them long enough to really soil them. He turned in his chair to follow me as I went. I pretended I wasn't paying much attention.

"Now you have something that would benefit me. Two things. You shall give me the first, and I shall take the second myself."

"Yeah?" I asked, my back still to him. "What things?"

He leaned forward and said, "You are going to give me the name of your demon. You are going to tell me how you summoned it, and you are going to show me exactly how you did it."

I thought about this, then turned back toward him. "How are you going to *take* that?"

He shook his head, lifted his hand again. "No, no, you misunderstand. Or rather, I miscounted. First, you will tell me everything I want to know regarding your demon. You will show me how you achieved mastery over him, and give that mastery to me. That is the first thing. For the second thing…" He was out of his chair more quickly than I'd have expected. He caught me by the shoulder and leaned in close. His fear was very distant now. What colored his scent was something like anger, but not quite, and lust, but not quite that either. A little of each, perhaps, with the fear feeding both of them. "For the second thing, when the next full moon comes, I am going to wait until the change comes upon you, and then I am going to take your soul from you." He let me go, looking up at his treasured collection. "A wolf soul, imagine. I wonder what difference it will make, to my thoughts, my senses, when I imbibe yours slowly. I wonder if your powers will become my own?"

Well, he would wait a long time for the change to come upon me if I didn't damn well feel like changing. Why did he think it mattered which of my two natures I was wearing when he took my soul? Not that I was going to ask him that. I didn't want to give him any ideas.

"What makes you think," I asked conversationally, "that I'm going to tell you anything?"

Well, that was a mistake. He reached down and yanked up hard on the chains around my ankles. He may have been an old guy, but he was strong enough to pull my feet out from under me with the right leverage, which he held in his hand. I landed hard, on the same hip I'd hit before, but this time he followed up with a kick to the stomach that I was not expecting. That knocked the wind out of me. I lay there breathless, my mouth open, aching, waiting to be able to breathe again, holding away that stupid panic that I wasn't ever going to breathe again, while he turned me onto my back with his foot and then stood looking down at me. "You probably realize by now that I have been alive for a long time." His gaze lifted, his eyes rose to the vessels above us, and they lit his face softly as he spoke. "In that time there have been many things that I have needed to know, from people, and other things. Long life brings patience, you see. And patience is all one needs to convince such as you to tell me all I wish to hear. Patience, and an understanding of persuasion." He waved to his son, who came and hauled me to my feet just as I drew air into my lungs again. This time, when his fist hit my stomach just below the diaphragm I was a little more prepared. I tightened my stomach hard and flung myself backwards, riding the blow. The son stood aside and I fell once again, backwards this time, and conked my head against the floor before I was able to save myself. Having my hands manacled behind my back was not helping. That hurt.

He came and stood over me again, looking down into my face and said, "Then, too, you must understand that the means of extracting your soul need not be delicate. It may be crude, and difficult, and, yes, very painful indeed. Some people, in fact, even some of my own children, still cringe at the sight of me. Is that not so?" He reached out and lightly patted the cheek of his son.

The son hauled me to my feet again. I stood warily, a little hunched over. The fact was, I felt like shit right then. My head hurt, stomach hurt, my back hurt, and I was just hoping that if I threw up I could project far enough to spray his clean white robe.

He held out his hands. "You see? These cruder methods are so distressing. Distressing for everyone, myself most of all. You dislike these methods just as much as I do. That is how I know that you are going to tell me whatever I wish, without further ado."

He lifted a finger. The door opened again and a procession entered. Six of his children came in two lines into the room, and between them, in the center, they escorted a boy of about sixteen, fair haired, smooth and new as though he had just been made. He wore nothing but a tiny chain around one wrist. He looked up at me as he came in, and his eyes widened but he spoke not a word. He turned like the other children to attend the father of the house.

Ibrahim al Hassan raised his hand with gentle beneficence. "Amyas," he said. "Come here to me."

Richard moved obediently. The chain on his wrist glinted in the soft light, and my anger rose up in me like bile. "Richard!" I said, hard and clear. "Take that fucking thing off!"

Without hesitation Richard flicked one finger under the chain and pulled it from his wrist. His face lit up suddenly with hope, with happiness, and with something like glee. He turned to me as though asking what to do next when Ibrahim al Hassan answered with a roar like an explosion. Something struck me hard, and I fell into darkness.

❧❧❧

CHAPTER EIGHTEEN

I woke up in the dark, but that didn't faze me. I was leaning against some pipes along the wall where my handcuffs had been chained. My back ached as though the pipes had made permanent indentations in it. My head was pounding, and my stomach hurt. My arms ached where they were being pulled behind my back. My feet were drawn tight across the floor by the chain around my ankles. This was not so good. I was sitting on some pipes running parallel under me. Someone had been doing some soldering recently. I shifted and tried to make myself more comfortable. Fat chance.

I was in the far corner of a large room, probably an underground room because the floor was damp cement, and smelled of dirt and mold from not being cleaned very often. And Richard had been here, not right here, but nearby. There were traces of him, new and old, in all directions. I lifted my head, turned it from one side to another, my mouth open, breathing in with short breaths. I couldn't sense him now, but no one else was here. I thought perhaps he could hear me.

"Richard? Come over here, can you?"

In a moment I smelled him quite close to me. He reached out and touched me without speaking. I smelled his fear, like a layered coat, and sweat. I sniffed for blood, thinking they might have hurt him, but there was none of that. Strangely, in this filthy room he smelled clean.

"Richard?" I said, "Are you all right?" I reached for him but my hands didn't move very far. He found my hand then and squeezed it. I pulled a little and he came closer. I could feel him shaking. I reached out as far as I could and touched his side. He crouched on the cement floor beside me, and his skin was bare and cold. "Did they take your clothes? What did they do with them? Didn't they give you anything to wear?"

I reached out again and this time I felt a layer of cotton covering his side. "Well, thank goodness. Can't have you freezing to death. Is there any way we can get a light in here? I wish I could see what they've done to you."

I didn't feel him go, but a moment later I saw a dim glow, and when he turned around he was carrying a thick candle, cupping the heat of the flame with one hand. He sat down beside me, and I saw that we were occupying a square cage in the large dark room, and that the pipes beneath me were bars, and my handcuffs had been looped around the bars behind me. I couldn't see how he had gotten in to the cage. He hadn't been there when I woke up. I looked for the opening, but didn't see it. I had to smile when I saw that the bars were silver. That's what they'd been soldering. A brand new cage, just for me. Well, that should take care of me! Sure.

I struggled to sit up further, and bumped my head on the top of the cage. Richard was wearing a pair of his jeans, and a black sweatshirt that almost looked like one of mine. Strangely, the jeans looked quite clean. Maybe they weren't treating him as bad as I thought. But his feet were bare. They looked cold. I smiled at him, reaching out my hand as far as it would go. He didn't look at me, but he took my hand, and bent and kissed it.

I shook his hand where I held it. I don't know what I expected, but this wasn't it. Thanks for coming to find me? Thanks for trying to rescue me? How did you get here? How good to see you? He wouldn't even meet my eyes. He was different enough from what I remembered, from what I expected, that I sniffed him over carefully before I spoke. It was him all right. His cleanness was strange. He hadn't used any soap.

I pressed his hand. "So, Richard. You all right?"

He still didn't look at me. He nodded at the floor, still holding my hand.

"A fine kettle of fish," I quoted briefly, looking around. I couldn't see very far into the dark beyond the candle flame. The small light glinted off the silver bars of my cage. I looked back at Richard. "You've met this guy before," I said. "This is the guy you were so afraid of. The Eater of Souls. Did you know he's not really the Eater of Souls, the real one? He's something different, some perverted magician or something. Richard? What do you know about him?" I tightened my grip on his hand. What had they done to him? "Richard, talk to me."

He looked up at me then. His face was as smooth and unlined as a boy's. It was as beautiful as an angel's in an old painting, but it bore no expression, as though it had never been used. But his eyes were old and haggard, and scared. The little scar beneath his eye was gone. My throat felt tight. I watched him swallow once, twice, and open his mouth. I reached out to touch his lips, to stop his effort, but my hand was jerked back by the chain. He said, "I…"

I felt tears in my eyes. I blinked hard. I *don't* cry. I don't. "He killed you. Didn't he? He *killed* you." I felt the blood roar in my head. That was the second time in as many days I came close to changing involuntarily. I was enraged. I held on, clutching Richard's hand, until my anger collected itself, cold and hard above my heart. Richard was trying to smile, as though it was something that he had forgotten how to do.

He shrugged awkwardly in answer to my question. "Once or twice," he said. "He killed me in front of you. Yesterday. I tried to make you understand. I tried."

The fly. No wonder it had smelled like Richard when I got outside. It was Richard. "I'll kill him," I told him. "I'll tear his head off, and you can watch him die. I promise you."

He shook his head. "I just... I didn't want him to hurt you. I'm sorry. It's my fault." He was looking down again, clutching my hand in his. His pale white skin glowed in the candlelight that caught up highlights in his golden hair.

"It's your fault?" I wondered why he would say that.

Richard nodded. "I sought you out... not you. Someone. Someone who could help me."

"Because you knew he was after you." I sat up a little more, which I couldn't actually do because my head already touched the top of the cage, and my legs were extended as far as they could reach, chained to bars on the far side. I couldn't lie down any further because my hands were cuffed behind me through the bars. I was really uncomfortable. But I shifted until I was uncomfortable in a whole different way, to ease the places that ached enough already. "You took that soul from him." I'd concluded this already.

He didn't raise his head. "I needed it. I thought it would help me to get away from him, find out what I needed..."

"All right, back up. When did you meet this guy? And how?"

Richard took a deep breath. When he spoke, his words were tentative, as though he tasted each one before he set it before me. "When my last master died—I told you, the earl—I found myself bound to his son, together with the rest of his property." He smiled a little as though at a private joke. "Entailed... But then he died young, and without an heir, and left me to a friend who was abroad at the time, in Ceylon, and he died there, without leaving me to anyone." His voice grew less hesitant, and he raised his head. "And so, for the first time, I found myself free. I had no master. But I was still here. And—I didn't want to stay here. But I didn't know what to do, how to get my release. I went looking for someone, a sorcerer, a mage, who could understand what I was, how I came here, and could counsel me on how to get free. I heard there was one adept in such matters in Cairo. So I went there. But he was there. In Cairo. He has demon traps, you see, and they found me out. He wanted a demon. He has always wanted a demon, but he is not one of those who can raise them himself. He captured me."

"So you belong to him?" I asked.

He shook his head vehemently. "No. I never did. And I won't, as long as…" He met my eyes. "As long as you don't give me to him."

"Don't worry," I said. "I won't." He held my gaze as though he was going to say something else, but then he didn't. I prompted him, "So, what did he do with you?"

Richard dropped his eyes again. "He spent a number of years trying to learn my name. He experimented with what he could do to me without killing me. He did kill me, once. The time I died of hunger? That was him. He went away once and forgot about me."

"How long did he keep you?" I asked.

There was a short pause. Richard looked at me sideways. "One hundred and twenty-four years."

I stared at him. "All that time?"

He nodded.

"That's…" I didn't know what to say. "A long time."

"Yes," he said. "It was. A long time. Then I heard he had been killed. There was—chaos. A riot. His house in Cairo was burned down. That's when I escaped, and I took… the soul from him. The child it had come from was dead. I knew that because I saw… I took that one…. No one else needed it. And I did. When I have it, I am immune to demon traps. I can't be caught that way. I can pass other wards as well. And I can disguise my nature from those who can otherwise sense… I believed, for a long time, if I could some how take in the soul, make it mine, I might find a way out of here. But I never could. Some time later I learned that he was still alive." He clutched my hand hard. "I didn't lie to you. I thought he was the Eater of Souls. I heard that name in Cairo, and I have seen him.... I've seen what he does. I thought he was..."

"All right," I said. "Hey, calm down. I believe you." His breathing softened at once, and he met my eyes steadily. "This has just been one big mess from the start." I shifted again. This was getting on my nerves. I could get out of these chains, of course. My wolf feet are a lot smaller than my wrists. Well, not a lot. But enough. But Ibrahim al Hassan didn't know I could change at will. He seemed to be under the impression that he'd have to wait till the next full moon before I became a wolf again. And he also seemed to be under the impression that I couldn't change if I was in contact with silver. How I love those old myths! They've saved the asses of my kind a bunch of times.

So I was in for some discomfort. But that was better than having my soul ripped out, or being subjected to whatever methods of persuasion he and his big old dysfunctional family could come up with to get me to cough up Richard's name and a transfer of ownership. I wasn't going to give Richard to this guy. He was mine. Besides, even if I did, it didn't mean for a second that he'd let me go, no questions asked, on with my happy life.

So I was stuck. But at least I had good company.

"Tell me," I said, looking for distraction as much as anything, "what is it with this guy and souls? What does he do with them?" He didn't answer me all at once. The information came out after question upon question. It was like getting meat off an animal with too many bones. I had to work for every piece. Richard held my hand all through my questioning, like a lifeline.

This is what he told me, piece by piece. "A long time ago he learned how to take people's souls out of their bodies. It's a crude piece of magic; it isn't easy. It doesn't take long. It's like taking an oyster from its shell. There's always some left behind. He doesn't mind that. They mostly don't die then, his victims. The younger he takes them, the more he gets. When they're just born, when they're babies, he can get a whole soul. And the child is left alive, but just… empty. They'll die later. But not for a while."

"Where does he get these children? Does he use his own? I hope?"

"Yes. Usually. Sometimes he can get an infant or a child through the local black market. He doesn't care if they're ill, you see. And he'll give them back, still alive, without a mark on them, for disposal."

"What he does, the extraction, doesn't leave a mark?"

He shook his head. "It's painful. I've seen him do it. I've heard the sounds they make. But the bodies are unmarked. You've seen his children—all of his servants are his children. He takes the souls from most of them when they're young. He allows a few to keep theirs into adulthood, because he needs some servants who aren't fools. They know what will happen to them if they disobey him. That's how he keeps them from killing him, and getting free from him that way. The others, the empty ones, obey him implicitly. Your will goes with your soul. You've seen his collection?"

"I sure did. What a nice guy." I scooted around again, trying to get comfortable. "How many children has he had?"

"He was old when I first knew him. He had hundreds then already. And he has hundreds now."

"And grandchildren? And great-grandchildren? He could have peopled a whole country by now."

"No," Richard said. "He doesn't allow that. They don't leave him. Once he has you, he doesn't let you go."

"Well," I rubbed his hand. "We'll just see about that."

Richard was different. It was almost as though he, too, had lost something precious in the sorcerer's workshop. But then, I don't know how smart I'd seem, or how cleverly I could hold up my side of a conversation after I'd been killed a couple of times. God knows what else that piece of work had done to him. I stroked Richard's hand with my thumb as though I could will some of the spirit back into him that he'd had the week before. The more he talked, the more he seemed to come back to the way he had been before.

"What happened to you, Richard? What did he do to you?"

He avoided my eyes again, looking at the floor, but he answered me. "He remembers me. He's angry with me for getting away from him, all those years ago. And when he's angry, you have to pay. So, I have been paying. And he's thought of a few more ways, in the time I've been gone, to make me do what he wants. And to make me tell him my name. And he's been trying those, when he has time."

"And have you? Told him your name?"

He frowned. "No. It isn't allowed. I can't—except to you. He doesn't understand that."

He kept reaching for information as though it were outside of him, separate from him, and he had to find his way there. It was as though my questions were leading him through a maze.

"Richard, did he take something from you? Part of your brain or something?"

He thought about that, and then shook his head.

"You're different."

He looked up at me then. "I don't mean to be. Tell me how to be, and I'll be the same."

"You don't remember? How you were?"

His eyes were open, blank with realization. "I can't remember anything, until you ask me."

Once again I had to fight back tears. I'd never felt—I'd never let myself—feel about someone the way I felt about him. Not since my dad had disappeared, and my brother didn't come back. And my mom and other people in the family started acting so strange, and caring for people was suddenly pointless. I wanted to take Richard into my arms and kiss him until he changed again into the companion, the friend that had stood at my back through all our adventures together. That wild, marvelous creature I'd had in my bed. I felt a powerful sense of loss, that some important part of him had been battered into oblivion, that though he might not have a soul, his spirit, or whatever he was made of, had been damaged. But I couldn't hold him unless I wanted to give up the pretence that I couldn't get out of my chains, and I didn't think that would be wise if I wanted to get close to al Hassan again. So I went on talking to him, asking him questions, because that had worked so far. Besides, it doesn't hurt to know everything you can about your enemy. If there ever was a guy that needed killing, I thought, this was one. And his whole family, living and dead, and living dead, would probably thank me for it.

"Are the souls that he keeps in the jars just his children?"

"No. He stores others there too. He uses them when he needs power. He eats them. They're what keep him alive and strong after all these years. When he's doing a great working, he'll consume a few more. He's not a very strong sorcerer. He's been searching all his life for an adept that he can make his slave, someone who has the talent for magic, who will obey his will. Anyone reasonably adept can usually avoid him, however."

"Not always." I told him about how I met Darius, and what had happened to him. I told him how I went to the dance studio where the Thunder Mountain Boys do their magic. I saw his face change as he remembered the place. I didn't ask him about what exactly had happened there. I knew too much already. When I told him what had happened to Marlin, what he'd been like when I last saw him, Richard said, "Good." And that was his only comment.

"Is Darius's soul in one of those bottles? Is Marlin's?"

"I don't know."

I stiffened suddenly as my arm and back cramped up. I clamped my teeth on what I was going to say and tried to move to ease the cramp. Richard sat up and eased himself closer. Tentatively, he reached out and touched my shoulder. I could hardly feel the weight of his hand, his touch was so light, but the cramp faded and vanished in moments. "Hey!" I said. "Thanks."

He moved his hand to my neck, and an aching stiffness I'd hardly been aware of eased and disappeared there as well. His light hand on my forehead quieted my headache, his gentle fingers on my side seemed to draw out the pain in my stomach and from my bruises. Moments later, I felt almost comfortable. Richard looked better, too. At least, his eyes were not so frightened and his face was starting to hold some expression. More like the Richard I was used to.

"Why don't you move that," I pointed at the fat candle with my chin, "and come over here?"

After a moment he grasped my meaning, and I saw him smile a little. He lay down with his head on my lap, turned so he could hold my hand in his. Aside from being chained in the cellar of a mad sorcerer who wanted to steal my demon and rip out my soul, it wasn't bad.

"I missed you," I said. I couldn't quite lean over to kiss his cheek, but I saw his smile.

"You came after me," he said. "Thank you."

I told him how I had tracked Honey and marooned him on top of the building, and felt him shake in silent laughter against me. So for good measure I told him how I almost made a wolf pancake of myself jumping off that same building, but he didn't think that was funny at all. He sat up suddenly, his eyes darkening, and he leaned forward and kissed me. Well, that was nice. He scooted forward and put his arms around me and kissed me again. Let me tell you, if you have to pass the time while you're caged in a dark cellar, this is the way to do it. So we did this for quite awhile, until I heard a noise.

"Someone's coming."

Richard sat up, tense and scared and suddenly he seemed very young. He stared at me as though he couldn't hear the noise that I knew distinctly was coming from across the room and beyond. I nodded the direction and he looked that way with blank, frightened eyes. I remembered then how I couldn't smell when I was in this house before. I could smell now just fine, thank you, so I assumed the token that Tamara's mother had magicked for me was still around my neck.

"Richard, are you under some sort of spell so you can't hear things, or understand things in this house?"

He looked back at me, still frightened, hardly hearing what I said, but he tried to answer. "I… I don't know."

The door was opening on the far side of the room. A light flashed. Someone had a flashlight. I said softly, "I've got something around my neck. Put it on for a bit, why don't you? Maybe that will help."

I had my eyes on the figure across the room but I felt Richard's light fingers find the cord on my neck, draw out the talisman, and lift it over my head, disentangling it from my hair. Until that second I'd known absolutely that it was Suzie coming toward us across the floor. She'd left the door open behind her, where a pale light shone, and a small amount of air preceded her into the room. Suddenly, I could smell nothing, as though that part of my brain was erased, and my hearing was dulled as well. I sniffed hard, franticly, even though I knew what had happened, and that sniffing harder wasn't going to make it any better. My senses were deadened, so I didn't know for a moment why all of a sudden every hair I had was standing on end, but I said to Richard, "You'd better get out of here—" I looked over at him.

He was squatting on the ground next to me, the cord looped over his head, holding the talisman in his hand, and I thrust myself back from him so hard that the cuffs on my wrists and ankles dug deep in my skin. He was human and darkness at the same time. He was a mass of wild, seething energy rising from depths I couldn't fathom, overlaid by the form of a beautiful human youth, and I saw in an instant why John Dee had kept him in a cage for those years, throwing everything he had at him, trying to contain him. Richard turned to look at me at the sound of my voice. His eyes were wild—and yet the same. And as I jerked back from him, his whole being softened and for an instant he was the Richard I knew again.

The flashlight beam hit me in the face and I turned to it, just as I remembered why for a second I'd been unaware that Suzie was almost upon us. "Richard, give me that—"

But Richard was gone.

Richard had left the candle, and it was out of my reach. Suzie bent over the cage, looking in, and then squatted down to peer inside the bars.

"Hey, there," I said. I hated not being able to smell her. My shoulders and back were beginning to ache again. But it was hard to concern myself with what Suzie was up to when my hair still felt electrified by whatever it was that Richard had been possessed by that last moment before he disappeared. I did wonder where he had disappeared to. And how he had gotten in and out of the cage in the first place.

"You must be a powerful sorcerer indeed." Suzie was staring at the candle.

I thought I'd go along with that. I didn't think it would be a good thing for them to know that Richard could get in and out of the cage when he—or when I—wanted. "Yeah? Your dad already knows that. That's why I'm here."

She shifted along the bars, moving closer. I squinted as she trained the light in my face, and she lowered it again. "I have come to ask you for help."

I almost laughed out loud. "Sure," I said. "I'll help anyway you want as soon as I'm unchained and out of this cage."

She looked at me solemnly. "I cannot unchain you. The moon is not yet down. I know that as a werewolf you could not help killing me—"

For the gods' sake! I opened my mouth. I almost bit back at her. Did she think there would be any of the wolf kind left if we were that undisciplined? Honestly! But I didn't say a word. I just let her jabber on.

"—and that unless you are kept in contact with the purest silver, you cannot help but change, until the last light of the full moon has departed the Earth. But I swear to you, as soon as it is safe I will release you, if only you will help me."

"Help you?" With all my senses dampened again, since I no longer had the talisman, I couldn't tell what she was feeling, so I couldn't tell if she was lying her head off. But I was pretty sure I'd be a fool to trust anyone in this house.

"Tell me the name of your demon, and I will set you free."

"Oh, I see. So you can pretend to your dad that you're the talented one he's been looking for to be his heir."

"He wants no heir!" she hissed at me. "There will never be an heir. He tests us for the talent as soon as we are able to speak. The ones who have even the smallest ability, they are gutted of their souls, and killed. He wants no one near him to have power but himself. No one. And once he possesses the demon, he will not even want us as his slaves."

"Where is my demon?" I asked.

She looked across the cellar, flashing her light as she did. Across the room, on the floor, I saw the outline of a small rectangular box. A rage rose up in me. It didn't look big enough to hold a man.

"That's—not very big," I sputtered. I wondered again how he'd gotten into the cage with me.

"Upstairs, in his rooms, my father has in his possession the tools of a diviner. He is teaching the demon to diminish himself, so that he can fit into a certain bottle." She added bitterly, "My father has always coveted a demon in his service, that he could keep in a bottle."

"He's been making Richard smaller?"

"With the correct tools, one can force a demon to shift its shape," she said primly. She looked smug. I didn't need wolf senses to figure out she'd been playing with her daddy's tools, or guess what she had done to him.

I threw myself at her so hard the cage shifted even as the cuffs bit. She leaped back. When she was sure I was still chained, she came and stood over me. "You may have power, you may bear the wolf's curse, but I have stood in your rooms. You are no practitioner! You are not the one to wield such a weapon as the demon can be, for the right master." Her eyes lit strangely in the darkness as she bent over me. "With such a tool I could scour all evil from the face of the Earth. I could weigh the souls of the righteous and reward them as they deserve. I could bring a golden age to the world and reign over it for all time."

"You're kidding," I said. The idea of this girl in charge of anything was scary. Besides, "How does the demon do all that?"

"The demon must do whatever his master commands. Quickly! Give me his name! Everything will be for the best, if you tell me—" She glanced back to the door, where a flash of light revealed the opening. "My brothers. They are coming." She dropped her voice. "I have lost my father's favor. He has spared me this long because I am dutiful and obedient, but now... if you don't help me, I will become like them." She bent close to me. "Please!"

Her brothers arrived at the cage. Two of them were holding what looked like cattle prods. I stayed perfectly still while the cage was unlocked, and the whole roof of it was lifted up on hinges, like a big box. Well, Richard certainly hadn't gotten in and out that way. I would have noticed that. But now I could guess how he had managed it. Suzie pretended to her brothers that their father had sent her to me, and was giving commands right and left to prove she was really in charge. They put a new set of silver chains on my hands and feet before they removed the old ones. They were sure being careful of me. Now that's what I call respect. I went with them. I didn't want to be zapped. I was pretty sure I wouldn't enjoy it.

Suzie clasped my arm when I stood up, and put her face close to mine. "Please! I beg of you...."

I wondered if there was any way I could get the talisman back without giving up every card I held at this point. I had the feeling that every single separate one was going to be necessary if I was going to get out of this house without becoming another of al Hassan's mindless slaves.

"Bring me my demon," I told her.

She shook her head. "I cannot." As we passed, she pointed her flashlight at the heavy metal box on the floor. There was a sword on top of it, crossed with some kind of wand. It was surrounded by a pentagram sketched in chalk, and that was surrounded by a circle made up of some kind of grain. There were bunches of magical signs and symbols in and between the points of the pentagram. I supposed that was a kind of respect for Richard. Then I noticed there didn't seem to be any air holes. I felt an emptiness inside as I wondered suddenly just how many times Richard had died since he'd been brought here.

We climbed the basement steps, and emerged in a wine cellar. We climbed those steps and came into a passageway that led to a larder, and then walked through a large kitchen, where more of al Hassan's happy children, clad in aprons and little white hats, were working away, methodically chopping, mixing and cooking what was probably food, though I couldn't be sure, because I still couldn't smell a thing. We went out the kitchen door and down a few corridors, and through the heavy door into Daddy's work room.

I was taken straight to the table. No pretence that I was an honored guest or just a visitor this time. I wondered if he'd changed his mind, and thought he should go ahead and get my soul now. I wondered if he'd decided that was more important than getting the name of my demon from me.

I hesitated at the table. I thought I was already under enough restraints. There's no way I was going to be laid out on that stainless steel operating table if I could help it. So I stopped walking. The guy behind me pushed me forward. I rocked forward and then back again and stood my ground. One of the guys with the cattle prod stepped up, and I dropped and rolled under the table to the other side.

"You fools!" Ibrahim al Hassan swept in through the other door, accompanied by some more of his children. He made a gesture and they came for me, two diving under the table while the other two went around it.

It's fun when they're stupid and slow. And when they dive at your feet it's like they're practically begging to be kicked, and I like to oblige, when I can. I aimed a good one at one of their heads, which turned out to be not such a good idea as I'd forgotten the length of the chain between my ankles. My kick was shortened by a good foot and I fell backwards, tripping myself. This gave me a wonderful view of two of the soulless children meeting over my head in a classic double head-crack as they tackled me from either side of the table. I fell down laughing. It didn't last long, as one of them fell on top of me, the two on the floor hadn't stopped, and two more were coming. They got me, all right, but it took six of them. By the time they hauled me up and had me pinned, al Hassan was glaring.

They dragged me towards the table, and I made up my mind that if I was going to go down, I was going to kill a few of them first, and al Hassan if I could, so I was going to have to blow my cover and change—but al Hassan said, "Not that one!" He turned and pointed at Suzie, who waited in a submissive posture by the side of the room. "Her!"

She looked up at him, appalled. "But, Father—No!"

Two of her brothers grabbed her. When they had her fast, al Hassan stalked toward her. "Do you think I do not know of your rebellious thoughts? Do you think, after all the children I have raised, I cannot tell when the mind of one begins to stray from my service?" His hand came up as though to strike her, and she cringed, but the gesture changed as it reached her head, and he caressed her hair briefly. "Oh, my little one, do not be afraid. I do not discard you utterly. You will still serve me, but in a new way. And see? Your two sisters have arrived. Do not fear that I will have no one at all in this great house to talk to." He gestured through the door where two small dark heads, covered with black shawls, peaked through the doorway, tentative and scared. "Come, little ones. Yes, come to me, now." He raised a finger, and two skinny little girls scuttled to his side. He put an arm on each of their shoulders. "You must attend now, my dear daughters. This is Maryam, your older sister, and she has disobeyed my will. She has dreamed of departing my service without my leave. I do not tolerate insubordination. Behold her fate, the fate of any of my children who disobey me. Or who are slow in learning to serve me."

He gestured, and Maryam was the one who was lifted onto the table. She cried and yelled, she begged her brothers to wake up, to stop what was happening, to help her. She begged her father to listen to her, she told him that he was mistaken, that she had never had a thought but how to please and serve him. He paid no attention to her. Her brothers fastened her to the table with cuffs and straps that were molded into shape from long use.

Al Hassan went over to the shelf and made a show of consulting the little girls as he chose a bottle. He picked up a round, clear, cut-glass bottle, one that wasn't shining like the ones on the upper shelves. One that was still empty.

"My little birds." He gestured the two girls to the counter behind the table. They scrambled to follow him. He lit the gas burner that stood on the counter and adjusted the blue-white flame. He selected a little white ceramic cup and dropped in it a short length of silver wire. He picked up a lump of wax and handed it to one of the girls. He fixed the cup in a pair of tongs, and handed it to the other. "Now, I depend on you to do this carefully. Heat the crucible until the wire is just hot enough to begin to soften. Never take your eyes off it. It must not become too hot. When the wire just begins to lose its shape, take the cup off the flame and drop the wax into it. Use this little prod to mix the wire into the wax. Do not fail me," he said, patting their heads in a kindly way. He handed the empty bottle to one of his sons who had his hands free. And then he approached his older daughter.

"Be still, my little sparrow. Be quiet." He stroked her head and she was quiet, but no less panicked, staring up at him with huge, frightened eyes. "You will serve me yet. That's what you want, isn't it? Of course it is. Every child longs to please her father.

"Listen, I have made a new plan. Why should I keep that—" he pointed at me, the pig "—alive in my house? All I need for my experiment is the soul. It is her soul that makes her change. I have studied the phenomenon all night. If you carry her soul, I will be able to make my experiments without any added danger to my household. But, you say, there is one small problem." He waved his hand across her face. "You already have a soul. There is no room for another. But for that, I have the answer."

He took the top off a big jar on the counter, reached inside and drew out what looked like a handful of glittering white sand. He murmured some words over it and then he sprinkled the sand over the girl's body, from her legs to her head. Maryam whimpered as the sand touched her face, but he silenced her with an admonishing finger. Her form began to luminesce with a pale, rose light, as though it were one of his bottles.

Al Hassan brushed off his fingers over her chest. He reached up and took from around his neck a thin, golden chain. He drew it up and over his head. At the end of the chain dangled a tiny pair of golden scissors. He opened his hands and intoned some words in a language I didn't know. On the table, Maryam began to scream, and then he reached out with the scissors, and seemed to reach into her throat. He made small, delicate cuts from her throat down toward her heart, and in these incisions, which did not bleed, the luminescence of her body began to pool. Where it pooled, it became darker, almost purple. He gathered this light into his free hand, wound it like a cord through his fingers, and then as he cut toward her belly he leaned down and took the tendrils of light into his mouth. Maryam screamed and screamed as her father sucked the light of her soul into his mouth like someone eating a long piece of errant pasta. All the while he continued cutting, across the shoulders, then along the spine, winding the tendrils of light into his hand, and drawing them into his mouth. The luminescence of Maryam's body faded, and as this light was drawn out of her, her screams changed. He finished with a few cuts at the back of her head, and the sound she made became breathless, and then breathy, and then stopped.

Al Hassan continued sucking and working something in his mouth. He reached out his hand for the bottle and his son offered it at once. Al Hassan put his mouth to it. He worked his mouth again, pushing something out into the mouth of the bottle, and very slowly, the bottle began to glow with a pale pink light that intensified to a fiery purple, and then faded again to a pale rose. Al Hassan continued working his mouth and moved over to where his little daughters were still assiduously bent over the melting wax. He reached into the pan, picked up the globule of wax and wire and rolled it into a ball in his fingers, and then stuck it in the mouth of the jar, which sat in his hand now, glowing as luminously as any of the others.

Maryam lay on the table as limp and quiet as though she were dead, but her eyes were open, and she was breathing calmly.

Al Hassan turned to me, his eyes as kindly as ever. The hair rose on my neck and body. It's a good thing he wasn't a dog. He would have smelled my fear.

∞∞

CHAPTER NINETEEN

"You see how easy it is for me? You see what fate awaits you?" He waved a hand at his older daughter. "You may release her, my sons. I am finished with her."

Maryam's arms and legs were freed from the restraints and she was lifted off the table. She went and stood beside her brothers with her head bowed. The light was out of her eyes. I guessed she'd be a really good girl now.

"And now," al Hassan waved the air again. "It is the turn of our honored guest."

The boys started pulling me toward the table. I pulled back and for a moment, stayed where I was. "I thought you wanted the name of the demon?" I asked. I was pleased to hear my voice sound hard and cold. It's not, the gods know, what I was feeling at that precise second. But he didn't need to know that.

"Ah." Al Hassan lifted his hands, one still holding the small rose bottle, in one of his theatrical gestures that made me want to cut his goddamn hands off. "My memory," he cried. "What was I thinking? The excitement of possessing the soul of a werewolf—"

"Not yet you don't." The sons had begun to pull again, and I was losing ground.

"That I shall soon possess the soul of a werewolf," al Hassan amended, "has made me forget my purpose."

"Yeah, right," I said. "You held that demon a hundred and twenty-four years and all of a sudden you forgot that you're trying to possess it." I leaned to one side and grabbed the closest guy's shoulder in my teeth and bit down hard. I felt flesh tear, I tasted blood, but the guy didn't even slow down. It was depressing.

Al Hassan said, "You may as well release him. They hardly feel pain in that state."

I had reached the table. I wrapped my leg around one of the corners, trying to hook my chain on something so I couldn't go any further.

"Tell me." He waved a hand, and the guys stopped pushing. "How is it that you gained possession of that which I have so long desired? What book, what incantation, whose grymoire did you use to learn the creature's name and bind it to you?"

"Wouldn't you like to know?" I asked.

He stepped another pace toward me, he met my eyes full on, and this time all the kindliness was gone. The illusion of a middle-aged man slipped for just a second, and I saw him, old, hard as nails, crusted with cruelty and malice, greed and power. He let me see him like that, and he smiled. His hands lifted, and the illusion of the middle-aged, kindly scholar was back in place.

"You do not yet take me seriously," he said. "But I assure you, you should. Perhaps, if you see a little more of my power, you will be convinced." He peeled the stopper out of the bottle that he held in his hand. Maryam cried out as he raised it to one eye and pressed it there. His eye lit up with a rosy glow, as though a light had come on inside it. Behind me, Maryam whimpered one more time, as her father stoppered the mouth of the bottle with his thumb, and then moved it to his other eye and held it there, until the light in the bottle was entirely gone.

He turned back to me then, his face illuminated unnaturally

from within. He looked younger, vibrant, powerful. Even his beard was black again. He lifted his hands and his sons stepped back. He spoke some words and pointed at me hard—and I felt a concussion as though I'd been hit all over at once with a big stick. I slammed back into the wall. The luminosity died from his face. Maryam, too, was leaning against the wall, crying as though she had just witnessed her own death.

He glared at her for a moment. "I don't usually let them see that. It's better to allow them to hope."

I was still trying to breathe, waiting for the pain to subside. He kept talking. There was a drumming in my ears, far away.

"They understand just enough to know that they could be worse off than they are now. They do have something more to lose. Maryam, unfortunately…" He shook his head sadly. "Now, I'll have no further use for her. A pity. She was a good girl. One of my favorites. And her mother…" He smiled in reminiscence.

I thought it was time to move on. I took a breath. "So what you're saying is, you'll trade me my soul for the name of my demon."

He looked surprised. "Is that not what I have been saying all along? But now you know you must obey me, that you have, in fact, no choice at all."

My heart was pounding hard in my ears as the realization reached from my gut to my brain that this guy was going to cut me apart. It sounded like drumbeats. I could call Richard to me now, just by that name, but what would come? The new-made boy who had died in this house at least once already? Or the creature of darkness he'd been the moment before he disappeared? The vision of Richard as I'd last seen him, pulsing with darkness, his eyes as wild and knowing as death, grew in my mind, and with the picture I understood: I'd really had no idea what I was dealing with. But this kindly old fraud in front of me probably would. And this critter was the last thing on Earth that I'd want something like that working for. He already had way too much power. Any more, and he'd probably do for us all.

Between the rock and the hard place, the frying pan and the fire, there is still the choice. There's the choice of what kind of end you want to make. Do you want to sizzle, or do you want to dance? Do you want to give in, or take your chance?

"Lay her on the table, my children," al Hassan said gently. He lifted the chain from around his neck and took up the little scissors once again. "I will make the first cut, and we will see if you still remember. I will make the second cut, and I will ask you again. I will make the third cut, and you will call upon your demon to save you." I was fighting with the guys as hard as I could. They were falling over themselves, but I had the table between me and some of them, and my foot was still holding onto to the table leg for dear life. But at this I met his eyes. He thought he had me. I saw it in his face. He knew that before I let him cut out my soul, I would call my demon to come and save me. And when I'd pronounced his name, al Hassan would have it, and then he would kill me. I smiled. I guess he didn't know everything after all. He didn't know me. I changed.

I had to pay attention, as I never had before, to where my feet were as they changed shape, and as my joints changed their orientation. I didn't want to get caught up or twisted or broken as my alteration became inevitable. But it still had to be fast, and it was. I unhooked my foot from around the table, stepped out of my manacles, took a huge chomp out of the arm of the guy who was holding me the hardest while shrinking away from the other, and slipped my handcuffs at the same time. And then I leaped at the nearest child of al Hassan, expecting at any moment to find myself at the bottom of a pile of his sons and daughters, attacking me from every direction and holding me down by their sheer weight. I made my way through the press of people, snapping here, tearing there, clawing four ways at once, trying to reach al Hassan, which was the only way, I thought, to prevent my death in that little room. The pile-up I expected didn't come. A lot of al Hassan's servants and protectors did not seem to be facing me when I attacked them. There was a banging and a crashing in my ears, and all the shouting and screaming I anticipated—and more—and then through a clear space in the crowd, I saw a bear.

It is said of the bear kind that they are brave and strong, as cunning in battle as they are tenacious, and that it is best, on the whole, not to incur their wrath. All this I know to be true. When I had a moment to notice such things, I saw that the door to the workroom that led to the hallway was torn from its hinges—bears are strong—and that there were two piles of al Hassan's children, one lying at the feet of the bear to his left, and one to his right, and none of these people were moving. The bear was on his hind legs, batting one way and then another, which accounted for the distribution of his fallen opponents. The door that led to the library was rocking, there was more noise, and another bear fell into the room onto all fours, carrying with him a pile of men who seemed to have been trying to bar his entrance. He rose to his hind legs as well, and began to dispose of all who came in his way.

I decided then that I like bears very much.

Crowds of people poured into the room from both doorways. I continued to tear up anyone who came near me, but more and more I had leisure to look around because no one was coming near me. The people, I realized, were not trying to attack the bears. They were trying to get past the bears, and once past, they did one of two things. They attacked the shelves that held all those luminous bottles, dragged them down and smashed each shining vessel so that the crashing of glass was a constant percussion beneath the screaming, the shouting, the roaring of the bears, and the beat of the drums.

Drums? I could hear them now, pounding away in a fervent heartbeat and riding the upbeat against the cacophony of the riot. More troops were beyond in the hallway then, I realized. That left me with one more task to do. I looked for al Hassan. When I fixed on him as my prey, something broke open inside me with a roar, and I was riding a riot of my own as I tore around the room hunting for a sign of where he had gone. I didn't have to go far. I found his hand on the floor. There was another pile of the bodies of his children, but this one was writhing and intent and alive, and beneath it lay their father, Ibrahim al Hassan, who had enslaved and devoured them. They had turned on him at last. I saw his hand clawing for purchase. I saw it convulse. I saw it relax, and flap easily one way and another as his burden of children pounded at him with their fists, and tore at him with their fingers and their little teeth.

His two small daughters, their veils askew, were the first to burrow out of the melee. His other children, soulless, were slower to realize that they had accomplished their task. The first little daughter waited for the second, and when that one emerged, stood looking at her speculatively. Tangled in her fingers was a slender golden chain from which still dangled the tiny pair of golden scissors.

That was it. I changed. I walked over to that cute little girl while she was still sizing up her sister, and pulled the scissors and the chain out of her hands. She cried out and turned to me, to find herself facing someone—something—a lot bigger than her, and pretty darn mad. She threw herself backwards in terror against her sister, and then both of them, screaming high and hard, scurried away.

When I turned back, Jacob the bear was standing next to me in the form of a man. He nodded in greeting. "Was that necessary?" he glanced again at the two girls screaming their way out of the crowded room and back at me.

"Yes, it was," I told him. "It absolutely was." I twisted the golden scissors in my hand, trying to ensure that they'd never cut anything again. It wasn't enough. I went to the counter and lit the gas burner to heat up the little ceramic bowl. I held it close to the flame to get it hot as soon as possible. "Don't let any of them come near me," I told the bear, "or we may have to do this all over again some day."

I didn't notice how many of al Hassan's more ambitious children had to be batted away. I was intent on my task. I melted down the scissors and the chain until you couldn't tell one from the other. Then I spilled the gold in droplets over the counter, onto the floor, onto the clothes of those who had finished fighting and were just lying around, until gold mingled with the blood in the room, so you'd think maybe a griffon had been fighting.

"We should make sure all those bottles are smashed," I told Jacob, while I was making sure the evil little tool could never be made whole again.

Jacob looked at me with his head to one side. He kept glancing from my face to the top of my head and back. He was smiling a little, but he also looked impressed. "You should perhaps put your head on straight, first?"

I looked down, and up, and started laughing. "It's your fault," I said to Jacob. "You showed me that trick. I didn't know I'd learned it so well already." I was wearing both my aspects, my wolf and my human one, simultaneously, one above the other. No wonder those little girls had screamed. And I thought it was my natural authority.

I pulled myself together, looked at Jacob. "All right?" He nodded. "Very good."

Al Hassan's children, those still on their feet, were assaulting the shelves that held the luminous bottles. I was about to join in the grabbing and smashing when the drums from the corridor reached a crescendo, and a familiar face appeared in the doorway. I found myself smiling. I realized I did have a co-worker smile. Or maybe, this was my friendly smile.

Yvette was wearing a stylish African cap over her many beaded braids. The closed, hard look was gone from her face. She looked happy and powerful. She wore her drum on a sling at her front, and as she pounded it, she danced. She came into the workroom, glanced at the bears, glanced at the piles of bodies, at the blood and the gold and the broken glass, and she finished her drumming with a articulation that sounded like a comment on the whole event. Then she beat out a final phrase and stopped, and silence fell.

Silence, except for the groaning, the shouting, the moaning, and the smashing of glass. Over all this she saw me and beamed. "Amber!"

I thought she was going to hug me when she reached me, but her drum was in the way. She grasped both my hands. "Why didn't you wait for us? I told you I would help you."

"The bears brought you," I said foolishly, smiling. Through the corridor I could see a third bear, lumbering after his fleeing prey, and two more drummers, Yvette's friends from the Wicca circle.

Jacob came to stand beside her, put an arm around her shoulders in a way I could see wasn't new to her. Yvette looked awfully smug. "She brought us," Jacob amended.

"I thought you'd be needing help. We would have got here sooner, but you left too fast. So, it took us awhile to find out where you'd gone. Didn't I tell you I was going to help you?"

Maybe she had. I didn't remember. Wolves don't hunt with other kinds. It hadn't occurred to me that her offer was serious. But I was in a new place, and I was learning new ways. Perhaps these were the ways of the humankind. "Thanks," I said. "You were in the nick of time."

Yvette grinned and beat out her pleasure on her djembe.

We smashed the rest of the bottles. The luminosity in each of them held in the scattered shards on the floor for a long moment, and then went out like a falling star.

"I hope," I said, almost to myself, "they find their way home."

The third bear joined us when there was only one bottle left. He metamorphosed into Aaron before my eyes as he kicked aside the broken door with a bear's foot, and shoved a crawling young man of his way with the foot of a man. "Are we finished here?"

"One more thing," I said. I took off at a run, reaching out onto four legs instead of two, since that would be faster. I had to know.

The spells that kept me from smelling inside that house were wafting away in the fresh air from every broken window and smashed door. I tracked my way down the passageways, through the kitchen, to the wine cellar, to the basement stairs. I charged down headlong, caught myself up at the bottom, stood up onto two legs, and went to the box where Maryam had indicated that Richard was kept. The circle, the pentagram, the signs of ward and restraint, the sword and the wand, seemed suddenly justified to contain that being of writhing darkness that had worn Richard's form, the last moment I saw him. I hesitated. Richard had come to me when I called for him. The talisman that had preserved my senses against all the spells that al Hassan had laid on his house, had released the dark energy that might well be his true form. I'd come down here to make sure Richard was all right. If he was in that box, he was not all right. But what if it was not Richard in that box?

I kicked aside the circle, smudged open the pentagram, and tossed the blade and wand aside. I fumbled a few moments with the complicated latches, and then opened the box. He had been there. I smelled his scent, and I smelled his desperate fear. But the box was empty. I tried to believe that was good.

Just to be sure, I made my way through the house all the way to the rooms at the top, but the children had already been there. I found the room where al Hassan had done his experiments, because Richard's sweat and his blood were still evident. The sumptuous rooms were wrecked. I didn't find any tools. I went back downstairs.

I joined up with my rescuers after that. Yvette and her drummer friends from the Wicca group were standing in a circle in the hall while the three bears loped around, chasing the few remaining children of al Hassan who had not hidden or fled. Then we walked out of the house and into the morning light, and the free air, and all the scents that tell the tales of the world. The drummers were laughing, giddy and proud of our success. The bears,

Jacob, Jonathan, and Aaron, and Sol, whom we met up with in front of the house, seemed pleased and satisfied with their morning's activity.

I made sure, before we left, that al Hassan was dead. Richard had believed him dead too, at one time, and it had proved untrue. I supposed a sorcerer such as al Hassan would have defenses and illusions to help him in a pinch. I guessed his children knew that too. When I went to look, there wasn't enough of him left to make a meal for a puppy. I couldn't have done a better job myself. I wished I had done the job, for Richard's sake, but I knew justice when I saw it. Al Hassan had raised up his own executioners.

The gates stood wide open, never to be closed again without a whole lot of repair work. They had come in two cars, and they piled back into them, while I trotted down the street to find my car where I'd parked it a few blocks away. From a trot I slowed to a walk. From a walk, to an amble. I was really, really hungry. I was more relieved than I cared to admit that al Hassan wasn't going to do experiments on my soul or on my body to extract my demon's name. I was tired. And it wasn't over yet. In my pocket I held, hidden in the palm of my hand, the last remaining bottle, a small one, sky blue.

I followed the others back to Tamara's shop, where we celebrated with pizza and soda and coffee and beer. The coffee was awful. And there was drummer boasting, and bear boasting, and bear boasting will beat any other boasting in the world. To hear the bears tell about it, each one of them had separately taken Ibrahim al Hassan's house apart, beaten off the hordes of his children, and torn out the sorceror's throat. The drummers told their side, in higher voices against the background of the bears' unceasing gloating, how their drumming had opened a hole in the defenses of the house that had enabled the bears to break down the gates and the doors and scatter the children. I didn't know what the defenses were, except the one that kept me from using my chief senses. I nodded and smiled and thanked them and agreed again and again that they had come just in time. They'd earned their celebration. It was the least I could do. You wouldn't believe how much pizza a bear can eat.

When the twelfth large pizza box was opened in front of me, Yvette came and sat down beside me, the better to reach for her share, I thought, before the bears got in and there was none left.

"Great hat," I told her.

She glowed. "Tamara gave it to me. She says…" She leaned forward to tell me, out of hearing of the others. "She says I have power in my drumming, that the ancestors speak through my hands. She says it's a gift I have, and I'm always welcome here." She took a huge slice of pizza, with four kinds of meat on it, in both hands. "This is the best time I ever had in my life." She bit off the pointed end. "You ever need help again, you tell me."

"I will," I said. "And, thanks."

She flapped her full hands at me. "Anytime. Next time, though, you tell us where you're going, and we won't have to haul a diviner out of his bed to find you."

"Tamara knew."

"Yeah, but she was sleeping."

Tamara's sleep was more important than the diviner's, it seemed.

Tamara was back at the hospital with her mother that morning. The store was open, with friends running the shop. We sat in the back room until the pizza was gone, and then I thanked them all again, and made my excuses, and drove home.

Richard's scent, though faint now, was still discernable in my apartment. The smells he'd made in the kitchen were still there, as were those that remained from the things we'd done on the bed. I took a long shower, set the alarm clock, and lay down. After a while, I came conscious long enough to climb out of the blankets and change my form, turn around until I found the right configuration, and lie down again. I didn't want human thoughts, or human dreams, right now.

I slept wolf-style, in short naps. When the moon rose, I changed again and reached out to turn off the alarm clock before it buzzed. I got dressed, put on my jacket against the cold, and slipped the shining blue bottle into my pocket. I drove up to Hellman Park as the gibbous moon was lifting off the horizon. The park closes at dusk, so I left my car a ways down the street and, holding the little bottle safe in my hand, inside the pocket, I climbed the steep hill and walked back along the ridge and down into the bowl where the Wiccans met.

ℬℭ

CHAPTER TWENTY

There were clouds in the sky blowing in from the sea. There were not a lot of stars because the night was hazy and the moon was close to full. The Wiccans weren't there tonight. I knew they wouldn't be. Yvette and her friends would have told me if there was a working on for that night. I wanted to do what I planned in the open, under the sky. And this place had the resonance of all the previous magic that had been raised there. I might need all the help I could get.

I took a stick and drew a circle in the dirt, more than big enough to stand in, and a pentagram inside it. If I'd known any symbols of guard or protection, aversion of evil, I'd have written them between the points of the star. If I'd known the proper prayers or invocations, I'd have offered them up, sealed with lit candles at the points of the pentagram. Richard hadn't been Richard anymore, the last time I'd seen him. He was a demon, an actual demon. I needed to talk to him, but I did not want to be eaten. So I did what I could. I drew the basic sign of containment, and the open gate, which was as much as I knew. And then I spoke Richard's name, his true name, and called him to me.

He was there in the center of the pentagram on the last sound of the last syllable, clothed in darkness upon darkness that moved, and only a shadow of him was the Richard I knew. I stepped back and, once again, all the hair rose on my neck and back. A half-familiar form was traced over the figure, like the reflection of a friend seen in water, among other forms. I hadn't been mistaken. It really was a demon. This was the form that had been spilling out of Richard the last time I'd seen him.

He saw me and turned, and knelt down inside the center of the pentagram. "Mistress." He bowed his head without taking his eyes off me.

That wasn't Richard. Richard had never called me that. I could feel this creature's will, huge and deep and dangerous. "That's not what I wanted," I said. "I want Richard."

"It is what you called." It spoke with many voices, like whispers in the darkness. One of them was Richard, but hardly distinguishable from the rest.

I shook my head, trying to separate the voice I wanted from the others. "It's not what I asked for." And I commanded, "Richard!"

And he was there, shaking with cold, bent and bowed before me.

And that pissed me off. "*With* clothes," I demanded. I wasn't going to have this conversation while I watched his body turn blue. And I was pretty sure he knew this, and was trying to distract me, one way or another.

He was clothed almost instantly in jeans and the blue silk shirt all clean and new, and the used leather jacket, and the worn boots that I was used to seeing him wear. He looked up at me with wild, unregenerate, rebellious, and completely foreign eyes.

"No," I said. "*Richard.* That's all I want to see."

And there he was, his dark blue eyes troubled as though by a storm. But it was him, all of him, and only him. He lifted his hands to me and said in his own voice, "Do you know what you are asking?"

I thought about that for a second. I was beginning to think I did. "First," I said, "give me back the token I gave you in the basement last night." I held out my hand for it.

He moved then as though he was struggling in someone's grasp, as though he were trying to find his way around my direct instruction. Finally he said, "What are you going to do with me?" And in his voice I heard Phaedrus, and Amyas, Jack, Philip and Stan, and other names that I probably hadn't been told, since he hadn't told me everything. He'd certainly forgotten to mention earlier a hundred and twenty-four years of imprisonment by Ibrahim al Hassan. But I understood that he didn't have to answer anything that wasn't a direct and specific question. And I understood, too, that he could be tricky. So I didn't answer him, and I didn't negotiate. I just held out my hand.

And the token was in it. I smelled it. There were scents upon it that I couldn't identify or describe, but beneath those, which it carried lightly, it was the same. I slipped it over my head. It didn't seem to make any difference here to my senses, but then, I wasn't inside a mad sorcerer's bespelled fortress.

"What did it do, when you put it on?" I asked. "You changed. I saw you. What happened?"

I sat down on the ground in front of him, so I wouldn't loom over him anymore. He sat back on his knees. His face was smooth. He looked new again. He looked the same, and yet not the same, from when I had first seen him. He was frightened as he'd been then, but that had been an old fear that he trailed behind him like an exhaust fume. This was new, and it was large, and it nearly pulsed the air like the darkness that was his true form.

"I remembered," Richard told me. He looked at me from under his brows to see what I understood from that.

He was afraid of me. Of what I might know, or learn, or understand. The more I knew, I thought, the more power I'd have over him. And that was odd. Didn't I already have all the power over him I could possibly imagine?

"What did you remember?"

He paused, and I thought he was trying to find a way to phrase his answer to explain as little as possible, while telling the exact truth. And when he answered, I was pretty sure I was right. "What I was."

Tamara had warned me to be careful. So I took her warning. Some wolves are so proud they don't listen to advice. A wolf alone must be wiser than that, if she's going to survive. So I didn't ask the question he wanted me to ask, "What were you?" I thought for a moment, and asked instead, "What did you remember about what you were?"

He drew in a breath, and he dared to say, "You wouldn't understand."

"Richard. Tell me so that I do understand."

His eyes began to empty of hope. He drew another breath, lifted his hands again and let them drop. "I remembered what John Dee caused me to forget. What I am, where I come from, and... what I can do."

"Ah," I said, and sat back on my hands. I saved up the next question, and asked a different one. "And how did he do that? How did John Dee make you forget?"

"He was terrified of me. He spent years and years of his life trying to raise a demon, and when he finally succeeded—by accident, and with help—and I would never have been caught in their flimsy, ridiculous wisp of an invocation if they hadn't happened to have done it on a day at an hour that was propitious to a certain bend in the roof of the Halls of Air, and if I hadn't just happened to be passing by at just that exact particular—"

"All right," I said. His voice had changed, drawing on a new timbre. He might look like the Richard I remembered, but all the rest of him was still there, just out of my sight. At times I caught a whiff of it, and my hair stood on end. "So he caught you—"

"By accident," he muttered, like a schoolboy who was going to have the last word.

"Right. How did he make you forget?"

He looked at me then with his eyes so full of pain, human pain, that I almost put up a hand to ward him off. "Please—" he began.

I wondered if he'd try to fool me, or tell me in a way that was so garbled I couldn't make sense of it. I wondered long enough that he stopped trying for a reprieve and answered my question as I had asked. It really seemed to be completely true, that he had to obey me. Like it or not.

"He began by using every spell of ward he could find, against every part of me that looked frightening to him. He commanded that I may not do this, and I may not do that, and I may not go here and I may not think that, and then he said I may not remember…" He looked at me for a long moment. I almost thought his passion would break through his human form, and he would cry, or rush at me, or yell or something. But he just took another deep breath and then continued. "And I obeyed him. As you know I must. And I no longer remembered." He gave a slight shrug. "The trouble was, by the time he finished there was so little I could do for him, within all those strictures that he spent two years laying down—"

"While he kept you in a cage?"

He nodded, looking at the ground. "All I was good for in the end was housework. Stable work. Servant's work. Card tricks."

"And sex," I added. I couldn't help my smile.

He nodded again, his head lowered still more. "And sex, of course."

"And he had you without term or limit, even beyond the end of his life."

He didn't reply to that, I guess because I'd said it all. But he raised his head then and gave me a look. I got what he meant.

I shifted my legs in front of me and made myself more comfortable. It was chilly up there on the hill. The clouds crossed the moon again and again. The ground under me was wet, but what the hell. There was no way I was bringing this conversation indoors.

"You played me," I stated.

He didn't deny it. "Slaves do," he said bitterly.

"You used me."

"I did. And a good thing, too."

"Why?"

"Imagine a world where al Hassan has a demon at his command," he suggested. "I needed a shield from that fate. He would have had me at once, if I hadn't already been in your service. He'd learned enough since he last had hold of me to bind me. He would have me now, if you hadn't come after me."

I grinned. We had been a team. And we'd done that much. I'd thought, once in awhile, that we were friends, companions, as well as lovers. I'd been playing at love. I'd known it wasn't real. Richard wasn't real. I just hadn't always remembered it. "It wasn't real, then. Our... friendship."

"Of course it was real!" he said, with that look in his eyes that I remembered, and his sweetest smile.

I smiled back. I knew he was lying, and the light faded from his eyes when he saw that I knew. "I have something I want you to do for me," I told him.

Miserable, sullen, and rebellious, Richard bowed his head and awaited my commands.

"The Eater of Souls. The real one. You know who I mean?"

"I know what you mean, Mistress," he answered, putting a bite into his words. I don't know if he meant that he wasn't stupid, or just that he didn't want to be here, which I already knew. I let it go. I'd be pretty pissed, too, in his place.

"Can you get rid of her? It? Whatever it is? Can you make it that she never comes here?"

"Never?" he asked, like a lawyer fingering a loophole.

"I'll tell you what I want, and you tell me if you can make it happen. All right?"

He bowed his head again.

"All right," I continued. "I want that thing that is known as the Eater of Souls to be gone from this place and never threaten a human again."

"That's two things," he pointed out.

"Yeah?" I was starting to get pissed myself. I didn't ask for this attitude. "And are you telling me that you can't do two things?"

"No, Mistress." He bowed again.

Funny, I was beginning to like the sound of that word. I shook myself. This wasn't supposed to be fun. "All right," I said. "Can you do that? What I asked?"

"Make the Eater of Souls be gone from the Earth and never threaten one of your kind again." He raised his head.

"Okay," I said. "No, wait. How long will it take you?"

He raised his eyes to me, laughing, and lifted a hand. "Mistress," he said grandly, but still with that hint of a bite in his voice, "it is already done."

Well, that was a little hard to swallow. "Are you kidding?"

He didn't answer that one. He just looked at me.

"Really? She's gone, and won't come again."

He bowed.

"How did you do that?" I said. "You didn't do anything."

His smile reminded me of the Richard I'd known. It wasn't an easy smile, and there was mockery in it, at him and at me. He might be enslaved all right, but he sure didn't have to like it.

"I live in many worlds at once," he said. "You don't wish to see that, and I no longer allow that in your sight. Thus, I can serve you here, and in another place, and never seem to leave you." He added, after a second's pause, "This is one of the things that John Dee forced me to forget."

"Well then," I said, "All right. Thank you."

He gave me that small twisted smile again, and bent his head.

"Next thing," I said. "The World Snake."

"Yes, Mistress?"

"I want it to go away. I want it harmless. I want there never to be a human city that is swallowed by the World Snake again." I leaned forward and asked him, "Can you do that?"

"Mistress, I cannot."

I couldn't believe how pissed that made me. I thought I'd figured it all out. "What do you mean?"

"You have asked me to do three contradictory things."

"I did not!"

"May I explain?" he asked.

"Yes," I said impatiently. "Explain."

"The World Snake is bound to the sinews of the life of this world. She is a part of them. The tracks she makes through the fires of the Earth, the trails she follows beneath the crust, are part of the lines of power of your world, like the veins of a leaf, or the blood veins in a human. To send away the World Snake will destroy those courses of energy. This world would die soon after."

"So, she can't be stopped?"

"She cannot stop," he amended.

"But she could turn," I realized.

"She could turn."

I almost smiled. He had offered me the answer on a plate. "Ah. Can you make it so she never swallows a human city again, without doing any other harm to the world? Of any kind?"

He almost smiled back. "Mistress, I can."

"Okay." I thought a second. "Tell me first: have I phrased it right? I don't want anything to go wrong with this. I want the World Snake not to bring destruction on habitation of any kind again. Do you understand? Should I say it to you any differently, so that I get what I want?"

"No, Mistress." He met my eyes appreciatively that time. "I understand your wishes, and I will obey them."

"All right, then," I said. "Do that."

He bowed and lifted his hands.

"That's it?" I asked. "It's done?"

"Wait for it," he said.

From the top of the hill, I could see the lights of the greater Los

Angeles area, all the way to where they blurred into the distant haze. The traffic roared, the pale stars shone, a pair of skunks waddled along the path below.

My arms began to tingle, the hair on the back of my neck rose, and I smelled ozone, as though the wind had blown in from the sea. The roar began in the distance. I put my hands on the ground and felt the earth tremble and then shake. I hunkered down as the hillside rocked in a series of sharp jerks. I looked up and saw Richard kneeling there unmoving in his circle, as though he really was in another world, while mine rocked and rolled, on and on. He grinned at me. He liked the big stuff. He really did.

Finally the rumble faded away, the shaking stopped, and the earth was still under my hands. Below the hill, we saw transformers spark and flame, and all across the city the lights went out. Down at the college people were shouting, horns blared, car alarms went off. In the darkened valley, pinpoints of light flared as generators started up here. In the distance, I heard the song of sirens.

"It is done," said the demon. "Your city is saved. The World Snake has turned. She will not come here." My city. Hm. Had a nice sound to it.

"That's it?" I asked.

He looked up. "Not entirely. She'll leave her mark for a while."

I followed his gaze. The stars were brighter now, and more numerous. To the west, a strange glow rose in the sky. As we watched, lines of greenish yellow light spread out like spider legs, then drew back, then drifted out again. The shapes grew brighter, then faded, turned, and grew larger. An aurora borealis. I'd only heard about them. I'd never seen one before.

"It's beautiful."

His eyes were untroubled now. He was smiling fiercely. The big things were more his size, I saw. They were what he was for. Mucking out stables must have been hard on him, all those years.

"Okay," I said. "The Eater of Souls is gone, the World Snake is no problem. You're absolutely certain? No fooling?"

"I swear to you," he said, and his voice filled again with other voices I could only partly hear. "By my name."

"Good enough." I rubbed my hands, and then my shoulders. It was cold. "Okay. Ibrahim al Hassan. You remember him?"

"Always."

"Could you check that he's really going to stay dead this time? And that scissor thing that he used to cut souls out is totally destroyed? And all traces of how to make it again? And the set of diviner's tools he had, those need to disappear. And could you check that his children are scattered and none of them is going to, I don't know, take up where dad left off?"

Richard's eyes shadowed for a moment. "It is done."

That startled me. I thought we were going to discuss the ramifications of what I was asking, first. I thought hard about what I had said, and wondered if he could have interpreted my words as some kind of command, a command he wanted to hear, and had since carried out. He met my gaze passively. I decided I didn't want to ask, and I didn't want to know. After all, a hundred and twenty-four years. I didn't blame him.

Richard knelt, waiting for my next command. His eyes held an unfamiliar glint of power and mischief. More than just mischief. And I thought, for a moment, what it would be like to walk in the door of my mom's house with this Richard in tow. And how the heads would turn. And they would smell him, but by then it would be too late. I was arrested by the realization that with Richard by my side, I could scour the world of evil. I could weigh the souls of the righteous. Forests would grow from one end of the continent to the other. Buffalo would roam the plains. Elk and deer would fatten in the grasslands. Goats would leap upon the mountains. The wolf kind would rule this world. And… I would be old enough, and strong enough, to rule the wolf kind.

Richard was gazing at me, and his eyes were bleak. I held my vision close for one moment more, picturing my stepdad and his sons running at the head of the pack, the pack led by me and Richard that was after their blood, and gaining. I let his yelp, and their screams, ring in my ears one more time. Then I reached in my pocket and drew out the little glass bottle that glowed in my hands like a candle. I set it on the ground between us. Richard looked at it, and then he looked at me. I saw hope rise in his face like the dawn coming.

"You told me—Richard, my Richard—told me he needed this in order to go free."

Mutely, he shook his head. "He—I—was mistaken. I didn't remember. All I need to go free," and his voice became a plea, dragging with centuries of loss and pain, carefully contained, "is your word. Nothing else. But nothing else will do."

"You don't need this?" I was dumbfounded. After the trouble I'd gone to, and the long walk up the hill that I could have loped up a lot more easily—I didn't want to take the smallest chance, not likely, but not impossible, that I might lose it out of my pocket if I changed, so I'd carried the bottle every step of the way, for the gods' sake. "What do I do with this, then?"

Richard looked down at the bottle with compassion. "Let it go, if you would. Or let me do it. I will free it gently, where it needs to go."

All I could do was nod. He lifted his hand, staring intently, and gradually the light sank in the bottle, and went out. Then he flicked his fingers and the bottle vanished before my eyes. Great. No recycling.

"So all you needed from the start was for John Dee to set a limit to your time here? And he didn't, so there wasn't one?"

He didn't try to answer. He started making terms. "Mistress, I will serve you, with all my powers, to the end of your tiniest whim, for all of your days on Earth, if you would set my term of service as your last breath. Mistress…"

His voice rose as I shook my head.

"Mistress, I beg of you—"

"That's not what I want," I said. "I'll tell you what I want," I continued, while his eyes bored into me like blue suns from another world, "and then I'll set you free."

The word emerged as though from his last breath. "Anything..."

I tried to say it. And then I had to stop. Wolves don't cry. I don't cry. And I don't show what I feel easily. But I had to, to have what I wanted. "I want Richard back. My Richard. For—for two weeks. Until the new moon. I want the Richard back that I knew. Just for that long. When the new moon comes, Richard can go. And so can you. And this will be so, whether I die, or the world ends." I added quickly, "Unless you've had anything to do with it."

And there was Richard, my own Richard, in his own clothes, and his short hair, with the little scar on his cheek and all, and the scent of him was the same. But the fear was gone. "You know," he said quietly, "that I am not allowed to harm you."

I reached out to him through the tears in my eyes, and in his arms I was warm.

₱⁂

CHAPTER TWENTY-ONE

All right, it wasn't the same. But I tried to pretend it was, and I succeeded most of the time in believing it. It was fun, playing at being in love. And if love is doing things together, and enjoying it, well, then that much of it was real.

Why didn't I keep him? My lightest whim granted to my last breath and all that? I am young and need to grow. I have things to learn and new powers to attain. If I am to be what I am meant to be, having my whims granted is just going to get in the way. Besides, wolves don't keep pets. We don't run with our prey.

Richard and I spent as much time in the next two weeks in wolf form as in human form. I liked that, because in wolf form I didn't have to think about anything but what was in front of me, and what was in front of me was great. I lost my job. What the hell. Sacrificing my job to be with Richard just made our time together it seem more important.

I fell asleep on the night of the new moon, curled up with Richard beside me, our mingled scent on the sheets. In the morning, he was gone. I lay there alone for a long time, and I was too happy to cry.

Why didn't I ask for my dad back? Why didn't I ask for my stepfather's head on a hubcap? Or my stepbrothers' entrails made into harp strings, and played while they were still alive? We made up a lot of possibilities, Richard and I, lying side by side on the hillside where we had run and played and hunted for hours. But I asked for none of these things.

I am a daughter of the wolf kind. What I want, I get for myself. And so it will be.

❧❧❧

ACKNOWLEDGMENTS

First of all, I must thank my side man, my true and all, best friend and husband, Eric Elliott, who can't find the place in the contract where it says he has to read all my drafts, but does it anyway. Keep looking, it's there.

To Doug, who opened the door, and my awesome agent, Laurie McLean, who knew the way, and is even more splendid than Doug said she was. And to Jeremy Lassen, Ross Lockhart and Night Shade Books for embarking me and the wolf girl on this wonderful adventure.

Thank you to Kit for her generous and thought-provoking notes, to Janna, and also Allan and Bill, for saving me from error, and grateful thanks to Deborah Ruth, for standing by in the middle of the night, down to the wire, with encouragement and wise counsel.

ABOUT THE AUTHOR

Carol Wolf earned a B.A. in History at Mills College, an MFA in Drama-Playwriting at Rutgers University, and pursued a life in the theater, which resulted in about thirty productions of her plays on five continents, including the feminist musical farce, *The Terrible Experiment of Jonathan Fish*, and the award-winning *The Thousandth Night*. She wrote the scripts for the blockbuster video games *Blood Omen: Legacy of Kain*, and *Legacy of Kain: Defiance*. She co-founded a micro-budget film company, Paw Print Studios, and produced and directed *The Valley of Fear* (a horror comedy, much more comedy than horror), and *Far From the Sea*, a drama. She studied broadsword fighting in the SCA, Uechi-rhu karate, and recently earned a black belt in Iaido. She has lived on both coasts, and in Europe, and presently lives in the Foothills of the Sierra Nevadas with her husband, two border collies, and a varying number of sheep.